BOYS IN BED

A collection of 20 gay erotic stories

Edited by Lucas Steele

Published by Xcite Books Ltd – 2013

ISBN 9781908766151

Copyright © Xcite Books Ltd 2013

The stories contained within this book are works of fiction. Names and characters are the product of the authors' imaginations and any resemblance to actual persons, living or dead, is entirely coincidental

All rights reserved. No part of this book may be reproduced, stored in a retrieval system, or transmitted in any form or by any means, electronic, electrostatic, magnetic tape, mechanical, photocopying, recording or otherwise, without the written permission of the publishers: Xcite Books, Suite 11769, 2nd Floor, 145-157 St John Street, London EC1V 4PY

Previous publishing credits:
Bananas originally appeared in Indulge magazine, 1998

Printed and bound in the UK

Cover design by Madamadari

Contents

Finished by Hand	William Anthony	1
The Hung Games	Elizabeth Coldwell	15
Chocolates at the Sun Garden Hotel	D.K. Jernigan	27
The Age of Indolence	Lynn Lake	34
Two in the Bed	Drew Payne	45
Paddle Boy	Landon Dixon	56
Bananas	Dominic Santi	65
Evolution of Attraction	Katya Harris	77
Happy New Year DJ Lawrence	Graham Benedict	94
Lay-by	L.A. Fields	109
April Showers	Michael Wells	121
A Queer Kind of Caring	Eve Ray	133
Valentine	Beverly Langland	145
Bustin' Our Balls	Landon Dixon	161
Memories	Michael Bracken	170
Spanking the Stripper	E.C. Cutler	177
A Bear in the Woods	Marcus Swannick	190
And the Crowd Goes Wild!	G.R. Richards	206
The Gamekeeper's Lodge	JY	214
A Year of Waiting	Andy McGreggor	225

Finished by Hand
by William Anthony

It had been a typically slow Monday afternoon down Porthmerry Lane, when a customer walked into Marquis & Delaney – Gentleman's Outfitters. Young Mr Grisham had wasted no time in giving him the once-over with his experienced menswear eye. It had been easy to tell from tall black gentleman's bespoke houndstooth jacket, white shirt with an autumn brown silk tie, gabardine slacks, and well-polished brown leather brogues, that he obviously possessed good taste and a timeless fashion sense – and he certainly wasn't afraid to spend a pound or two on clothing. The style was quite clearly classic Continental French, accentuating the gentleman's broad shoulders and chest, while at the same time cut to compliment his flat stomach and 34-and-three-quarter-inch waist.

Predatorily, Mr Grisham waited just long enough for the shop door to start closing before he glided around a rack of Hugo Boss cashmere and wools, well ahead of his other two colleagues, and made first contact with the commission – er, *customer*.

'Excuse me, but would sir be looking for anything in particular? We pride ourselves on carrying most of the classic, as well as the modern, designer names. So I am sure we could find something to sir's liking.'

The gentleman had regarded the shop assistant silently for several seconds. His large, warm brown eyes were set in an exotically dark face, which young Mr Grisham thought was Moroccan, or possibly North African. Then the gentleman had smiled broadly, a hint of gold flashing for a moment. 'I was just passing, saw some of the window displays, and decided to come in. I'm not entirely sure what I'm looking for – probably something casual yet adventurous in trousers. Oh, and a jacket would be nice as well.'

Mr Grisham had smiled warmly back at the thought of increasing his sales figures, and told the gentleman he thought he knew exactly what he was after, little realising just how true his words would turn out to be.

With the Moroccan gentleman in tow, Mr Grisham had headed toward the back of the shop where the more casual, rather than business, styles were located. He had also been more than pleasantly surprised when – on stopping short in front of a rack of Gerrals & Fletcher trousers – the gentleman had, seemingly accidentally, bumped into him from behind. It had not been the bumping which had been the surprising part, but the exhilarating feel of the Moroccan's strong hands gripping his waist as the gentleman steadied himself – apologising profusely as he did so.

'I'm terribly sorry, I was preoccupied for a moment and forgot where I was.'

Young Mr Grisham had turned around and, in light of the incident, had taken a more appraising look at the gentleman. He was slightly taller, around 6 feet 2, with a lean, almost athletic build to him. With his broad shoulders and inverse waist he appeared masculine, but not brutish. His hair had been neatly barbered, framing his handsome facial features, and he gave the appearance of being in his mid to late 30s, as best Mr Grisham could tell under the warm shop lighting.

Making eye contact, the assistant had asked, 'I don't suppose sir happens to know any of his measurements?'

He shook his head. 'I've lost a little weight recently since attending a club gym, hence the need for something new in my wardrobe.'

Without thinking, Mr Grisham had eyed the gentleman up and down several times, and, before he had been able to stop himself, said, 'Sir certainly appears to be in very fit shape to me,' then he had felt his face flush a little with embarrassment.

Instead of taking offence, the Moroccan had just tilted his head slightly to one side. 'Thank you. It seems rare to be given an honest compliment these days.'

'Now, sir,' said Mr Grisham, hurriedly trying to move things along, 'If you would care to follow me, we shall get you measured up. Then we can see what we can offer.'

They moved further back into the shop, stopping in the middle of a small space surrounded by various mirrors, and several wooden doors which led off to the fitting and changing rooms.

Picking up a measuring tape from a rack, young Mr Grisham asked, 'If you would care to raise your arms up?' As he did so, the assistant had moved closer, slipping the tape around the gentleman's waist – and almost laying his head on the gentleman's chest in the process. At such close range he could smell the warm, inviting musk the Moroccan was wearing.

It had been an intoxicating scent which brought back recent memories of holidays full of illicit adventures. Quiet, sandy coves under a hot Algerian sun – the taste of olive oil and herbs, licked off a dark brown hip, then his tongue travelling across a seductive stomach to the glistening base of the thick-veined tower …

Blinking several times to help dispel the images, young Mr Grisham quickly wrote down the measurement in his little top pocket notepad. Thirty-four-and-three-quarter-inches. It had been gratifying to know he hadn't lost his touch. Turning back to the gentleman at hand, he had pursed his lips, smiled, then knelt down in front of him. Placing one end of the tape measure against the right shoe, Mr Grisham had slowly moved up the gentleman's inside leg seam. The tape unravelling as he went, it seemed as though he had been greeted with the faintest of gasps when it – along with the back of his hand – had brushed up against the inside of the gentleman's crotch.

Looking back on it, as young Mr Grisham would recount later, the sound had taken him by surprise and he couldn't for the life of him be sure who it had come from.

However, try as he might to focus on the tape measure, Mr Grisham's eyes were repeatedly drawn to what had become a rather large and prominent bulge – unmissable by dint of its size and the position of Mr Grisham's eyeline. For a moment he had remembered Algiers again – the lithe and oiled African body underneath him, the firm feel of muscular buttocks, the way his hands had felt as he ran them along the supple back, and the incredible feeling as muscular resistance had melted away and he had slipped into the realms of physical ecstasy.

Looking upward, young Mr Grisham had seen the Moroccan gentleman looking down at him, a knowing grin raising the corners of his sensuous lips. A pink tongue had darted out and back momentarily, leaving them moist and glistening, and young Mr Grisham had felt his heartbeat speed up, which had led to an increase in his blood pressure which, in turn, had led to a painfully similar bulging of his own.

Mr Grisham stood and added the gentleman's inside leg measurement to the notebook. 'A respectable 31 inch should hang well, provided the cut isn't too restrictive. Seeing as though sir obviously dresses to the right, may I suggest you consider this rack over here?' He had guided the Moroccan to the racks nearest the changing rooms, and waited while the gentleman picked out three pairs of trousers.

Looking at Mr Grisham with a smile and a twinkle in his eye, the gentleman said, 'I believe the changing rooms are this way?' And with that he proceeded to head toward the back of the shop once more. Over his shoulder, he added, 'I take it you will be able to give me assistance if I encounter any problems?'

Young Mr Grisham had nodded reassuringly. 'I shall be right outside the door, sir. All you need do is call.'

A few minutes later, while Mr Grisham had been idly rearranging some sports jackets which, in all honesty, didn't need rearranging, he heard the gentleman's soft voice call out for him.

'Could you please come in for a moment? I seem to have a problem and I could do with some advice.'

Young Mr Grisham had discreetly opened the changing room door and, after a hurried glance to check on the other staff, he had backed into the changing room. Without hesitation, Mr Grisham had turned round, expecting to find the customer close by. To his surprise, the Moroccan gentleman was standing on the narrow wooden bench against the far wall of the changing room. Naked from the waist down and only wearing his white shirt and tie, his impressively sized black cock had been protruding between the front tails of his shirt, pointing directly at the bemused sales assistant. Over his warm smile – and Mr Grisham's happy amazement – the Moroccan gentleman explained his predicament in regard to putting the trousers on.

'The problem is this erection I have.' He pointed to it, possibly on the off-chance that Mr Grisham had somehow failed to see such a prominent member poking through two pieces of brightly laundered material. 'It keeps getting in the way and makes it particularly uncomfortable whenever I try and do these trousers up. Is there anything you might be able to think of which could help alleviate the problem?'

Young Mr Grisham's knees went momentarily weak and he had felt another rush of blood flow to his groin. As best he could remember, he'd never seen a bigger, or blacker, member in all his cottaging life, and to his expertly trained eye he had estimated it to have been at least nine and a half inches long. It had been straight and true, with a beautifully classic upward curve to its profile. The foreskin had naturally rolled back part way to reveal the tip of the exotically dark head, bobbing slightly in time to the gentleman's heart rate, and as seductively black as a length of old-fashioned liquorice! Without taking his eyes from it, Mr Grisham had stumbled into the changing room, barely remembering to shut and securely latch the door before anyone else could catch an eyeful.

The gentleman had remained standing on the wooden bench. Looking directly toward Mr Grisham, he had continued to stroke his incredible schlong, seemingly hypnotising the shop assistant with his slow forward and backward movements.

'No matter what I seem to do with it,' the gentleman had said in a half whisper, 'I don't seem to be able to appease it at all.'

Young Mr Grisham had eyed the thick length of meat like a mongoose preparing to tackle a large cobra. He had sucked on a lot of dicks in his time, but none quite this long and certainly none as gloriously black as was being presented to him at that moment in time. Still, he knew he was more than up for the unexpected challenge.

'I am pretty sure, sir, there are many ways of dealing with such a problem. In fact, at the moment, I can think of several immediately. So it will just be a case of trying to find the right method which works best.'

He had moved in closer, still fascinated by the slow movements of the Moroccan gentleman's hand. Without looking up, he asked, 'May I?'

'Please, feel free.'

The gentleman had released his cock from his hand, watching intently as Mr Grisham carefully wrapped his supple fingers around the dark shaft. It had been hot and twitching to the touch. The velvet smooth softness of the outer sheath moved gloriously over the iron-hard centre, and in one slow movement he had drawn the dark foreskin back, completely exposing the glistening head. Mr Grisham had leant forward and, as he gently blew on the tip, his thumb came up to massage and rub at the base of the fully exposed head.

Above him, he had heard the gentleman groan softly, pushing his hips forward, toward Mr Grisham. Continuing to position his head closer, Mr Grisham had moved down so that his lips were barely an inch away from the smooth and inviting glans. Seconds later, he had started to tease the slit and the swollen head with the firm, wet tip of his outstretched tongue.

The gentleman had stifled another collection of sounds as he arched his back and pushed his shoulders against the wall of the changing room. With hurried hands he had loosened his tie, unbuttoned his white shirt, and pulled the loose ends around his back, holding them there with his hands. It had exposed a glorious mat of pubic hair, and above it, the flat, slightly muscular stomach and smooth black chest. As he looked back down again, below his fingers young Mr Grisham had seen the slightly parted legs, and between them the pendulous, dark scrotum – its contents clearly outlined as they hung down and bounced against the gentleman's inner thighs.

Breathing heavily himself, the shop assistant had moved his hand down so that it was wrapped around the base of the wonderful shaft, then he proceeded to tongue-whip the head – teasing the sensitive underside, slapping his tongue across the top and sides before licking the shaft up and down in long, hard, wet strokes. Reaching down with his free hand he had carefully cupped the beautifully dark sack from below, taking the weight into the palm of his hand and rolling the contents gently with his fingers.

The Moroccan gentleman had brought one of his hands back around in front of him and pushed his fingers into Mr Grisham's hair, urging his head further into the gentleman's exposed groin. As he thrust his hips forward, he bit at his bottom lip, then whispered, 'Perhaps if you were to suck on it ...'

Without pausing, the young sales assistant had opened his mouth slightly and guided the swollen top to his lips. Slowly and deliberately he had popped the bulbous head in and out of his mouth until its rich blackness gleamed with saliva under the muted changing room lights.

In response, the gentleman again ran his fingers through Mr Grisham's hair, his voice cracking as he strained to keep it to a whisper. 'Yes. Ah, yes!'

Spurred on, young Mr Grisham had slowly worked more and more of the shaft into his eager mouth, his other hand now gently tugging on the Moroccan's scrotum, feeling it contract and its contents draw upward as he worked on it. As he repeatedly brought his head down he found the air around him becoming heavy with the smell of musky maleness. The sensation had made him work his jaw and lips all the more, his tongue sliding up and down the shaft as he started to take more and more of the glorious meat into his mouth with each head-bob. Then Mr Grisham had removed it completely, stroked it rapidly half a dozen times with his hand, then pushed it up so that it pressed firmly against the Moroccan gentleman's belly.

Bending further down, the sales assistant then started to lick and suck on the tightening sack – lapping at his heavy pouch and bouncing the contents around on the tip of his tongue, before sucking first one and then the other into his hot mouth. They had seemed so large that he felt he could only manage one in his mouth at a time! For a fleeting moment he had moved even further down, licking underneath, then digging his tongue in between the gentleman's legs. The sensation set the Moroccan gasping and moaning all the more, and he had spread himself wider, which allowed Mr Grisham to run his fingertips over and up the exposed flesh. Glancing up, he saw the gentleman's face and his expression of shocked ecstasy, his eyes half closed and his tongue flicking repeatedly over his lips.

With a feeling of pleasure rushing through him, Mr Grisham went back to work on the shiny black shaft. The gentleman's breathing had become steadily more rapid and heavy. In a frantic whisper, the Moroccan said, 'I don't think I can hold out much longer!'

Little did he know that the best was yet to come.

Mr Grisham had pushed the twitching, jerking shaft back into his mouth, worked on it with his lips and tongue so as to ensure it was properly wet and lubricated, then he began inching his lips further down the magnificent meat. He did his best to make his mouth into a vacuum and slowly sucked more and more of it in until, when he'd managed to take almost half of it, he had felt the tip of it as it banged up against the back of his throat. Consciously he had then relaxed his muscles and kept right on gulping and swallowing.

Above him, he had heard the Moroccan gentleman catch his breath several times, an incredulous expression on his face as he finally realised what was happening. Within seconds, Mr Grisham had felt the Moroccan's thighs flex, his buttocks clench and his scrotum pull itself up tight against his body as the sales assistant continued the pleasurable task of working his way down the midnight black shaft. Inch by swollen inch, he had taken more into his mouth and down his throat, enjoying the sensation as he slowly rocked his head back and forth.

Then young Mr Grisham knew it was time for the final push and eagerly thrust his head forward, gulping down the remaining few centimetres of this fantastic ebony prick. It slid down easy – the customer's entire cock now packed into the warm, wet tightness of the assistant's mouth and throat, his firm tongue sliding out under the shaft to poke and lap at the tightly constricted scrotum.

The sensations had finally proven too much. The Moroccan clenched his teeth as he did his best to choke back the sounds of his release, but his body jerked quite strongly as his load of hot come gushed down the young assistant's throat. He must have been saving it up for some time, because his body spasmed over and over, and with each twitching jerk came yet another load of hot jism. The sensation was exhilarating for Mr Grisham and sheer ecstasy for the Moroccan.

Eventually, his body stopped trembling, his knees regained some of their strength, and his cock shuddered with the aftershocks of joy. Dazed and disoriented for a moment, he finally let go of Mr Grisham's head and he watched in wonderment as the sales assistant slowly eased the softening shaft out of his throat, one delicious inch at a time. Finally, he had left only the head of it in his mouth. He sucked hard on it, milking it and swallowing the last few drops of the salty-sweet goodness, before letting it slip, deflated, from between his lips.

Standing upright, he had taken a clean handkerchief from his pocket, dabbed several times at his mouth, then proceeded to help the Moroccan gentleman down from the wooden bench.

As the gentleman had seated himself, still panting from the exertion of his release, young Mr Grisham said, 'I think sir will now find the trousers will fit much better than before. However –' he paused and glanced down at himself '– I seem to have developed a similar problem of my own.'

The gentleman had smiled broadly, again flashing the hint of gold amongst the whiteness of his teeth. 'It is an uncomfortable thing, is it not?' He raised a hand and stroked at the now prominent bulge at the front of Mr Grisham's own trousers. 'As you so kindly helped me out, I feel I owe you a debt of gratitude. If you would allow me to repay that debt?'

He had then slipped a hand underneath Mr Grisham's jacket, hooking his fingers over the waistband of his trousers, and had gently pulled the young sales assistant so he was standing directly in front of him. Still seated, the Moroccan had reached up and carefully unbuttoned Mr Grisham's jacket, pushing it wide so as to expose the neat waistcoat. Several more buttons later and the young assistant's belt buckle had been deftly undone. With the palm of his hand, he had again cupped the prominent bulge, and had felt it twitch and jerk in response.

With aching slowness, the Moroccan had teased and pulled at the zip, popping it open one tooth at a time, until completely undone. Then his hands were back up again, either side of Mr Grisham's hips, the thumbs hooked around the waistband of the trousers and Mr Grisham's underwear. He had slowly pushed the garments down beyond Mr Grisham's knees, then ran the flat of his hands back up his legs and thighs, slipping both thumbs between his legs, until his dextrous black hands slid in and around Mr Grisham's groin, the Moroccan's thumbs tucked up behind the sales assistant's hot scrotum.

He had opened his mouth wide and, without touching the shaft, he had brought his head over the top of the young assistant's erection, deliberately engulfing it in a cloud of warm, sweet breath.

Looking down, Mr Grisham had sighed involuntarily at the sight of the Moroccan's head close to his crotch, his own dark-veined shaft seemingly vanishing between sensuously wet lips. Then came the sweet sensation of thumbs rapidly tapping, rubbing, and vibrating against his scrotum and the root of his shaft, closely followed by the incredible heat as the Moroccan's mouth closed tightly onto his achingly hard cock.

Within moments the sales assistant had felt the tingling starting in his groin, his heart rate quickening, and his breath catching at the back of his throat almost every time in inhaled. The Moroccan's tongue had danced around, over, and even teased into the slit, but then the Moroccan had suddenly pulled his head back, allowing the young man's shaft to slide free.

Confused and frustrated, Mr Grisham had been about to say something when the Moroccan had firmly grasped the jerking shaft in his hand. Almost in a blur, his dark fist moved up and down, squeezing and pulling, his thumb sometimes coming over the top to be almost swallowed up by the young assistant's foreskin as the Moroccan worked the ball of his thumb against the sensitive head.

The sight from above and sensation of the dark hand wrapped around his cock had been enough to push him over the edge, and the tingling from around his tightened scrotum had given him barely enough time to say, 'I'm coming!'

But, instead of pulling away, the Moroccan had moved his face closer, his fist slamming firmly into the young man's groin before sliding itself upwards again in quick succession, squeezing and pulling as it went. It had been too much even for him to control, and when the Moroccan's other hand had slipped hotly between Mr Grisham's legs he had been left with little choice but to shoot gobbet after gobbet of white-hot come across the Moroccan's dark face and into his eagerly open mouth.

Some ten minutes later, once Mr Grisham had readjusted his clothing and helped the Moroccan gentleman wipe his face and get dressed again, they had exited the changing room one at a time so as not to attract attention.

Over by the till, young Mr Grisham had the pleasure of ringing up several items for the Moroccan gentleman, now back in his flattering houndstooth jacket, shirt, tie, and slacks. As the sales assistant had processed the gentleman's credit card he had also reached into his jacket pocket and pulled out a slim, silver business card case. He had extracted a card and, before presenting it, he turned it over. On the back, in a flourish of penmanship, he had written a phone number.

Smiling broadly, he handed the card over, saying, 'If you have any further problems with any of your new purchases, sir, please do not hesitate to call, and I will see what I can do to help. It's all part of the Marquis & Delaney experience. We consider customer satisfaction to be the biggest part of our aftersales service …'

The Hung Games
by Elizabeth Coldwell

The chain feels heavy in my hand. I stroke the cold metal links as I wait, watching a watery sun rise over the city's broken skyline. I would've preferred rope as part of my armoury – more flexible, lighter to carry, especially when you've been on your feet for two days straight – but that had already been allocated, so you just have to make the best of what you're given.

My stomach rumbles, but I resist the urge to unwrap my last protein bar. Physical hunger doesn't bother me so much, nor thirst; the appetite I'm really aching to satisfy is the one that has my cock swelling, aching to bury itself in a hot mouth or the tight crevice of a welcoming arse. I thought I'd prepared myself for whatever the game could throw at me, but the one thing no one ever told me was just how horny I'd get. It's my own fault, I suppose; when Wade was taken while I crouched in my hiding place in the bushes, a matter of metres away, I should have resisted the urge to watch.

Though it still surprises me that Wade went down with so little of a fight. When we all came together at the starting line, everyone had him pegged as the winner of this year's game. The TV and live streaming crews fighting to stick their microphones under his nose clearly seemed to think so. Who could blame them? He had everything the audience loves. A professional footballer in the days before everything fell apart, he'd retained a fit, athletic body well into his late 30s. With bulging muscles, velvet-smooth black skin, and chin-length hair woven into dozens of tiny braids, who couldn't fail to be attracted to him? My cock had given an appreciative twitch as I watched him shrug into the earth-toned combat gear that was the standard uniform of the games, admiring the broad, sinewy expanse of his back and his round, firm arse. If I was to meet my fate at the hands of any of the men here, I'd rather it was Wade, confident in his abilities but not too cocky, than Darien – cold, arrogant, and never less than completely in control. Darien had been the champion for the last four years; here was the man who seemed destined to dethrone him.

Except it hasn't worked like that. One by one, all the challengers have been hunted down and dispatched. Now I am the only one who remains, and I don't know how much longer I can stay a step ahead of Darien.

Though I can't see them, I know cameras are on my every move, relaying feeds from across the length and breadth of the arena. This place was once the site of the Olympic Games, back when I was a kid, but it has long since fallen into ruin. The huge, formerly state-of-the-art stadium is now a ruined steel and concrete shell, while the formal parkland is overgrown with straggling weeds, and home to feral dogs that are every bit as much of a threat as the human competitors in this game. I'm certain eyes are on me now, the director cutting between Darien and me as the final battle, the climax of this eagerly watched contest, approaches.

Hearing what sounds like the snap of a twig beneath an approaching foot, I press myself against the weathered trunk of an ash tree. As skilfully as I've tried to conceal my tracks on my way down to the relative sanctuary of the riverbank, with its sheltering reed beds, it seems Darien has found and followed them. A conversation floats back to my mind; one I had with the boys as we sat crowded round the computer monitor in Fox's apartment, watching the coverage of last year's games.

'That Darien, man,' someone – it might have been Mickey – had said, helping himself to another couple of fingers of Fox's bathtub gin. 'The way he finds them all, it's like he's got superhuman powers. Whatever they do, wherever they hide, they just can't get away from him.'

'That's 'cos it's all a fix,' Fox had asserted, voice slurring slightly from the potency of his home-made booze. 'There's someone watching the feeds, telling him where the other contestants are. If the guy wasn't so popular with the audience, he'd have been taken down long before now.'

'How do you know this?' Mickey sounded scornful, even though he loved a good conspiracy theory as much as the next man.

'One of the other guys in enforcement, well, his ex-girlfriend used to be a runner on the show. She told him everything, but swore him to secrecy, and not just so she wouldn't lose her job. I mean, people would go mad if the truth got out. They love the idea that someone's going to come along and take Darien down, but they love the fact he always wins in the end even more.'

I bite back a sour laugh. At the time, I'd been just as sceptical as Mickey, but that was before I went for my annual medical assessment. Whatever notes the doctor scribbled on my form led to my being called up for this year's game. I hadn't been able to refuse – not when the alternative was three years' prison time – and I duly took my place alongside the other seven hopefuls hoping to dethrone Darien. Now, as I crouch among the reeds, tired and in dire need of a hot shower, listening to those soft footfalls come ever closer, I can't help wondering if Fox was right. Has someone told Darien where I'm hiding and, if so, what chance do I have of escaping him?

Keeping my wits about me is half the battle. I clutch the length of chain tighter in my hand, partly for reassurance, partly because it's the only weapon I have. Darien has the rope – and now I wonder if he really did get it through random chance, or if that too was preordained. He wields it like a pro, just like he does everything.

'Hey, Venness, I'm coming for you!' It's Darien's trademark cry, guaranteed to strike fear into the souls of his opponents when he calls their name. Usually, it's the last thing anyone hears before he bears down on them, and I know he's got to be almost on top of me now. But he hasn't yet spotted me, as I flatten myself a little closer to the boggy ground, feeling dampness seep through my combat gear to add to all the little miseries that make surviving the game for any length of time such a challenge. The TV helicopter is circling, its blades making a relentless chopping sound above my head. They have night vision, thermal imaging; they must know where I am. And if Fox is right, they can relay that information to Darien any time they like.

Peering out from my hiding place, I see booted feet, squelching in the mud. He's so close, and still he doesn't see me. I've only got one chance here, and I've got to make the most of it, because once he knows where I am, it's all over. Somewhere close by, a bird lets out a raucous caw. Darien turns in the direction of the noise – whether he thinks it's me, calling in an attempt at parley, I have no idea, but he's distracted just long enough for me to throw the chain across his path in a haphazard loop. When he steps forward again, his foot lands in the circle of links, and I tug hard, pulling the chain toward me and sending him sprawling.

Seeing the big man lying in the mud is shocking, having built him up in my mind into some invincible stalking machine, but I know I've only got a moment to press home my advantage. Leaping out from the reeds, I fling myself on top of him, using my full weight to hold him down while I wrestle the rope from his belt.

'Venness, what the fuck do you think you're playing at?' he roars, wriggling beneath me in an attempt to shake me loose. But I'm running on adrenaline and pure exhilaration; the feeling of having brought the champion low gives me a strength I never knew I possessed till now. Wrestling first one of his wrists, then the other, into the small of his back, I loop the rope around them, tying it almost painfully tight. Having caught him, there's no way I'm letting him slip free.

But having him trussed and helpless on the ground is only half of what's required. I have to finish this.

'Get up – now,' I order him in a voice rich with sudden authority, smacking the end of the chain on the ground to emphasise the urgency of the action. He looks around him, as if expecting someone to emerge from the neighbouring bushes and come to his assistance, and for a moment I actually wonder if he does have unseen help to call on. Nothing would surprise me any longer, in the light of Fox's claims about these games. But, at last, he gets to his knees, mud smeared on his craggily handsome face and bits of twig caught in his thick, golden-red hair. I don't think I've ever seen the man look more vulnerable – or more attractive. My cock pushes at the crotch of my combat pants as a strong thrill of power and arousal runs through me.

'OK, over to that tree.' I gesture to a sturdy-trunked oak. When he doesn't immediately move to obey, I kick at the back of his leg to encourage him. It's a petty little action, sure, but I'm not just doing this for me any more; this is for Wade, and all the rest of the fallen, this year and every year that Darien has dominated the game.

He takes the hint, shuffling over with his arms roped securely behind his back. A long, thick branch extends out, a little more than head height from the ground. I loop the chain over it once, twice. If Darien wondered why I'd left plenty of rope free when tying his wrists together, he wonders no more. Those lengths are quickly secured to the dangling ends of the chain. It's an unorthodox way of holding him steady, and hardly the most secure, but it doesn't need to be. The relative lack of fight from the big man, and the look in his eyes as I stare at him, tells me he's accepted his fate.

Even though I can't see them, the cameras will be trained us on now. I can't imagine what people are saying in the studio, or in their homes. Everyone's been waiting for the moment Darien finishes this, and claims his rightful place as winner of the game; now here we are, with the roles reversed. This is my moment, and I'm determined to enjoy it to the full.

Grasping the neck of Darien's shirt in both hands, I start to pull. The material's more flimsy than is really practical in the circumstances, designed to tear. It takes almost no effort on my part to rip the garment in two, exposing the tanned, hairless expanse of his chest. His pecs and abdominal muscles have been sculpted through endless hours of working out – as champion, with the financial backing of the channel's sponsors behind him, his full-time job consists of bulking up his body and practising his combat techniques – and the ridges are so deliciously defined, I ache to run my tongue along them. But not just yet.

Darien issues a little moan as I reach for his pants. They present more of a challenge than the shirt, but with a yank that sends his fly button pinging into the undergrowth, I tear those to shreds too. He wears nothing beneath them – none of us does, it's one of the rules of the game – and his cock is immediately exposed to me, and the eyes of the watching millions. We've all seen it before, as it breaches the arse of some vanquished contestant or other, and we've acquainted ourselves with its impressive dimensions, but in the flesh it's even more magnificent – long and thick despite only being half-hard, its juicy, purple head peeping out from the covering sleeve of flesh.

This is the true point of the games, the reason viewers tune in year after year. Not so much for the thrill of the chase, the relentless pursuit of weaker prey by a truly dominant male, but to see one big-cocked stud after another brought low and stripped bare. That the man who now hangs obediently in his bonds, displayed for all to see, is Darien, the seemingly invincible, must only add to the thrill.

Aware of their need for flesh, I peel out of my own combat gear. The morning isn't warm, and goosepimples rise on my skin as I toss my shirt to the ground. The pants follow, leaving me standing in nothing but my heavy black boots, the leather scuffed and worn from two days of running and hiding. But it's not my boots the audience will be interested in. I pause for a moment, giving so many unseen eyes the chance to absorb the sight of me, and compare me to Darien. I may stand a head shorter than him, but in the department where – for the viewers at least – it really matters, I know I'm his equal. Already beginning to stiffen, stirred by my victory and the thrilling prospect of giving Darien the hard, masterful fuck we both know he needs, my cock is, I'm sure, what prompted the doctor's excited scribbling and my subsequent call-up to this year's game. In the end, it's not bravery that matters, or skill in combat, or even the easy good looks that the likes of Wade possess: it all comes down to how well hung you are.

Darien's tongue flickers out, wetting his lips, and I'm certain he's eyeing me with the same greedy speculation as the audience at home. Only they'll have to imagine how it feels to have my cock sliding into whichever orifice I choose, to touch and taste it; Darien will have that pleasure first-hand.

I hunt in the concealed pocket of my pants, and fish out the lubricant we're all given as part of our supplies. The first couple of years they broadcast the games, they gave the contestants condoms too, until they started getting complaints that they were spoiling the experience for the viewers. So now we're all subjected to tests beforehand, letting us fuck each other bareback without fear of any consequences.

But sexual diseases aren't the most immediate of my problems. There's the small matter of a significant height difference to overcome if I'm to fuck Darien in the standing position that will give everyone watching the best view of the action. The solution is to haul over a heavy, flat-topped chunk of rock and place it behind him. When I clamber up on it, my groin is pretty much level with his luscious arse. It might not be dignified, but it's practical – which has been my strategy throughout the game, when I think about it.

I spend a long while lubing myself up, wondering if the cameras are lingering on the sight of my fingers as they spread the slippery goo along my shaft. If not then, they certainly do when I turn my attentions to Darien's arsehole, repeating the process there.

'You want this, don't you?' I murmur into his ear, not caring whether I've pitched my voice at a level the microphones will pick up.

Darien barely hesitates before replying, 'Yes.'

My finger pushes at his pucker, meeting only a token resistance. 'Yes what?'

'Yes, sir.'

Those words do deserve a wider hearing. 'I can't hear you.'

'Yes, sir,' he repeats, louder this time. That's the moment I know I'm the champion. Darien has acquiesced to me; the most successful contestant in the history of the games finally conceding that he's been mastered.

I drop my voice to a whisper, ensuring only he can hear. 'Then let the real game begin.'

My finger probes deeper, exploring his tight, dark passage. As I feel him begin to relax, slowly opening up, I add a second finger. This isn't what the audience might have been expecting; Darien's tactics have never involved this kind of slow, almost loving build-up. Hard and rough, that's the way he's played it till now. But I want both of us to enjoy this, and forcing myself into a hole that's not ready, even with the aid of lube, doesn't get me off. Maybe they've cut to commercials, planning to come back when the serious fucking begins; I don't care. All I know is that when I grasp Darien's cock in my other hand, easing lube-sticky fingers up and down that fine, upstanding length, he groans.

'God, Venness, that feels so good.'

'You like that?' I ask. His only reply is a nod and another groan, this one sounding like it's wrenched from a place deep within him. 'Yeah? Well, it's going to feel even better when my cock slides into that hot, slick arse of yours.'

'Don't tease me,' he begs. 'Just do it. Fuck me. Fuck me, please, sir.'

What has happened to the dominant Darien from all the previous games? The man who fought and fucked without mercy; who took what – and who – he wanted? Vanquished and gone, it seems. Am I seeing the man's true character, as he submits to my desires so willingly? Whether that's the case – that he's just been playing the part the games' production company required of him all these years – or not, I'm revelling in the power I now have over him, power he has ceded up to me from the moment I brought him low and roped his wrists.

'Are you sure?' I ask, tormenting him with the slow back and forth motion of my wanking fingers. 'Don't you want to wait just a little longer?'

'God, no!' he blurts. 'I need you inside me. Need to be fucked with that huge cock.'

The urgency in his tone sends a fierce jolt of desire through my body. My balls feel heavy with seed, and I know just where I want to discharge their potent load. I pull my fingers out of Darien's hole, and guide my cock into place. He registers the sensation of something big seeking to enter him, and writhes in his bonds. But he's not pulling away. Instead, he's pushing his arse back at my helmet where it seeks to enter him, desperate to be filled.

One firm thrust, and I'm inside that clutching chute, caught in its tight, hot embrace. With short, stabbing movements of my hips I bury myself as far as I can, amazed at how much of my length Darien can take. My hand still grips Darien's dick, and as I start to fuck him, it slides in the slick tunnel formed by my fingers, giving him all the stimulation he needs.

Even though I know millions are watching us at this moment, somehow it still feels like it's just the two of us; me shunting hard into Darien's arse, him bucking back, seeking to have even more of me inside him. Sweat gleams on the vast, muscled expanse of his back, and his breathing is as shallow and tortured as mine. The silent parkland resounds to the noise of our bodies slapping together, the grunts and moans and throaty exhortations from Darien for me to give him everything, shoot my load into his hungry arse.

Knowing this is the only chance I'll ever have to fuck him, before he disappears into whatever life awaits the losers of this game, I want to make this last. But I can't hold back a moment longer. Every nerve-ending feels like it's screaming at me to give in to my orgasm. Pulling out so I can give the audience their money shot, even though I desire nothing more than to fill Darien with my spunk, I come instead over those firm arse cheeks, branding them with streaks of thick, hot come.

A few tugs of my fingers is all I can manage as post-orgasm languor threatens to overcome me, but they're enough to make Darien come too, his seed jetting out to paint the rough ground at our feet. I cling to him, hearing his heaving sighs subside and his heartbeat slow, then I take charge of the situation, ready to bring my prize scalp home.

'Thank you,' he murmurs as I release him from his bondage. 'For giving me my life back.'

'I'm sorry?' It's not what I expected to hear from him, to say the least.

'I've had a good run, but I'd decided it was time. The production company wanted me to come back for another year after this one, but I don't need this any more. I'm set up for life as it is.' The implications of what he's saying must register on my face, because he laughs. 'Come on, Venness, didn't it occur to you when you pulled that stupid little stunt with your chain that I could have put up more of a fight if I'd wanted to?'

He stands, rubbing his wrists to ease the ache that's built while they've been held in one position for so long, but he makes no move to dress. It's another of the rules – the vanquished have to make their way out of the arena naked, just to complete their humiliation. Though for some reason I get the feeling Darien doesn't mind that too much.

'Believe me, you're still a worthy champion. After all,' he continues, tone almost thoughtful now, 'for a guy of your size you've got a hell of an endowment. The audience is going to love watching you pound the losers' arses with that thing.'

For the first time, I realise this isn't over. Yes, I've defeated the mighty Darien and won the game, even if I've done it on his terms. But that's only the beginning. They'll want me back next year to defend my crown. I'll be forced to chase down a group of hot, well-hung young men and fuck them all into submission if I want to win again. And I'll get to find out what advantages are handed to the reigning champion to aid him in that process. Fox might be right; this game might well be fixed. But if it's fixed in my favour, I think I'm going to enjoy playing by those rules.

Chocolates at the Sun Garden Hotel
by D.K. Jernigan

Traffic on 42nd Street began to open up, and a car pulled out of a space right in front of the hotel at just the right second. I parallel parked my delivery car with practiced efficiency, ignoring the assholes who felt that honking might encourage me to hurry out of their way.

The chocolates I was delivering to room 1436 of the Sun Garden were some of the best we sell. I may not be much more than a glorified delivery boy yet, but the confectioner I worked for was teaching me the ropes, and the cocoa-dusted truffles in the box I was carrying were some of the best. Ever.

I hopped out of the car, gathered up the correct box, and went straight to the bank of elevators on the far side of the lobby, nodding politely to the concierge as I walked by.

Outside the correct door, I gave my uniform a quick once-over, brushed out a wrinkle, and stood, fastening my best smile on my face and presenting the box before me as I knocked. I stood frozen that way for a long moment, and just before I would have raised my hand to knock again, the door cracked open. I bumped up the wattage on my smile and took a deep breath to announce my delivery when the sight of the man behind the door knocked the wind right out of my chest.

Everet, my boyfriend of three years, stood behind the

door in all his naked glory, his gorgeously dark cock jutting out in an elegant sculpture of arousal and virility. I couldn't suck enough air into my lungs and, as the blood drained from my face, I thought I was going to faint.

'This is how you break up with me?' I whispered. I was conscious of the dozens of potential witnesses hiding behind the doors that lined the hall.

Everet's face turned upside down as his saucy grin slid into shock and dismay. 'God, no!' He grabbed me by my shirt front and pulled me into the room, slamming the door behind us, and me into it, a second later. The breath I had started to draw huffed out of me again as the door, then Everet's kiss, folded my lungs neatly shut.

'This is how I get you all to myself for a whole afternoon,' he purred against my neck, kissing his way from my collarbone to my earlobe and back again. Since most of my blood was already pooled in my stomach (after draining from my face a moment ago), it didn't have far to go to get to my cock. I moaned and let my head drop back against the door, surrendering to the sensations. Everet zeroed in on my weakness – a spot just behind my ear – and my knees turned to water even as my cock pulsed harder.

'You're going to get me fired,' I managed. I was still trying to wrap my head around the sudden reversal of fate that had sent me from despondent to horny in record time.

'No, I'm not.' He nipped at my earlobe. 'Because *I* –' nip '– called Ricardo –' nip '– and arranged for a little surprise time off.' He backed away and grinned broadly. 'Surprise!' Only someone who knew him as well as I did would have seen the apology in his eyes for the way his good deed had gone slightly awry.

'What about the car? My deliveries –' I began, not

wanting to go down the road of responsibility, but knowing I had to.

'He told me he'd send Sammi with the spare set of keys,' Everet said, leading me toward the bed. 'She's probably already down there driving away. Which means you're stuck with me ...'

'It's her day off,' I murmured, dazed with pleasure already. He ignored me.

He stopped in front of the bed, but, before he could so much as reach for my first button, I was on my knees, devouring his cock as if it were one of the chocolates that lay neglected where I had dropped them, just inside the door. Funny, I thought, I don't remember letting them go. But for the moment his cock was all that mattered.

He moaned as I took him deep into my throat, swallowing around him as the smooth chocolate flesh slid over my tongue and past, into the back of my throat. I took one deep, steady breath, then held it as his cock moved deep enough to block my airway – until he was all the way inside me, groaning and rocking his hips into me. My face was buried in his wiry curls, and I eased back enough to breathe deeply, taking in his unique masculine scent mixed with the cocoa aroma that I carried with me.

Then I slid onto him again. The muscles of my throat contracted and squeezed as I swallowed, milking him and teasing him, suppressing my urge to cough or gag with practised will. It was sublime, feeling him in me that way, knowing that I was welcoming him in and giving him the gift of pleasure. His gasps and moans confirmed that I was hitting all the right buttons, and I resisted the urge to grin around his cock. Instead, I licked and teased with my tongue, making love to his shaft as my throat gripped and massaged his tip.

'Stop it,' he said. 'I'm not ready.' He leant back, but he was already standing against the bed, and couldn't step back any farther. I was going to have to take a breath soon, anyway, but until I did ... I sucked harder, making my whole mouth caress him. 'Stop! I'm gonna come. Jonah!'

But it was too late for him. I eased back, sucking and caressing all the while, inhaling deeply through my nose as he cleared my throat. That meant that I could tease his tip with my tongue, flicking against the rim of his head and teasing at his slit. I was rewarded by a flood of salt and heat across my tongue, flowing down into my throat, and by Everet's cry of pleasure as his orgasm took him. He threw back his head and cried out, and I didn't let him go until his knees buckled and he sank to the bed, pulling his cock free of my mouth with the movement.

'Damn it, Jonah, I wasn't ready yet,' he said, but he was smiling as he said it.

'Seemed pretty ready to me,' I answered with a cocky grin. He snorted and swatted at me, and I stood up and quickly shed my clothes as the combination of relief and arousal made me light-headed and giddy. 'So, Sammi has my shift.'

'Uh-huh,' he answered. He'd flung an arm over his eyes and was breathing deeply, soaking in the pleasure, perhaps, or regaining his equilibrium for a second go. I took a moment to enjoy the sight of him limp with pleasure, his dark body stretched across the sheets, powerful muscles relaxed and gorgeous.

'And I have the whole rest of the day off?' I bent over him and licked a trail from his belly to one dark nipple, and he groaned in what I assumed was an affirmative. 'Sneaky bastard,' I teased. I bit down on his nipple, just hard enough to make him groan, and then got up and walked away. He grumbled a complaint at my retreat, but his tune changed a moment later when I returned with the box of chocolates and held one cocoa-dusted treat to his lips. He opened his mouth with a much happier sound, and his entire body reacted with pleasure when the chocolate melted in his mouth.

'Holy shit, Jonah, this one of yours?'

'I helped,' I answered, ever modest. It *was* one of mine, though. Ricardo has supervised my efforts, but this particular batch had been my handiwork, and it was a fine bit of chocolate. I popped one into my own mouth and groaned as I bit down, the experience almost orgasmic as the bitter and the sweet blended perfectly on my tongue. My cock was hard, aching, and somehow the chocolate only intensified the erotic feelings coiling in my belly.

I bent over Everet again, helping him scoot his way up the bed as I climbed on top of him. 'I want you,' I said.

'Of course you do.'

I shut him up with a kiss, hot enough to sear me to the core. He reached between us to circle my cock with his fist, pumping gently, and I moaned and rocked my hips in time to his attentions. His mouth tasted of cocoa and sugar, and our tongues twined and explored, lazy and content, even as our bodies told a different story of tension and need.

My body won the argument. My balls were tight against me, my cock rock-solid and fiery with demand. I shifted until I was between his legs, and reached for the little bottle of lube and the box of condoms Everet had left on the nightstand. Obviously my boy had come prepared ... I knocked the box over in my haste but managed to snag one strip of condoms and tore one off, rolling it on in careful haste as Everet shifted and moaned, lifting his hips to offer himself to me.

'Shit.' I was so aroused that I could barely think – so ready for him that my cock burnt under my touch as I slicked myself with lube. 'Shit, Ev, you look so good …' Like my own personal gourmet chocolate – and I was about to eat him up.

My cock slid easily into his passage, and we both groaned as I thrust slowly into him, past his tight ring of muscles and deep, deep into his body, until the curls of my pubic hair tickled his ass. His cock stirred, not hard yet, but swelling as I rocked back and thrust deep within him again.

'How do you want to do this?' I asked, teasing him. I pulled out, slowly, slowly, and buried myself again just as slowly. 'You want to take some time? Take it slow?'

'God damn it, Jonah!' Everet never wanted it slow. Everet wanted to be pounded into the mattress, and fucked until his teeth rattled. I pulled back again, still teasing, and he opened his eyes enough to glare at me. 'Damn it, fuck me!'

'You didn't say please,' I said. I pulled all the way out to tease my cock against his hole, making him growl with frustration before I pushed my way in again, penetrating him slowly.

He tried to push back against me, but I put a hand on his hips and held him at bay, keeping my pace teasing and torturous. To be honest, it was almost as torturous for me, but it was worth it to see him writhe and moan as he grew ever more desperate for me. Served him right for scaring me out of my mind, earlier.

But my desire for him was burning hot, and I wasn't going to be able to hold off for ever, however satisfying it was to tease him.

'Please! Fucking please, OK? Fuck me. Please, fuck

me!'

It was all I needed to hear. I plunged forward, spearing him on my cock and thrusting deeply into him, again and again. He groaned beneath my assault, bringing his knees up for a better angle. My cock throbbed with the desire to let loose, but I held myself in check, forcing myself to take my time and enjoy every moment as I slammed into him.

He clenched around me, gripping me with his inner muscles and teasing me closer to the edge. My body responded, and I fisted my hands in the bedding, desperately holding back as Everet cried out beneath me.

'Fuck! Yes!'

His eyes rolled back as he surrendered to the fierce sensations, and I gasped as I did the same, finally losing my grip on control. My balls tightened and pleasure washed through me, over me, drowning me as if a truffle had melted on my tongue, carrying me away in a flood of endorphins and a rush of adrenaline. Fuck. Yes.

I eased back from him a moment later and got rid of the condom. When I returned, I placed another truffle against his lips, and he sucked it into his mouth, sighing in pleasure. 'All day, you said?' I asked him. At that point it was bravado, since I was fucking exhausted, but if we had all day …

Everet gave a chuckle. 'We've got a Jacuzzi in the bathroom,' he murmured without opening his eyes. 'And I'm almost ready for round two.'

I wrapped my hand around his thickening cock as I curled close against his body. 'So you are.' All day …

The Age of Indolence
by Lynn Lake

I knew I was in for quite an evening when the four young men greeted me at the front door of my friend's home and promptly stripped off my clothes. They were starkly naked, themselves.

'Clive, how good to see you!' my friend, Bertrand Toddy, exclaimed, rushing out of the parlour to warmly clasp my hand in his. His lips found mine, as well, wet and writhing.

'That's quite the welcome!' I gushed, nodding at the four young men who had now assembled behind my totally nude host in the hallway of his home.

'They *are* a delight, aren't they?' Bertrand responded proudly.

He swung an arm around my shoulder, clapped a hand to my cock, and gently tugged on the swelling appendage, both of us admiring his new men. 'I discovered them in the country, not far from here. They were working on a farm – well, sunning themselves like Grecian gods around a pond, truth be told – and I knew for certain they'd be perfect for my next play, *Gaily Go the Boys Through the Countryside*. They're all of legal consenting age, I assure you.' He licked his lips, mine, smiling broadly.

I returned his smile, and his lick, just as excitedly, the man's hot, tugging hand on my cock hardening me to pulsating proportions below the waist. I well knew that Bertrand Toddy was skilled with his hands, being an erotic playwright, equally adept with his mouth, being an erotic orator. His skills as a pornographic photographer were renowned, as well, especially in the more open societies of Greece and France.

Victorian Britain embraced him too, mind you, though on the sly; which only served to make things naughtier. A big man, with a shock of red hair and a rubbery face and expressive body, he had an absolute passion for the finer, perverted things in life. Which I shared with him, as often as my work as an MP allowed.

'You shall have to invite me to the opening,' I declared, planting the seed. The sensualist's homoerotic hospitality was notoriously legendary.

He nodded his head, as we stared at the naked young men, his hand swirling the length of my pulsing rod.

The boys were of almost uniform height and weight: that is to say, lithely built, slender, and supple. Their youthful bodies were bronzed from the sun's caresses, their pretty faces blushing immodestly from the caress of Bertrand's and my combined gaze. Two of them had dark hair and doe-brown eyes, the other two were blond and blue-eyed.

'Allow me to formally introduce you!' Bertrand suddenly ejaculated, releasing my cock and springing in behind the young men. He examined their derrieres, then winked at me.

'This is Thomas,' he said, grasping the shoulders of the brown-haired lad at one end of the line-up. He caressed the slim neck of the blond next to Thomas. 'And this is William.' He stroked the smooth arm of the black-haired boy standing to William's left. 'And Everett.' Bertrand moved over and playfully slapped the ass of the young man at the opposite end, then cuddled the blond's cock with his hand. 'And this is George,' he informed me happily.

I received the information joyously, though I dare say I had a difficult time memorising the names, what with those glowing, nude reflections of young manhood all in a row right in front of me, dizzying and delighting my senses. My cock twitched from my loins as if I were aboard the male express from Donnybrook, my pink-hued nipples protruding, body warm as though before a roaring fire.

'You will get to know them better, fear not.' Bertrand further heated my ears and harkened my heart. 'But first, we dine!'

We supped in style, for sure. Garden salad, beef barley soup, battered cod and rice, roasted game hen and potatoes, fresh fruits and hand-poured chocolates, rich, steaming coffee. The food was salivatingly satisfying, the sight of the boys serving us even more so. My erection rattled the dining board almost continually, watching the young men enter and leave, hungrily eyeing their clean-cut, bobbing cocks, their rippling, mounded buttocks, the rest of their sinuous, sensuous bodies and pretty, pleasing faces. I ate with ferocious appetite, till my belly and balls were both full to bursting at the conclusion of the awesome repast.

We repaired to the parlour, where, clutching glasses of fine brandy in one hand and fully engorged cocks in the other, Bertrand regaled me with scene descriptions from his new play, had the four young men act out what he intended. My attention was riveted, my cock in my pumping hand aroused to epic proportions, as the boys playfully wrestled with one another in the "discovery" scene; then tentatively kissed in the "awakening" scene;

and, at last, intensely stroked and sucked and frotted in the "coming-of-age" scene.

Their gleaming pink tongues twined eagerly together, their urgent young hands excitedly exploring their bodies, their impassioned, wet mouths consuming swollen, hard cocks, using those cocks to superbly shift up and down downy cracks between divinely piled-up golden buttocks. Their acting was strikingly realistic, hitting me hard in the groin, as they truthfully captured the wickedly intense emotions and movements of blossomed gay lust.

I mouthed "Bravo!", fisting my manhood, as Thomas and William, and Everett and George, curled up in separate 69 positions on the parlour floor and sucked one another's cocks with obvious pleasure for one and all. Their plush, red lips pulled pneumatically on swollen shafts and swelled-up hoods, silky hands grasping firm young buttocks and thighs, gilded heads bobbing with the erotic enthusiasm of youth.

I applauded with one hand, stroking my vibrating dong and squeezing my boiling balls and tingling nipples with the other.

'This will surely be your finest play yet, Bertrand!' I exulted.

He tilted his head modestly, jacking his own towering erection with breathtaking speed. Then he arose from his chair, set down his snifter, and set free his cock. He walked closer to the huddled, sucking young men and looked down at them. 'Yes, I think so too.' He turned to me, his cock meeting my eye a split second later. 'Shall I recite my latest poem to you – *Cock of the Walk*? I'm afraid it's the boys' bedtime.'

I feared that. I slowed my hand on my raging hard-on, and swallowed with equal difficulty, as the four young men disengaged and stood up. Their succulent pricks glistened with saliva, their beautiful faces were flushed with the fever of performance. 'Yes, yes ... Of course, of course,' I gasped.

'Bid the gentleman goodnight, then, boys.'

They swarmed around me in my armchair, kissing me on the forehead and cheeks and lips and nipples, the cock and balls. Tongues flashed wetly around scrotum and shaft, the naughty young sprites. I surged and shimmered, filling my grasping hands with as much hot flesh and heated appendage as I could, before Bertrand slapped their bubbled bottoms and sent them scurrying off up the stairs of his home.

The eroticist then assumed a position of oration by the mantelpiece, his new poem in his hand. I assumed a position of aural posture at his cock, the better to suck on his member as he mouthed his latest explicit creation.

He began reciting, and I took his cock in hand, stroked the turgid, purple-headed tool, gripping its heft and groping its length. And as his obscene rhymes rattled in my head, I twirled my outstretched tongue around his cockhead, lapped at his shaft; then sucked up as much of his massive manhood as I could and tugged with my lips and mouth and licked with my tongue.

I must confess, however, that even as I rejoiced at his words and cock, my addled mind was still upon the four young men, replaying in my brain their erotic entreaties of earlier, picturing their perfect young bodies and faces and maturely hard dongs. The stunning scene I'd witnessed was one I just couldn't shake, no matter how in how bellicose a fashion Bertrand spoke or how belligerently I sucked on his throbbing cock and twisted his shaven balls and jutting nipples.

The man soon read my dirty, dizzy mind, being the

pornographer par excellence, empathetically realising that my mouth and hands were just going through the motions. He broke off his seductive soliloquy to shrewdly observe, 'My boys made quite an impression on you, eh? Perhaps you would like to wish them a more intimate goodnight in their room?'

I popped his cock out, licked up some of the stringing slobber. 'Oh, I say, Bertrand, I'm terribly sorry if –'

He waved his hand and his cock. 'Go ahead, old boy. Go ahead.' He bobbed his wise head and wettened dong. 'We'll be waiting for you down here, fear not.'

I sprang up out of my crouch and turned tail and raced up the stairs. Gaining the second floor hallway, I streaked down the carpeted length to the open bedroom door at the end. The young men were not in the blissful grip of the sandman at all. Rather, they were grappling with one another again, naked on the spacious feather bed, their bronze limbs flinging and flailing, bold cocks bouncing and banging against each other, pressing into hot flesh. My sharp intake of air caught their ears, and they instantly flung themselves inert upon their stomachs, four golden boys with four sets of cheeky buttocks all in a row.

'I – I just came to – '

'Kiss us goodnight!' they chimed as one, giggling into their pillows. They all then reached back simultaneously and sunk their slender fingers into their taut buttocks, spread the caramel mounds, revealing four pert puckers.

It was a sight to put starch in the sturdiest of even a straight man's phallus. The boys' smooth, slender, sunkissed bodies laid out on the bed side by side, bum to bum, their cute, curvy feet and tapered, tender toes tilted upwards, their stretched back-hillocks clasped between burning white fingers, their bared, blossomed buttholes ablaze with virginal pinkness. I swallowed the lump in my throat and trembled to the thump in my chest, my cock snapping almost straight up into the air, rigid as the flagpole on the *HMS Himafore*.

I approached the bed of boys on quivering limbs, mounted it, straddled my weakened knees in between William's legs on one side and Thomas's on the other. Then I relieved the pressure, somewhat, of William's hands on his buttocks with my hands, bent my creaking neck and blood-thundered head down and kissed the lad's delectable starfish. He shivered and whimpered. I sent my tongue in after my lips, rimming his adorable bumhole, squirming my wet appendage inside his anus, exploring the young man's ass-tunnel with writhing excitement. He responded with rapid shaking and breathing, his fingers flaming beneath mine on his quivering rump-rounds.

I lifted my head and licked my lips, ogling the young man's rosebud, which I'd made glisten. Then I thrust down my head and stuck out my tongue a second time, targeting Thomas's pink manhole this time. I painted the outer pucker and inner tunnel with my tongue, delighting in the taste and tremble of this boy. He pushed his bum back, burying my eager, flaming face between his hot, wholesome cheeks. I burrowed as deep into his sexual depths as I could with my licker, worming it around in his rectum to his obvious pleasure and mine.

Everett and George were next, anxiously awaiting my most intimate kiss. I tongued Everett's asshole, making him spasm with joy, his pucker wink round my pink probe. Then I gripped his hands on his cheeks still harder and licked up and down his bum crack, lapping the soft, sensitive cleft between his buttocks, bathing the zone with my tongue over and over again. Until his impudent young globes shivered spasmodically in my damp clutches, his downy butt valley gleaming with my ardour. I tongued all along one final time, deep and dragging and achingly true, from the base of his fuzzy balls to the tip of his cute little tailbone; and then, at last, moved over to George.

The boy tensed when I tickled his opening with the tip of my tongue, then bucked up into my glowing visage when I buried my oral appendage right into his bottom. I stuffed his rectum with warm, wet tongue like I had Thomas's. Only now, I quickly, tantalizingly withdrew it, stuck it back in, pumping the boy's bum with my slippery sticker.

My mouth-organ was formed into a hard, pink spear that stabbed into George's spread asshole, struck deep, reeled back up. I fucked the young man with my tongue like one would with his cock. He squealed and thrust back, to the rhythm of my thrusting down. I must've delved into pink delight three inches or more, repeatedly, plugging willing young bum with a wicked pleasure I was only too happy to mete out.

'There's lubricant on the nightstand, sir,' William informed me. 'Bertrand's own concoction.'

I furled my tongue out of George's gaping, wet anus and smacked my lips. My friend, Bertrand, was a sexual aid inventor of some note, as well as an accomplished all-male smut purveyor. I reached over and grabbed up the indicated jar, uncapped it, dipped two fingers into the gelatinous substance inside. It smelled of something, was as slippery as the devil himself. I coated my erection in the goop, stroking strong and thoroughly, my orbs full of the waiting young asses and unblinking, shining pinkeyes.

George was the first to feel the full impact of my

manly lust, as I went up the row of buttocks in reverse now. I plunged my gleaming hood into his bumhole, burst through his deliciously resisting ring, shot glistening shaft into his chute with a hearty, heady outpouring of my hips. I half-draped over top of the flaxen-haired boy, pressing my thighs into the trembling hills of his buttocks, spraddling my hands out on either side of his curved back, filling his anus with my immensely engorged cock.

I wallowed in the wonderful sensations of stuffing a man's ass full of meat – a young man's hot, gripping ass. Then I pumped, bouncing the bed and the boys, banging into George's buttocks with my body, plugging his bung with my dong. I shafted to the hairy balls and back out again, back in again full length and width, stretching, stroking the young man's anus. He convulsed his ass muscles, whether deliberately or instinctually I know not which, so his bum was actually sucking on my plunger even as I plumbed it. I shimmered with an ecstatic warmth, boring into that furnace-hot, screw-tight back-tunnel of love.

I fucked Everett's torrid anus next, bloating the raven-haired lad's innocent rump with my rod, then blasting it. The bed creaked and jumped, my tensed thighs clapping against rippling buttocks, my cock cleaving ass and reaming chute. Hard, heavy panting was the order of the day, grunting and groaning, sounding even above the other noises of sexing in progress, as I ploughed into Thomas and William, delved their pink, molten depths and the limitless fathoms of my depravity. I fucked boy after boy, slamming their bottoms, pistoning their anuses, my frenzy knowing no bounds.

And when I wasn't ramming one young rump with my cock, I was pumping the one next to it with two or three of my fingers. It was a difficult sexual balancing act, which I executed – dare I say? – to perfection; pounding into one steaming hole with my cock while I stoked another with my fingers. I only wished that my head was off down by my hips somewhere, so I could lick and lap a third boyish anus as I fucked two others with digits and dong.

The young men revelled in the wild rutting just as much as I did, their erections shifting against the sheets to the raucous rhythm of my cocking efforts. And it was not too long, by gad, before George squealed and shuddered convulsively, squirting into the bedlinen. I tore my fingers out of Thomas' rectum to steady myself, rolled George over, took a hold of his pipe and pumped sizzling semen out with my hand. As I kept drilling Everett's anus.

To feel, to see, to almost taste the young man's orgasm, to encourage the spasming of his cock and the expression of utter bliss on his face, was enough to make my blood and balls boil, my cock seize up with imminent release in the clasping sleeve of Everett's ass. And then Everett shivered violently and spectacularly beneath me, his glorious glutes gyrating with a force more than that generated by my spanking thighs. He was striping the sheets with his sheer ecstasy. I pulled out of the lad, plunged into Thomas, rolled Everett over, and took a hand in his fountaining glee.

William and Thomas quickly followed semen-spraying suit, my frenzied chute-chuffing sending them into sticky, shrieking rapture. I bellowed myself, forsooth, yanked my cock out of William's gesticulating rear-end and jacked my jerking joy all over the breathless boys one and all, raining down my giddy appreciation of their beauty on their faces and chests and cocks;

emptying my balls and soul until I didn't have so much as a knee to soundly stand on. I collapsed into the overheated, overwrought mass of come-streaked young manhood. And the boys and I rolled around in our sticky, hot reverie.

'I couldn't persuade you to stay the night, could I, old chap?' Bertrand greeted me on my shaky return to the parlour. 'I've got some orgy photographs I'd love to get your opinion on. Fancy you're up to it?'

I dropped down to my knees at the man's still fully inflated cock, and grabbed on with hand and mouth once again. I'm one of the greatest admirers of Bertrand's body of work, you see, and not about to refuse any request that he makes.

Two in the Bed
by Drew Payne

When I opened my eyes I didn't know where I was. It was only for a minute, but it felt so weird. Guess it was being hung over but I didn't even recognise my own bedroom, my head was so thick. The next minute I knew where I was, but it still felt strange; something was wrong. Then I knew it. I wasn't on my own in bed.

There was someone in bed with me, some guy. He was lying behind me, his chest pressed up to my back, his face in my hair, his legs all wrapped up in mine and his arm around my chest. Now, I still had my Calvins on, and even though his crotch was right up against my arse it felt like he still had his on as well. Guess we hadn't done anything. It felt good lying there with that guy wrapped around me, but who the fuck was he?

Then I woke up some more and remembered. It was Mark.

Mark and I were best mates all through school. We'd gone around everywhere together as kids. After we'd left school, though, we'd lost touch. Mark had left for college and I'd stayed put to start working for a wholesalers. That had been a few years ago, when we were 16.

Last week, Mark had turned up at the garden centre I run with my brother, Jack. He recognised me straight off, even though I've now got a goatee and my hair in a ponytail. It took me a minute to recognise him. His black hair was in this smooth and shiny number three crop, he had a gold earring in his ear, and his chin was covered in black stubble. His body had beefed out too, pecs and a six-pack pushing his T-shirt out; no one could call him a wimp any more. But his eyes were that same bright green. Eyes I could get lost in, still.

The strange thing was it was like we'd last seen each other only the other week, not six years ago. We were soon talking and laughing, like he'd never been away. That's when he said we should go out together for a drink, which is what we did last night.

Guess he was still sleeping from the way he was breathing, sort of slow and deep, so I lay there and enjoyed being in his arms. His breath on the back of my neck, his arm around me, and what felt like his morning hard-on pushing at my arse. I felt comfortable and turned on. I didn't want to move. I just lay there enjoying it.

All the while at school I'd fancied Mark. As I grew up I realised how much he turned me on. I used to love going swimming with him because I got to see him naked in the showers afterwards. It was beautiful to see. Then we left school, and I found men who wanted me as much as I wanted them. I sort of forgot about how much I'd lusted after Mark.

Mark moved in his sleep and began to rub himself against me. His groin moved up and down over my arse, and it felt good. A warm feeling in my groin. My cock, which was half hard from lying there, now hardened up, pushing out the front of my Calvins. Mark's breathing was still slow, so I guessed he must be doing this in his sleep. I didn't know who he was dreaming about, but I wasn't complaining.

Mark and I had gone on a pub crawl around the best ones in town. About halfway through we passed a gay bar, one of my regulars, and Mark said we should go in for a laugh, but I said no. I'm known in there and it would have been awkward. What the fuck would I tell him? Anyhow, we didn't go in there.

We were really pissed when we got the taxi back to my place. We sat in the back of it nearly pissing ourselves laughing at the dumbest of jokes. At my place we were way too pissed to get the sofa bed out for Mark. So Mark or I, I can't remember, said we should share my bed. I don't remember going to bed, I was so out of it.

Mark's hand began to move over my chest, stroking it. His hips were still slowly humping away at my arse. His hand stroked the hair I've got between my pecs, running his fingers through it. My cock was so hard and I was so turned on I wanted to start moaning but I had to stop myself. I didn't want to wake him up and it all to stop. His hand began to play with my nipple. His thumb ran over it, making it stand up hard. I had to bite my lip to stop myself moaning, I was so fucking turned on. Then his hand left my nipple and moved down to my stomach. When he reached my belly button he began to stroke my stomach in slow circles. It was nearly too much for me; my cock was so hard it hurt. All I wanted to do was moan and start wanking till I came. I didn't. I lay there and enjoyed it, especially my hard cock.

Mark's hand seemed to stroke my stomach for ages. It was frustrating and exciting all at the same time. I was loving it, and hoping Mark wouldn't wake up too soon, because then it would stop and we'd be embarrassed and awkward and everything.

Then his hand reached the top of my Calvins. He ran his thumb over the top of them a couple of times, then slid his hand down over the front of them and took hold of my hard cock. It jumped in his hand and I could feel the precome oozing out of it.

'Shit, you've grown up since I last saw you,' Mark whispered in my ear.

The bastard had been awake all the time, but I wasn't complaining.

'Fuck! Don't stop!' I moaned.

But the bastard did. Mark's hand stopped; just lay on the front of my Calvin's, covering my hard cock, and he stopped humping my arse.

'Won't,' Mark whispered in my ear.

'What?' I said.

Fuck, had he got cold feet? Fuck, I was so turned on. Fuck, had this screwed up everything?

'I won't do anything until you kiss me. There's got to be a bit of give and take around here,' Mark said.

Fuck, was that all? I'd always wanted to kiss him.

'Try and stop me,' I said.

I rolled over and we jumped on each other. We didn't start with any kissy-kissy little kisses, all coy and lips closed. We went straight in for a deep snog. It felt like Mark's tongue went right down the back of my throat. His mouth did taste like an armpit crossed with an ashtray but I didn't care; I bet mine tasted the same, but I was finally kissing Mark. He knew what to do with that tongue of his. One minute it was almost down my throat, then it was filling my mouth and then it was pulling mine back into his mouth, and I tried to copy everything he did to me.

We didn't lie still as we snogged. Our hands were all over each other and our bodies were pushed tight together, I don't think you could even have got a bit of paper between us. Our cocks were squashed up together, even more so than our bodies, pushing at the other's through our undies. My cock felt hard and hot and moist and good as it oozed precome into my Calvins. Fuck, it felt good like that.

Then, and I don't know how he did it, but he didn't break our kiss or stop our cocks being pressed up close together, Mark pushed me onto my back and rolled over with me so that he ended up on top of me. As I said, we didn't break our kiss for a second.

We lay there for ages, kissing and groping each other, and I loved it. We kissed and rubbed our cocks together through our undies. My hands were all over Mark's back, running up and down his spine and stroking the muscles running off it. Mark's hands were playing with my hair, which drives me mad, or stroking my neck and shoulders.

Fuck, it was good.

'This duvet's hot,' Mark said as he broke off our kiss and sat up.

'Yeah, sorry,' I said.

'Don't worry.' Mark threw the duvet on the floor.

He then looked down at me, smiled, and touched his finger to the wet patch on my Calvins, which was right over the head of my cock.

'Why don't we get more comfortable and get our knickers off?' Mark said.

'Sounds good to me.'

Quickly we pulled off our own undies and threw them on the floor.

Mark's cock, which stood up hard and straight out of his thick, black pubes, was about an ordinary length but thick. It was so thick it looked shorter than its good six inches. His cockhead, all bright red and moist, pushed its way past his short foreskin and a clear drop of precome hung off the end of it, but only for a moment.

His cock was different from mine. My cock is thin but long. One guy measured it at nine inches. Even when I'm rock hard my foreskin still hangs down low over the end of my cock. Also my balls aren't as large and low hanging as Mark's, and my bush of pubes is sandy brown, same colour as my hair.

Sitting there, on my bed, now stark bollock naked, we didn't say anything; we didn't need to, because at the same time we reached for each other's cocks. My hand took hold of Mark's cock and slid up and down it. It was hard and it really filled my hand, but it felt good. Mark's hand closed right around my cock easily and he slid his hand up and down, just like I was doing to him. Without any trouble he slid my foreskin almost all the way back and right up over the head of my cock.

We kissed again, but not as madly as before. We bought our lips together and slipped our tongues into each other's mouths. We sat there, slowly wanking each other off and kissing, our tongues playing around with each other's. Mark's hand had a good hold of my cock and his strokes were slow and steady, making my balls all tight and excited. I wanked him off just the same way as he was doing to me. It felt so fucking good I wanted to do the same for him.

I could have sat like that for ages until I came, but Mark had other ideas.

He broke off our kiss and stopped wanking me. So I did the same. Mark said, 'Bryan, I've got this thing about arses. Can I see your arse?'

'OK,' I said.

I got up onto my knees and turned round, giving Mark the full view of my arse as I stayed kneeling with my legs open.

'Shit! You've got a great arse. A great and hot arse. Don't move, Bryan,' Mark said.

I felt him start to stroke my arse. Running his hands

over my arse cheeks, stroking the hairs there. His fingers going around in these tiny circles. Just that was getting to me; it felt like his fingers were connected straight to my pleasure centre. It was fucking marvellous.

'Oh God!' I moaned.

'Yeah,' Mark said. 'Some more?'

'Yeah, please.'

He ran his finger down the crack of my arse, brushing over my arsehole. Then he did it again, again and again. It was even more exciting than his fingers just stroking my cheeks. His finger running over my arsehole was driving me crazy; my cock was rock hard and dripping precome all over the sheets and I was moaning my head off. This was now really getting to me.

'Shit, you're turned on,' Mark said.

'Yeah, fuck, yeah.'

'Good.'

Then his finger stopped and left my arse alone. I was about to shout at him for turning me on and then stopping, being a prick-tease, but he had other things in mind. Slowly he pushed me forward, his hand on my back, until I was down on all fours, then he parted my arse cheeks, then I felt his tongue licking at my arsehole. He licked around it in small circles, driving me even crazier. Then his tongue pushed inside my arsehole, just the tip of his tongue but it was inside me and it went in easily. Fuck it was amazing. No one had ever done that to me before and I loved it.

Mark did it for ages, fucking me with the tip of his tongue, and I loved it. My cock was still rock hard and making a mess of precome but I hadn't touched it. I was so fucking turned on. Then suddenly he stopped.

'Got any condoms and lube?' Mark asked. 'Because I want to fuck you so much.'

'They're in the bedside table, top drawer. Mark?'
'What?'
'Go easy, I don't do this all the time.'
'OK.'

I stayed on all fours, waiting while Mark got the condoms and lube.

First he pushed a finger, well covered in lube, up my arse and held it there. Now I ain't no tight-arsed virgin but I ain't no Channel Tunnel either. I've been fucked before and enjoyed it, but not often. Mark's finger up there did feel good. After holding his finger inside me for ages he began to fuck me with it, slowly at first. As he fucked me he slipped that finger further up me. I loved the hot, rubbing feeling his finger was giving me. I let my head fall forward, my hair getting in my eyes but I didn't care, and I moaned loudly. I was so turned on.

Mark pushed his finger right up, and hit something electric inside me. The shock of it nearly kicked me off the bed. I yelled with excitement, tossing my head around. It felt like my balls and cock were on fire, and I loved it. He did it again and I yelled out again.

'Your prostate is hard as a golf ball,' he said.
'That's my prostate?'
'Yeah, your G-spot. Good, isn't it?'
'Fuck, yeah.'

So he stroked it again and I gave another yell. My cock was so fucking hard.

'You ready for me to fuck you?' he said.
'Yeah, please. Yeah.'
'Good.'

Mark slipped his finger out and pushed his condom-covered cock into me, but slowly because, as I said, I'm no Channel Tunnel. He had to push a bit hard to get his cock past my arsehole. I thought he wasn't going to make it at one point, but he gave my arse one quick slap and slipped right inside me.

He held it there, his cockhead just inside my arsehole, for ages. His cock made my arsehole feel really tight, almost hurting but good. The tight feeling made my whole body heat up and my cock was really painfully hard. I needed to, I had to come. It was all I could think about: fuck, fuck, come.

I couldn't take it any more and shouted at him, 'Please Mark, fuck me! You've got to. I need it. I need it.'

'OK. Anything for you.'

He then pushed his cock right up me in one go, hitting my prostate on his way up, and held it there, his pubes tickling my arsehole. My cock twitched up and smacked me in the belly. Then he pulled his cock out of me until his cockhead was the only bit of him left in my arse. That was a fucking turn-on as well. Then he slammed his cock back up me again, smacking into my arse cheeks, and just as quickly he pulled out of me, before smacking into me and pulling out again. Smacking into me and pulling out again, smacking into me and pulling out again, and again, and again, and again. It was fucking marvellous.

He quickly picked up speed and was soon going at me like a train, like a fucking machine. My arse was hot, was burning, and I loved it. My arse was hot and full, my balls felt like they were so full they might burst, my cock was so hard that it fucking hurt. All I did was stay there on all fours, taking Mark's cock as it pounded away at my arse, moaning my head off. I didn't even touch my cock. I was way too turned on to touch it or try to wank it or anything. But I loved what Mark was doing to me. No fuck before had ever sent me off the edge like this. None of the guys who fucked me before had ever done this to me. It was fucking marvellous

Then I felt Mark take hold of my cock and start to wank me off, fast. That was it and I lost it. I came like a fucking garden hose.

My whole body shook as my cock fired off come all over the place. My mind blacked out with the excitement of it all. Then my cock stopped shooting come. Guess it only went on a few seconds, but it felt like for ever. I slowly felt myself coming down to earth.

As I took deep breaths, I was so knackered; I found I was soaked in sweat, my hair plastered in my eyes and that. Mark was still in me but he wasn't moving.

'Oh God,' I moaned.

'Too right,' Mark said.

'You've come?'

'Come, I went right into orbit,' I said. 'That fuck was something else.'

'Shall we lie down? My arms are killing me.'

'Shit. Sorry. OK.'

Mark pulled his cock out of my arse with a plop and suddenly I felt very empty.

It took us a bit to lie down and get comfortable. I mean we were both covered in sweat and come, and so were the sheets. Anyway we did it but this time I lay with my head on Mark's chest.

We lay there for ages, in silence, enjoying it all, feeling comfortable together.

Then Mark started to play with my hair, even though it was all sticky with sweat. After doing that for a moment he said, 'I wish we'd done this years ago. It would have made things a lot easier.'

'What?'

'I fancied you all through school. Your arse always drove me mad, especially in the showers after we went swimming.'

'I fancied you too,' I said.

Mark laughed.

'There's irony for you,' he said.

'What?'

'One of life's stupid jokes. It takes us ages to find out we fancy each other. Anyway, I'd don't want to waste it. What you doing for the rest of the day?'

'Nothing much. Got to go to the supermarket and fuck like that.'

'How about doing it with me?'

'I want to stay in bed with you, fuck the supermarket,' I said.

'Good.'

Mark gently kissed the top of my head.

Paddle Boy
by Landon Dixon

It was a tight game, 20-19, for me. One more point and I'd finally beat Andy at his own game – ping-pong.

We were in the rec room of the frat house, just me and the tall, thin redheaded fraternity brother. His handsome face was flushed, beads of sweat dotting his tall forehead. He prided himself on his ping-pong, like some guys pride themselves on their beer pong, when they remember.

'Match point, A-man,' I taunted, raising the ball in my left hand, the paddle in my right. 'Your streak is coming to an end.'

'Shut up and serve,' he growled, crouching, bouncing side to side on the balls of his feet. He was wearing a white T-shirt and jeans, and an expression of intense concentration.

I grinned. Then I darted down my left hand, like I was dropping the ball, swung with my right. Faking the guy out. 'Ready?' I taunted, as he spasmed.

'Bring it,' he gritted.

I smacked the ball, cutting my paddle down across the white plastic sphere for maximum backspin. The ball bounced off my side of the table and onto Andy's side, within the lines. Then leapt backwards almost right into the net.

Andy rocked back, jumped forward. He'd been expecting me to try to blow a smashing serve right by him, like I'd done on the two previous points. By the time he recovered, it was too late. The ball pocked his side of the table a second time and was swallowed up by the net.

'*I* am the champion!' I sang out. 'Pong live the new king of table tennis!'

I danced around like I'd won miniature Wimbledon, pumping my paddle and fist into the air.

Andy stared glumly at me a moment. Then his expression hardened. He raised his paddle. 'Hey, Roger Frauderer, you know what week this is?'

I halted my moonwalk mid-heel and toe.

'Pledge week,' Andy went on. 'Paddling week.' An evil grin spread across his freckled countenance.

'Hey, just because you're sore, doesn't mean you have the right to make me sore.'

He wasn't listening. He was advancing, smacking the rubber-dimpled ping-pong paddle against the palm of his hand. 'Grab the table and take your punishment like a man.'

I dropped my paddle, filled my hands with the inch-thick green edge of the ping-pong table. Andy got in behind me, reached around me, unfastened my jeans with his free hand, yanked them down. He skinned my Jockeys down, to join my pants at my knees.

I looked back at the guy, my pale, smooth, mounded bottom exposed. He raised the ping-pong paddle up high over his head, slashed his arm downwards. I shut my eyes, tensing for vicious impact.

The red dimples just kissed my electrified skin.

'Ready?' he taunted, as I spasmed.

'Bring it,' I gulped.

He drew the paddle back, whistled it down onto my bare ass. The crack of rubber against skin went off like a gunshot, exploding inside my ears and body. I rocked forward, stung, heat and hurt flashing through my reddened cheek.

Andy whacked my other cheek, harder. I jumped at the fearful smack, sparks shooting all through me. He crashed the paddle down across both my trembling buttocks at once, raising me up onto my toes, making me moan.

'Hey, Andy!' Brent called from upstairs. 'We're going on a beer run. Get your ass in gear – you're the only guy whose driver's licence isn't suspended.'

'Lucky boy,' Andy hissed in my ear. 'Or unlucky?'

He gripped my rock-hard dick, and tugged. As he blasted my right cheek, my left, both together.

I jerked with the blows blistering my bum, with the ecstasy blistering my body. Semen jetted out of my prick, Andy jacking me, whacking me.

'See you later,' he said, tossing his instrument of recreational pleasure and pain onto the table.

He ran up the stairs. As my fingernails scraped the surface of the table, the last few spasms of sperm rocking my body. My butt smouldered, hardly ablaze, needing beating much worse.

Trevor and I were studying in the library, at a table way in the back behind the stacks. 'Hey, what'd you get on the chemistry quiz?' I asked, looking across at the big, blond, green-eyed guy.

He grinned, glancing up from his computer screen. 'Ninety per cent, ace. Not bad, huh?'

I nodded. 'Not bad. If you want a job cleaning test tubes at some high school chem lab. I snagged a 98 per cent, myself.'

His grin faded. 'Think you're pretty smart, huh?'

'Don't think it – know it,' I replied. 'Ninety-eight per cent positive.'

He glared at me, his big fists clenching on the table.

'He sassing you too?'

Andy, come up from behind.

'Yeah,' Trevor replied. 'He thinks he's pretty good.' His eyes glinted. 'Maybe we should knock him down a peg or two?'

'I'm game,' Andy said over my shoulder. He held a wooden ruler up in his right hand.

Trevor shook his head. 'I've got a better idea. You watch Poindexter.'

He got up from the table and jogged down the hall.

I looked back at Andy. He grinned back down at me, smacking his palm with the ruler.

Trevor was back in short order, clutching a pair of wooden measuring sticks; only way bigger, longer than the mere 12-incher Andy was gripping – yardsticks. He handed one to his frat brother. 'We'll see how you measure up now, pal.'

I opened my mouth to protest, was cut off by Trevor adding, 'It's paddling week.'

Andy pulled my chair back. I stumbled to my feet, gripped the edge of the table. Trevor unfastened my jeans, and both guys took a pants leg apiece, pulled. My briefs quickly joined my jeans, puddled at my feet.

My butt was exposed again, still a little sore from the spanking Andy had dished out the night before. It got a whole hell of a lot more sore, but fast, exhilarating.

The men took up position behind me on either side, Trevor being a southpaw. 'See anyone else around on this floor?' Andy asked the bigger man.

'Nope. Just us three.' He raised his yardstick. 'We'll have all the privacy we need – to beat the smart right out of this ass.'

I twisted my head around and gaped at him. He flicked the flexible stick against my butt, stinging my cheeks. I jerked. Then jumped, when Andy laid his lumber across my bum. The guy was obviously still warmed up from the night before, because he hit hard.

The table rasped against the cement floor, my breath coming in gasps, as Trevor swatted my behind again, then Andy. I bit my lip and quivered from tip to toe, inch-wide, quarter-inch-thick wood lashing across my buttocks, making my booty and body and brain boil.

The blows came faster, harder, the air singing with the slashing song of the three-foot rulers, exploding with the cracking reports of impact. They were well coordinated, one blow leaving off, leaving a stinging stripe across my tail; the other landing before the white-hot flash of pain and pleasure had a chance to subside, punishing me anew. My ass lit up a fiery red, criss-crossed with the markings of the brutal blows.

'Look who's enjoying this almost as much as we are,' Trevor said, tapping the tip of his yardstick against the underside of my wood.

I moaned. I was poled out as hard as those butt-beating devices, almost as long. Trevor ran the flat surface of his yardstick all along the swollen undersurface of my cock.

Then he cracked my ass. And Andy stroked the bottom of my shaft with his yardstick.

That's how they did it. One guy whacked my butt, the other ran his heated wood along my cock; vice versa. It was breathtaking, butt- and ball- and mind-blowing. They smacked and jacked.

I quivered up on my toes, taking the beating front and back. My butt cheeks blazed raw with painful pleasure, my cock seizing up come-hard.

'Fuck!' I cried, one man's wood whipping my ass, the other man's wood whittling orgasm out of my wood. Semen shot out of my cock and striped across the table, spurting in rhythm to the banging on my butt. I rode the waves of punishing ecstasy, blasting and getting blasted.

It was enough hard knocks education for any one man. If that man wasn't pain-greedy me.

It was Friday, end of the week. The successful pledges would be picked for brotherhood that night. I was leaning up against a tree in back of the frat house, holding court with some wannabes.

'Piece of cake,' I opined. 'The fraternity's short of guys. Too many flunked out of school last year, couldn't meet the academic standards. You guys have nothing to worry about.'

'Think so?'

That wasn't a pledge asking. That was Roger, head of the house; a small but powerfully built black-haired man with plush red lips and a dimpled granite chin, hard grey eyes. He was a leader, with a leader's strength and will.

He was flanked by five other brothers, Andy and Trevor included.

'Before we announce any successful candidates,' he went on, 'I think we better show these pledges just what kind of discipline and obedience this fraternity demands. On our big-mouthed friend here.'

He had his hands behind his back. All the brothers did. Now, on his word, they brought their hands out into the open. They were all carrying cricket bats.

I gulped. The pledges moved away from me.

Roger lifted his bat and rested it on his shoulder. The big, ball-hitting club had a foot-long handle, a three-foot-long, nine-inch-wide flat wooden blade. It looked like it could really do some serious damage, on and off the pitch.

'Paddling week isn't over yet,' Roger reminded me. Then, in a harder tone, he said, 'Turn around and grab some bark, while we see about tearing a strip or two off you.'

I stared at the grinning brothers, the varnished clubs they were wielding. I turned around, dug my fingers into the tree trunk, and shook like a leaf on that big old oak.

Somebody popped my jeans open, pulled them down. I was quickly bare-assed, *sans* briefs tonight. The cotton only cushioned the dull pain still throbbing through my butt cheeks from the previous two paddlings.

The pledges oohed and aahed, staring at the wicked red stripes on my buttocks. These were the dark sides of the moons, my sexual deviance revealed for all to see. My cheeks glowed in the starlight, flushing with the heat that was suffusing the rest of my body, in anticipation of the beating to come.

'Normally, we wouldn't go to this extreme,' Roger explained to the pledges, prolonging my agony. 'But this guy is an extreme case.'

He smacked my bottom with the cricket bat. My blistered ass burst with raw sensation. I gripped the tree trunk and waggled my war-ribboned bum at the brothers.

They formed a line, my exposed rear end at the front. Andy cracked me; Trevor, Ethan, Tony, Marcus, Roger again. They slammed me one after another, not so hard at first, really just tapping my derriere; then, as they got into the swing of things, harder, and harder.

I was jolted repeatedly, polished wood jarring my buttocks. My cock jumped along with my body, hard as any one of those bats. It was a warm, humid night, and sweat poured down my face and armpits, my ass getting burnt, bashed.

The blows kept coming, rocking me over and over, each smack uncorking electric agony and ecstasy in my ass cheeks, sending searing currents of delight shooting through me. It went on and on, the men moving faster, striking quick and ruthless. The heavy air clouded with the wet splatting of wood against skin, the rasping of men's breath.

I clung to the oak, battered and breathless, white ridges rising up all over my butt cheeks – the tell-tale signs of a truly brutal, beautiful beating. My head swum and my body seemed to sail, propelled upwards into the night sky on the end of those paddling cricket bats. Only my cock kept me secured to the ground, and reality, hard as that tree trunk.

'Trevor, Andy,' I vaguely heard Roger call out, 'get alongside, lay some wood over the poor guy's wood and give it a log-roll. While we finish knocking some sense into his brains.'

Trevor appeared on my right side, Andy on my left. I looked at them through glazed, tear-filled eyes, barely conscious; and grinned. As my butt was thumped again, and again, and again.

Andy slid his cricket bat over top of my jutting prick, while Trevor slid his in underneath. The guys sandwiched my dong, squeezing me where it counts. I felt the sweet pleasure even over the merciless beating my bottom was taking.

Trevor pumped his bat back and forth one way, Andy the other, the men rolling my cock between their two flattened slabs of wood. My fingernails sank deeper into the bark, my balls surging from simmer to boil.

I shook with a thunk to the ass, shuddered with the

pressing roll on my cock. By now I could hardly feel anything, could feel everything. The savage ass-assault had catapulted me to a higher plane, where lay pure, molten joy never experienced by the faint of punishment.

I lunged, and yelled. Andy and Trevor tried to stem the tide of my ecstasy, by slamming my cock almost flat between their bats. But it was no use. I was coming, hard and heavy and heated, from far, far away. One more thud up the backside and I was shooting.

Semen spouted out of my prick, blowing my balls apart, rocking my body and soul more violently than any blow to the ass ever could. But the blows kept on coming, Roger wielding the thunder all alone now, destroying my derriere. As I poured out my blessed, bone-rattling orgasm, sticky starburst after starburst.

It took three guys to help me back to my feet afterwards, Andy and Trevor under my arms to keep me upright.

'OK,' Roger said to the stunned pledges. 'Now you see how we enforce discipline at our frat house.'

Pledges gulped, gaped.

'And – and the thing of it is,' I croaked, numb now from head to haunches, 'I'm not even a pledge, or a brother. I just hang out at the house, help the guys out during paddling week.'

I glanced from Andy to Trevor, at Roger, tremors of phantom butt-blows still rippling through the empty spaces of my deliciously wasted body and mind. 'Th-thanks for helping *me* out, guys.'

Bananas
by Dominic Santi

I met Mick at the beach. He and some of his buddies wandered by a volleyball game I was in. Man, did I fall hard. Instant lust. I'm from Southern California, land of buff, tanned, blond-haired surfers. But I saw Mick, and I did a double-take – totally missed a perfect set – as I looked up at the most gorgeous man I'd ever laid eyes on. Tall and slender, wavy brown hair, about my age – mid-20's. And he had the sexiest ass a pair of Dockers could ever show off. He was wearing a lot of clothes for the beach. I'm used to seeing skin, you know? But with Mick, it seemed like I was seeing his perky nips naked right through his long-sleeved white shirt. Even the hat and sunglasses seemed there just to emphasise his killer smile.

And me in a Speedo that was barely decent enough to keep me from being arrested – and that sure as hell wasn't hiding my reaction.

'Get a room!'

'Huh?' I said, tripping as I shook my head and tried to focus on my partner.

Karl laughed and shoved me into position so the other team could serve. 'I suppose we could just forfeit, lover boy.'

As the ball cleared the net, I sneaked a quick look back over my shoulder. My dream date was still there. I kept staring as the ball thudded next to me.

'Dammit, Jake!'

Karl's roar finally got my attention. I blushed all the way through my tan. I mean, I didn't even know the guy, and here I was lusting over him so badly the front of my suit was getting wet. Fortunately, Mick just laughed and cheered us on. So, I grinned back and started showing off for him – diving, taking wild power shots. Well, as much as I could without letting my hard-on escape from its totally inadequate covering. The other team beat the pants off us. All I could think about was getting naked with the hunk who was turning me on so badly my dick hurt.

When the game was mercifully over, Karl pulled me over to Mick, then grinned and said, 'I hope you're worth it, pal. When he's coherent, tell him he owes me the ten bucks I had on this game.'

After that, the only part of the conversation I remember was Mick introducing himself. That and the arousal in his voice.

The beach house he was renting fronted right up against the sand. We were kissing by the time he kicked the door closed. A second later, our clothes were on the floor. We were all over each other, rolling from the futon to the rug as our lips devoured every inch of bare skin we could find.

'Condoms. Lube,' I gasped, arching up over him as I straddled his body. My arms shook as I dragged my throbbing cock over the hot, hard flesh poking up from his belly.

'No,' he panted. 'Rub against me. Unh!' He shook as I slid over him again. 'Oh, God, yes. Like that. Again!'

I was right on the edge. I thrust again.

'Shoot your cream on me. Do it! Ahh!'

His cock twitched as he arched into my next stroke. I lost it. So did he. Our cocks jerked against each other like a couple of wild snakes, our come gorping out and smearing together between our bellies and chests. God, he was sexy. I collapsed on him, totally blissed out.

The whole night was like that. The sex was wild and hot. I came so many times I thought I'd never move again.

And that night, I learned the first of many lessons about sensitive skin – at the beach and otherwise. I'd figured everybody was like me, just slap on sunblock and go for it, you know? But not only did Mick sunburn easily, and badly, he was allergic to lubes – and latex.

I'll spare you the gory details. Let's just say that over the last couple of years, our attempts to find a way to fuck entailed a lot of trips to the doctor. Mick's reactions looked like they were as painful as he said they were. Thank God he wasn't allergic to spit. But we'd yet to find a brand of non-latex condoms that wasn't either too thick or too tight for my taste, or both.

I loved Mick to distraction, and my honey had the tightest asshole I'd ever met in my life, muscles like steel bands that just would not relax. Most of the time, I could only rub that pretty pink pucker with my fingertip while I tongued his cock. Even when we were sucking each other off, it took a lot of work and gobs of spit to get just one finger in him. Fortunately, he loved being finger-fucked. And I loved feeling him squirm against my hand, listening to him gasp against my cock about how his ass itched to have me crawl up it.

Every once in a great while, if he was really turned on, Mick would flip over and offer me his tight butt. Believe me, it was worth every minute of the time it took to slick both my poly-whatever-clad cock and his hole with as much spit as we could work up, then for me to slowly, slowly inch my way up inside him. I got hard just thinking about being inside him. But as much as Mick craved it, I could tell it still always hurt. He'd be sore and swollen for a long time afterwards.

Last Friday was our third anniversary. I wanted to do something special for him. I'd downloaded a really hot stroke vid. At lunchtime I borrowed an empty office and recorded myself reading an hour's worth of my favourite porn stories. Lots of sucking and frottage and ass-fucking. Yeah, I've finally gotten over my tongue-tied phase. I planned on letting the recording play while I gave him a full body massage, followed by a handjob that would make him remember those stories for ever.

When I walked in the door that night, Mick was putting the finishing touches on a full-blown Italian dinner. I handed him a long-stemmed rose. When I saw the flowers he'd put in the centre of the table, we both burst out laughing. He kissed me, his lips promising a hot night ahead. Then he took the bud from me and walked back into the kitchen to get another vase. I smiled as I watched his firm ass move against his jeans. Damn, just looking at him still made me hard.

Dinner was wonderful. Mick was really into cooking. By the time we finished eating, my tongue tingled from the flavours in the spices he'd used. My lips were itching to get at the tender shadows I could see perking up beneath his shirt.

Mick took another sip of his wine, then he pulled a box from under the table and handed it to me. 'Happy anniversary, Jake.'

'For *moi*?' I laughed, ripping off the paper. The way his eyes were twinkling, I wanted to get at my present fast.

I couldn't believe what was inside – a large bottle of banana-flavoured body lotion.

'I got it from the new herbalist at the health food store.' He grinned. 'The guy says it tastes great. He also guarantees it's safe for both condoms and human consumption. I figure if you keep it away from my skin, just put it inside the condom so you get extra friction, it should be OK.'

I didn't know what to say. Though I'd tried not to complain, Mick knew how frustrated I got with how we had to fuck. I opened the bottle and squeezed out a little bit of the lotion, rubbing it all over my lips and then sucking on my finger. It tasted more like banana ice cream than plain bananas.

'Mmmmm,' I said, smacking my lips like a kid eating an ice cream cone. 'I think I know just what I'm going to do with this.' I stared meaningfully at his ass.

When we stopped laughing, I handed Mick his present. It took him a second to figure out what it was. But when he saw the "narrated by" label I'd put on the recording, his clear brown eyes dilated so wide I knew my present was having the same effect on him that his had on me.

He didn't say anything, just walked over to my chair and kissed me, softly licking my lips and letting the growing bulge in his crotch brush against my arm. I was really getting into the kiss, when Mick stopped and stood up, licking his lips. All of a sudden I realised I'd had lotion on my mouth.

'Shit! I'm sorry!' I grabbed my water glass, shoving it at him so he could wash his face. I mean, that stuff was probably burning the hell out of his skin!

But, instead of taking the water, Mick picked up the tube of banana lotion, squeezed some on his finger, and rubbed it onto his lips. Then he licked his lips again, looking at me with this really strange expression. He rubbed some of the lotion on his inner wrist, slicking it back and forth with his fingers. I was too shocked to say anything. Mick is definitely not into pain. When he started laughing, deep, long belly laughs, I really started wondering what the hell was the matter with him. Then he held his wrist out to me.

'What do you see?'

I raised my eyebrows at him. 'Nothing.'

I didn't see anything. Just plain old pink healthy skin. Then it hit me.

'Oh God, a lube you're not allergic to.'

Mick just kind of hiccupped, nodding as he stopped laughing. I could feel the heat rushing into my cock just thinking of the possibilities. This time when Mick kissed me, I could feel his hot banana breath on my lips as he whispered, 'Put it any place you want, Jake.'

We left dessert sitting on the table. We took the candles into the bedroom with us, stripped the covers off the bed, and dove in.

We went slowly, in case there was a delayed reaction. I stripped off his shirt, rubbing the lotion on his nipples while he did the same to me. Then we took our long, sweet time licking and sucking it off each other, until our tits were hard and tender and we both had wet spots on the front of our jeans. Still, on Mick's lips and on his chest, there was only healthy, rosy, well-sucked skin.

We yanked our pants off and fell back on the bed together. Mick ripped open a condom, put a dab of the lotion in the end, and rolled that soft, tight fuck-skin down all eight inches of my throbbing erection. Then, smearing the lotion all over me, he started licking it off, massaging that banana cream into my tingling ball sack while he alternated between tonguing me and taking me deep into his throat.

I knew I'd blow right away if he kept that up. Nobody sucks cock like Mick does, and the unexpected friction from the lotion in the tip was driving me nuts. So I grabbed his knee and dragged toward me. He stopped what he was doing long enough to scoot around until our heads were resting on each other's thighs. He waited, shaking, as I took a handful of lube and carefully smeared it over his cut head and down his thick seven inches.

I stroked him once and he jerked. Then he smiled and leant onto his forearms, sighing. 'Damn, Jake, that feels so good.'

I slicked the banana ice cream all over him, and we both settled into some serious sucking. I was in heaven, licking that sweet creamy syrup off him, feeling Mick surge and groan in response to my mouth. But what he was doing to me was building way too much pressure way too soon.

I pushed his mouth away. Without arguing, Mick switched to gently tickling and stroking my ball sack. He knows I love that, but it won't bring me off. I licked my way down to suck and tongue the back of his balls, poured more of the lotion in my hand. Then I lifted his thigh and carefully slicked my finger up the crack of his ass, gently but firmly spreading his cheeks until they parted to show the tight pink rosebud they'd been protecting. He smelled so good, deep, musky, earthy scents I could almost feel on my taste buds along with the faint odour of his soap and the sweet creaminess of banana ice cream.

He groaned when my fingertip touched that puckered skin. This time my hand was so slick that he couldn't get tight enough to stop me. My finger slid into him.

'Jake, please!' he cried out as he bucked forward.

Mick's whole body was stiff. His face looked like he was in heaven. I suddenly realised that, for him, this was the first time he was getting what he really craved and having it feel only good.

I gently pulled my finger out of him, massaging the pucker for a minute to give him time to savour the sensation. Then I sat up, rolled Mick over onto his stomach, and stuffed a thick pillow under his hips, raising his butt up to just the angle I wanted. This boy had never really been played with before, not the way I was going to. It was time he learnt just how good his asshole could feel.

He reached out to rub my leg, but I pushed his hand away.

'Just lie there, babe. This time, it's all for you.'

With a groan Mick dropped his hand back onto the bed. Then he was all mine.

I started out licking the back of his neck. His whole body shivered as I worked my way down his spine. When I reached the firm, perfectly curved mounds of his butt, I smeared the banana cream all over them and licked up every drop, one slow stroke at a time. He was moaning into the sheets by the time I was done. When I'd tongued the last of the cream from the soft bottom curve of his ass, I knelt between his thighs and pushed them apart, running my fingers over the tender skin of his groin and down onto the back of his balls. Then I slowly rubbed his balls between my fingers, just looking at him. That tight, dusky rosebud was wide open and waiting for me.

Holding his thighs apart with my own, I took the cream and very carefully let one thick, syrupy drop fall right onto that pucker. Mick stiffened and tried to move, but I had him braced too well. As my fingertip started to massage him, he moaned again, pressing back against me.

'Relax,' I said, drizzling more lotion onto my hand and sliding my finger up and down his crack. 'This stuff is going to let me slip right up your ass.'

I slowly inched my fingertip back into him until I was in to the first knuckle. Mick was squirming against the sheet when, all of a sudden, his muscles relaxed the tiniest bit. I pressed and my finger sank in to the hilt. He cried out and writhed on the bed, but he didn't try to pull away. His head was resting on his folded arms. Each time my fingers moved, his smile got bigger. I started finger-fucking him, stretching and pulling, loosening those tight, hot muscles as I slicked the lube higher up into him and spread it around.

'Feels so good,' he gasped.

My grin was about to split my face. Without the pain, Mick was opening to me like he never had before. I poured more lotion on his hole and my hand. Very tentatively, I pressed the tip of a second finger to him. He gasped as I kept up a steady pressure, the finger inside him still wiggling and stretching while my other hand stroked a steady rhythm over his perineum and the back of his ball sack. He shifted his hips, and in the movement my second fingertip slipped in.

He groaned, but this time I moved more quickly. Squirting the lotion onto my fingers, I pressed, and in one steady slide the second finger went in, past the first knuckle, then the second, and then the heel of my palm was resting on his butt cheek. Mick was going wild on the bed, moaning and grinding his cock on the pillow as he danced on my fingers. The whole room smelled like bananas and sweat and Mick's ass. I loved it.

Slicking the lotion up his crack, I spread his cheeks even wider. I leant forward and licked the sweat off his ass cheek, watching up close as my fingers slid in and out and stretched him. Without any warning, I bit him. Not hard, but he jumped, and in one swoop I slid in a third slippery finger.

'Oh fuck, yeah,' Mick gasped, his hips surging back against my hand as his muscles clamped down hard around me.

Mick's breath was coming in short, hot pants. I knew he was right on the edge.

'Come if you want to, babe,' I breathed against his back. 'Let me make you feel good.'

I was really close myself, just watching that hot man finally take his pleasure. Suddenly he forced himself up onto his hands and knees, grinding his ass back onto my hand. I could see his hard cock waving below him, slick with precome.

'Fuck me, Jake!' The words came out in a voice so harsh I almost didn't recognise it as Mick's. 'Fuck the come out of me. Now!'

I almost shot from the sound of his voice. I felt like I'd waited my whole life to hear him say that. Rising up on my knees, I squirted that banana cream all over my sheathed cock and all over that rosy, hot hole that was stretched over my fingers. Then I pulled out my fingers, positioned my cock, and started to push into Mick's ass. I was so slick that I slid halfway in on the first stroke.

Mick cried out and stiffened as I popped in past his sphincter. Then he gasped, starting to shake as he let out a long, low, almost animal sound. I froze, thinking I'd really hurt him. Then I realised he wasn't hurt, he was laughing! His ass twitched as he shook.

'Damn, Jake.' He laughed. 'That feels so fucking,

fucking good!'

I couldn't help grinning myself. I rubbed my hands up and down his back, smiling as I felt the tension drain out of his shoulders.

Eventually his laughter gave way to moans again. As his ass relaxed enough for me to move, I started pumping slowly in and out, going a bit deeper with each stroke. He was so tight and hot, and fuck, that friction felt so good! When we'd fucked before, I'd always tried to come quickly, because I knew how much I was hurting him. Now I gritted my teeth and tried to concentrate on anything but how good his ass felt. I wanted our first real fuck to last a long, long time.

Finally, I pulled almost all the way out, and when I thrust back in, I sank in to the hilt. God, he felt good! I ground into him. Mick gasped my name. I felt him shaking under me. But this time he wasn't laughing. My cock was really stretching his hole. His ass lips kissed my cock like they wanted to pull me in even further.

'Let it happen, Mick,' I growled. I reached down in front of him and wrapped my fist around his cock. He was so wet with precome and lube my hand slid over his skin. His shaft was stiff and hot. I knew without even looking it was the deep purple red that meant he was getting ready to shoot all the way from his balls. I couldn't help grinning again. For the first time, our fucking felt nothing but good, and I knew it felt as good to him as it did to me. Hell, I hoped it felt better. After all, he had a lot of catching up to do.

Mick started to shake harder, then he arched his ass back onto me and cried out in that same hoarse voice. 'Fuck me, Jake,' he begged. 'Harder! Please!'

I straightened up and grabbed his hips. Then I ploughed into him; not the slow, shallow strokes he could usually take, but hard, fast fucking that made him cry out each time I hit his joy spot. My nerves were all shrieking toward orgasm, my balls climbing my shaft as Mick's hot, tight ass sucked the come right up out of me.

I felt the spasms starting deep inside him. With Mick's first clenching jerk he yelled and I went over too, roaring as I surged into him, pressing hard while his tight ass muscles milked me as I spurted. I've never shot like that before in my life. I just held onto Mick while we both shook, and when he collapsed on the bed, I fell on top of him.

We stayed in bed all weekend. Mick got to listen to his recording while I massaged him. I used the banana lotion while I jerked him off. By the time we ran out of that stuff on Sunday afternoon, we were both so sore we could hardly walk.

Mick says the herbal guy can make lots of flavours. We're going to try them all. But I already know what my permanent favourite is going to be. Bananas and Mick, every time.

Evolution of Attraction
by Katya Harris

Jamie's dick was hard. Engorged with blood, it throbbed behind the thin material of his boxer shorts, the swollen crest so sensitive even the touch of the soft cotton was a torment. Jamie bit his bottom lip and tried desperately not to move. Lying on his back on the bed, muscles locked tight, his breaths sounding so loud in the near-darkness, his hands curled into fists at his sides as he tried not to touch the throbbing length of his aroused dick. The effort made sweat break out on his skin and he shivered as the air-conditioning gusted over him. He wanted to get beneath the thin duvet rumpled up next to him, but he knew as soon as he was covered he would be tempted to touch himself, to wrap his fist around his cock and pump the ache away. He should just go to the bathroom and jerk off, but he couldn't bring himself to leave the bed.

Turning his head, Jamie let himself look at the figure lying sprawled out on the bed next to him. His chest ached, and warmth pricked at the corners of his eyes.

It was late, past midnight, but the light from the streetlight right outside the motel room pierced the thin curtains to bathe the room with a syrupy yellow glow, caressing the form that held Jamie transfixed. The murky illumination flowed lovingly over the sculpted muscles and smooth skin, teased along the strands of dark hair spilled across the pillow.

A breath shuddered past Jamie's lips. His erection jerked, hard, a drop of precome slipping free of the head in a blissful pulse. He couldn't remember the last time he had been so turned on, and that just confused the shit out of him.

When had this happened to him? When had admiration turned into attraction? When had everything he had thought he'd known about himself changed so drastically? Jamie loved women. It was one of the truths that had so far defined his life, but now it appeared that he loved something else just as much. If not more.

Bryan Foster. He'd been a friend for less than a year, since they'd met at work and struck up a conversation. Clever and quick-witted, possessing a humour that was teasingly sarcastic and often self-deprecating, Bryan had quickly become one of his best friends, his confidant. Jamie had often said he was like the brother he'd never had, but it wasn't brotherly thoughts that had been plaguing Jamie's mind the past couple of months.

Jamie's eyes drifted over Bryan's exposed body. His friend had only worn his boxer-briefs to bed and, like Jamie, had kicked the too-warm duvet away, leaving his torso bare to the cool air. Long and lean, his sculpted muscles softer in sleep – Jamie couldn't take his eyes from him. His gaze caressed the shadowed terrain of his friend's body, the valleys of his defined muscles, the impressions of his ribs pressing against his skin. It was strangely intimate to look at him while he was at his most vulnerable, and Jamie felt something in his chest tighten.

In his sleep, Bryan huffed out a deep breath. His head turned toward Jamie and the other man froze, hardly daring to breathe until he was sure he was still sleeping.

He had never really noticed another man's looks

before, had never really cared beyond whether they would give him any competition when it came to attracting women. With his tousled dark hair, finely carved face, and ripped body, Bryan would have given him a run for his money any day of the week, and that was without the impact of his eyes, dark as bitter chocolate. Women stared at him wherever he went, and Jamie might have been jealous if Bryan wasn't gay.

'Why aren't you sleeping?'

The sleepy mumble made Jamie jump so hard the entire bed rocked with the force of it, the headboard striking the wall behind it with a sharp *crack*.

Bryan's dark eyes smiled at him slumberously. 'Sorry, didn't mean to scare you.'

A weak laugh made it past Jamie's lips. Hoping Bryan wouldn't notice, he pulled the duvet over his lap. 'You don't scare me.' It wasn't a lie. Bryan didn't scare him; it was the feeling growing in Jamie that did. 'I can't sleep.'

Bryan grunted, rolling over onto his side to face his friend. 'Are you worried?' They were travelling to visit Jamie's sister in Kent. She was going through a bad break-up and, although she said she was fine, Jamie could tell she was more upset then she'd let on. He'd asked Bryan if he'd wanted to come with him to visit her and, when he'd agreed, decided that they could drive down from Edinburgh. A couple of beers at dinner had led them to grab a room for the night. Lack of funds had prompted them to share it.

Was it a shortage of money that had made Jamie suggest it, though? After staring at Bryan's sleeping body for the past couple of hours he wasn't sure.

'Jamie?'

Bryan's concerned voice distracted Jamie from his thoughts. He struggled for a moment to remember what

Bryan had asked him. 'Sorry. Yeah, I guess I'm a little worried. I don't like Rachel being upset.'

'Is that all?'

Jamie frowned at the tone of Bryan's voice, the look in his dark, dark eyes. Apprehension started to twist his insides into knots, and he was glad the dimness hid the blood heating his cheeks. 'I don't know what you mean,' he said nonchalantly, looking away.

'Really?'

Unable to stop himself, Jamie looked back at him and found himself entranced by the planes of his face, the quirk of his eyebrows. All traces of sleepiness had evaporated from Bryan's face and Jamie felt pinned down by his sharp stare. 'What else could be wrong?' He almost cringed at the hint of breathiness in his voice.

A smile tugged at the sexily plump curve of Bryan's lower lip. 'I don't know, but that hard-on you're packing looks like it could be a problem.'

Jamie froze. He could feel the blood drain from his face, before it all flooded back in a burning rush. His mouth dropped open, but no words came out as his mind scrabbled for something to say. He thought of denying it, but even he could see that was ridiculous with his erection still pressing insistently against the cover that was a far from adequate shield.

Bryan saw the distress on his friend's face, and the humour that twinkled in his eyes darkened with concern. 'Shit, Jamie, I'm sorry. I didn't mean to embarrass you.' His hand reached out to touch Jamie's arm and Jamie flinched beneath its warmth. Bryan snatched his hand back with a frown. 'Jesus, Jamie, what's going on?'

'I – I –'

Bryan sat up, reaching out to switch on the bedside lamp.

'No.' Without thinking, Jamie moved, grabbing his upper arm to stop him. The heat of Bryan's sleep-warmed skin scorched his palm and he groaned as the sensation shot straight to his dick. Jamie bowed his head as he struggled to control the desire that seized his body until he trembled.

'Jamie?'

Bryan's voice was soft. It stroked against Jamie's ears, a velvety caress. His hand flexed around Bryan's arm, tightening before he let go. Flopping onto his back, Jamie covered his arms with a forearm. God, he wished he could just disappear.

A rustle of sound. The bed dipped, levelled out. A tug on his hair and Jamie stilled. He didn't think even his heart beat as he realised that Bryan was touching him, curling a lock of his hair round and round his finger.

'Did you think I didn't know?' The gentle question, barely whispered into the night, electrified Jamie.

'I saw the way you started to look at me,' Bryan went on. His hand shifted and the feeling of his fingers sifting through his hair filled Jamie with a sensation like bliss. How many times had he lain awake in the night and imagined what Bryan's touch would feel like? Too many, and now it was like his brain short-circuited at the sheer pleasure of the simple caress.

Without uncovering his eyes, Jamie croaked, 'How did I look at you?' He thought he had hidden his interest so well.

'Like you look at a woman you want.' There was smile in the warm honey of Bryan's voice. 'Like you were wondering what I looked like with my clothes off.' He chuckled, a soft, indulgent sound. 'Then you'd blush, like a schoolboy.'

Jamie's cheeks burnt. 'Oh God.' He cringed with the

embarrassment that singed his insides, and tried to move away, but Bryan tightened his fingers in his hair and just that small restraint kept him in place.

'Don't.' The urgency in his voice made it less of a command, more of a plea. 'Don't hide from me.'

Something like despair tightened Jamie's throat. The whole world was changing and he didn't know if he wanted it to stop or rush headlong into it.

A sound must have escaped him because Bryan's hand was suddenly cupped around his neck, his shadowed face only centimetres away. 'Shh, shh. It's all right,' he whispered. His breath gusted, warm and faintly minty, across Jamie's face, as intimate as a kiss and he shivered.

'I don't know –' He had to stop and then start again. 'I don't know what to do.'

'Are you really attracted to me?'

'Yes.' The affirmation was a whisper of sound, almost lost in the night.

Bryan's thumb stroked across Jamie's cheek. 'Good, because I want you too.'

Jamie gasped, and Bryan swooped in to capture his mouth with his own.

For a moment, Jamie could do nothing but freeze in shock. Bryan was kissing him, was brushing his firm lips against his with teasing sips that coaxed and cajoled him to respond. Sensation electrified Jamie's senses and he kissed him back, exploring his male lips that were as silky as a woman's and as firm as his own.

Jamie had often fantasised about Bryan's lips on his own and now, with a soul-deep groan, he knew that the reality of it was so much better than his imagination. *I'm kissing Bryan. I'm really kissing Bryan.* The thought ran round and round in his head, and it was his tongue that slipped like a thief into Bryan's mouth.

They both groaned as they tasted each other. Jamie's hands came up to clutch at the smooth muscles of Bryan's back as the other man moved closer, coming over him so that their heaving chests touched. Their kiss deepened, tongues no longer hesitant but sure, aggressive as they undulated against each other. Teeth nipped and mouths sucked. They ate at each other with rapidly rising passion until, overcome, they both had to break away to take a much-needed breath.

'What are we doing?' Jamie panted. His head swam with lust and an amazement spiked with confusion. Nothing felt real, and his hands clenched tight on Bryan's shoulders to keep the reality of him.

Even in the dim light Bryan's wide grin gleamed brightly. 'We're acting on what we feel.' His hand coasted from Jamie's neck over his shoulder and along his waist. Rucking up Jamie's T-shirt, he boldly palmed the indentation of Jamie's waist, making him moan. 'So how does it feel?'

Jamie licked his lower lip, swollen from Bryan's kisses. 'Good.'

Bryan's hand travelled up until his thumb strummed over the little peak of Jamie's nipple. It hardened and Jamie pushed out his chest, silently demanding a harder touch, which Bryan gladly delivered. 'How good?'

Writhing, Jamie moaned. 'So fucking good I think I'm gonna come in my pants.' He sucked in a harsh breath as Bryan flicked the aching tip of his nipple with the sharp edge of his fingernail. 'Bryan!'

The other man's chuckle was as wicked as sin. 'I like hearing you say my name like that.' Bending forward, he licked and bit at the wrinkled disc of Jamie's nipple. 'Say it again.'

'Bryan.' Jamie was helpless to obey. More breathy

this time, his hips bucking involuntarily as his cock surged to even greater hardness. 'Please.'

Rubbing his lips over the smooth expanse of Jamie's hairless chest, Bryan asked, 'Please what?'

Jamie gulped, swallowing heavily around the desire that threatened to choke him. 'Please touch me.'

Tilting his head back, Bryan smiled at him teasingly. 'You want me to touch you, huh?' His hooded eyes gleamed darkly, bottomless black pools that drew Jamie, entranced him. 'Where? Where would you like me to touch you? Here?'

Jamie sucked in a breath as Bryan trailed his hand along the tense length of his muscled arm.

'Or here?'

His hand teased down Jamie's chest, the tips of his fingers dabbling in the shallow hollows between his ribs before he reached the softer planes of his belly. His stomach muscles trembled beneath that light caress.

Jamie's heart pounded so hard within his chest he thought it might try to break through his ribcage. Bryan's touch left a trail of fire in its wake, igniting his nerves and heating his blood until it felt like his veins were rivers of flame. That diabolically light caress circled around the dip of his belly button and Jamie couldn't stop his hips from tilting up, moving restlessly in invitation.

'Where do you want me to touch you, Jamie?' Bryan's low voice teased him as surely as his fingers did as they stroked round and round his navel. 'Tell me where you want to feel me.'

Jamie gasped. 'My cock. Please touch my cock.'

Bryan's eyes watched him carefully as his hand drifted lower. He licked his lips as his fingertips skated the elastic edge of Jamie's boxers, briefly dipping underneath it to brush against the very tip of his slick cockhead. Sensation burst through Jamie, bowing his spine. The sensitive crown of his erection plumped up even more at the too-light touch and he begged Bryan for more. 'I've thought about this so much,' he said tightly, struggling to control the vicious need blazing within him. 'Please don't tease me. I don't think I could bear it.'

Bryan didn't obey. Back and forth, he swept his fingers along the waist of Jamie's boxers. A maddening rhythm.

'I've wanted to touch you too.' Bryan's voice was soft in the darkness, but thrumming with an intensity that he did nothing to hide. It told Jamie just how much his friend had wanted him, and a thrill of satisfaction went through him from the tips of his toes to the top of his head.

'Then touch me.'

Bryan grinned down at him. 'Oh don't worry, I will.' But his hand didn't stop that lazy back and forth stroke.

'When?' He blushed hard at the whine his voice had become. He had never felt so desperate to be touched. No woman had ever had him this aroused. His erection was so full and tight, it felt like his skin would split open with the pressure.

'When I'm ready.' Bryan told him. Delicately, he tugged at the fine hairs that trailed from beneath Jamie's boxers up to his navel.

Jamie moaned at the delicious little pinch of pain. 'You enjoy torturing me.'

'You know me so well.'

A thought flashed across Jamie's mind. 'How long, Bryan? How long have you wanted me?'

The smile slipped from Bryan's face, his expression becoming something softer, more serious. 'Too long.' His hand suddenly dipped down, palming Jamie's erection.

Jamie hissed in a sharp breath, back arching. Pleasure streaked through him as Bryan squeezed his aching dick firmly in his hand, the pad of his thumb rubbing gentle circles over the sensitive head. It felt so good Jamie felt light-headed, his thoughts swimming in a viscous sea of pleasure.

'More?'

'More. God, please more.'

Bryan's hand left him and Jamie cried out with the loss before he realised that he was moving over him. Without being asked, Jamie parted his legs to let Bryan kneel between them. He watched, wide-eyed and hungry, as Bryan hooked his fingers into the sides of his boxers, drawing the soft material down his legs. When they reached his knees, he drew each leg up so that Bryan could slip them off him and throw them to the floor.

'Take off your T-shirt.' Bryan's voice was soft and rough, a purring growl.

Jamie hurriedly did as he was told. He held his breath as he lay back down, struck by a sudden fear that Bryan wouldn't find him attractive after all, that he would stop. But then Bryan's hand touched him, stroking the heavy globes of his balls, and all thought and worry fled.

'You're so beautiful, Jamie. God, I've always thought so. You don't know what it's done to me to think that you wanted me too.' A harsh laugh burst from Bryan's lips, at odds with his gentle touch as he explored the velvety sacs of Jamie's testicles, the sensitive skin behind them. 'Sometimes I thought I was just deluding myself. That I was just imagining the way you looked at me or that you'd decide you didn't want me after all. I couldn't bear the thought you'd change your mind.' Bryan's whispered confession, so close to his own fears, pierced the sensual fog he had wrought around Jamie.

Sitting up, Jamie cupped a hand round Bryan's neck. 'I won't change my mind.' His voice hitched a little before the words tumbled free from his mouth in an unstoppable landslide. 'I've never wanted anyone as much as I want you.'

There was a terrible vulnerability in Bryan's face as he leant his face into Jamie's touch. 'But the women –?'

'Don't matter.' Feathering his thumb over the sweep of Bryan's jaw, Jamie smiled at him. 'Nothing matters to me but you.'

The insecurity in Bryan's expression was not erased by Jamie's declaration. In fact, it only seemed to deepen as they looked into each other's oh-so-familiar faces. 'How can you say that?' He looked down and then back into Jamie's eyes. 'I know you, Jamie. I know what, who, you really like. I don't think that I could stand it if what you felt for me was just curiosity.'

'I am curious. But –' he said firmly when Bryan started to draw away from him '– what I feel for you is so much more than that. I wasn't lying or exaggerating when I said that I want you more than I've wanted any woman. You're all I think about, Bryan. All I see. I don't want anyone else.' Jamie smiled, warm and sincere, as he willed Bryan to believe him. He couldn't let him walk away now. 'Just you.'

For a long moment Bryan stared into his eyes as if his gaze could pierce the dimness and read the truth there. Whatever he saw must have reassured him, because the insecurity faded from his face, replaced with a dark heat that made the breath catch in Jamie's throat.

Their mouths met in a ravenous kiss, lust and desire and something neither man was ready to admit to, spicing it with a fiery sweetness. Their tongues danced and duelled as they learnt the contours of each other's lips, while their hands groped with feverish intensity at each other's bodies.

'I want you,' Bryan growled against Jamie's lips. 'I want your cock in my mouth.'

Jamie was frantic in his agreement. 'Yes,' he nearly shouted. 'Please.'

Bryan didn't tease him now. Burying his face in Jamie's lap, he sucked his erection into his mouth. Jamie cried out, eyes flashing wide as his friend swallowed his dick down the convulsing depths of his throat. 'Fuck,' he swore, a deep tremble invading his body at the ecstatic pleasure that tore through his system. His hands went to Bryan's head as it bobbed up and down, fingers threading tight through the silken mass of his tousled hair. Bryan groaned around his dick, the vibration of it bringing a gasp of pleasure to Jamie's lips. He couldn't help but use his hold on Bryan's head to control his movements as he thrust upwards into the hot, wet depths of his mouth.

Bryan's hand slipped between Jamie's legs. With his mouth sucking demandingly on Jamie's cock, he rolled and tugged his balls with long fingers. The globes were wet with his saliva that had run in thick rivulets down Jamie's dick. He massaged that wetness into the tender skin of his friend's balls and the sensitive patch just beyond them.

'Fuck, Bryan,' Jamie growled. 'You suck like a goddamned dream.'

With a long lick of his tongue up Jamie's rigid hardness, Bryan lifted his head to look at him. 'I don't want you to forget a single moment of tonight,' he breathed through gleaming wet lips.

'Not a chance of that.' Jamie grinned. 'Now suck my cock. I want to come in that wicked mouth.'

Bryan grinned back, and in that moment Jamie admitted to himself at least that whatever he felt for his friend went far beyond a casual, curious lust. A quiver of something between anticipation and anxiety went through him; to cover it, he pushed Bryan's head back down, pushing his cock between his eager lips.

Bryan's mouth was a piece of heaven and hell. He licked and sucked at the silk-covered hardness of Jamie's erection with relentless attention, each caress amping up Jamie's arousal until he writhed, lost to the sensations that coursed through him. Words fell from his lips, breathless pleas, growling praise until even words failed him and there were only moans and grunts left to express his pleasure.

His head tipped back, eyelids fluttering shut. Orgasm was so close, drawing his balls up tight to his body, and he fought to keep it at bay. He didn't want the pleasure to end, wanted to balance on the knife's edge of orgasm for ever, Bryan's silky hair tangled round his fingers, his wet mouth wrapped tight round his dick.

Bryan had a different idea. The hand that had been playing with Jamie's balls dipped down. Wet from his own saliva, his finger swiftly pierced the untried ring of Jamie's arsehole. Jamie stiffened with the unexpected intrusion, his muscles locking in rigid surprise before orgasm, stronger than anything he had ever felt before, tore through him. It hit him with the force of a freight train, a cry bursting from his lips as his come shot from his cock to be swallowed down eagerly by Bryan.

Jamie flopped back onto the bed, panting in desperate breaths. He didn't think he had ever come so hard in his entire life and, startled, he realised that his arousal hadn't abated even an inch. Bryan licked at the still-hard flesh of his dick, his finger flexing deep inside the depths of his bowels, rubbing a spot that had Jamie seeing stars, it felt so good.

'Oh my God, what are you doing to me?' he groaned. His spine bowed, the back of his head digging into the mattress.

Lifting his head, Bryan grinned at him. 'I'm showing you what you've been missing all your life.'

'You.' Jamie kicked his legs out helplessly. 'You're what I've been missing.'

Bryan's finger flexed one more time within him, massaging his prostate with dextrous skill, before slowly withdrawing it. Moving back off the bed and standing up, he quickly slid down his boxer-briefs, baring himself to Jamie's avaricious gaze. He stood for a moment, letting his friend's eyes roam greedily over his body, lingering over the long hardness that curled up to tap against his navel, before he went to his overnight bag, retrieved a couple of things, and returned to the bed. A bottle of lube and a condom.

Jamie's eyebrow lifted. 'What were you planning for the weekend?'

Bryan grinned at him with that devil-may-care smile of his. 'Whatever it was, it doesn't compare to this. Now watch me.'

With Jamie's gaze rapt upon him, he put down the bottle on the bed to open the condom's foil packet. Each movement as he slipped the latex sheath over his rampant erection was slow, graceful, and so unhurried that Jamie was almost gnashing his teeth before he was done. He grabbed his aching dick, pumping it lazily as Bryan's heated stare warmed him.

Still unhurried, Bryan picked up the bottle of lube. Squeezing a good amount in his hand, he rubbed it over his latex-covered cock. 'Spread your legs wider.' His voice was husky, and the dark command in it made a delicious shiver race up Jamie's spine.

'I'd thought you'd want me on my hands and knees.' When he had thought about this, fantasised about it, that's how Jamie had envisioned it.

Bryan shook his head, his eyes remaining locked on Jamie's. 'No,' he said in a growling whisper that made Jamie's cock jerk in a burst of arousal. 'I want to see your face when I put my dick in you.'

Jamie spread his legs, propping his upper body on his elbows so that he could watch the other man. Bending his knees slightly, he exposed himself completely to Bryan's hungry gaze. Anticipation, arousal, and fear swirled through him as Bryan moved onto the bed, walking up between his legs on his knees. Jamie couldn't look away, and he bit his bottom lip to keep from moaning when Bryan's lubed-up fingers tickled over the sensitive pucker of his arsehole, igniting the nerve-laden flesh with his teasing touch. Closing his eyes, his mouth open and panting, Jamie gave himself over to the sensations rolling through him.

With his slicked fingers, Bryan pierced the tight rosette of Jamie's arse with first one and then two fingers. The bite of pain as he carefully stretched the virgin hole spiced the pleasure that rocketed through Jamie; he shamelessly pushed his hips into Bryan's invasion. 'More,' he begged hoarsely.

Another finger joined the two already in his arse. Jamie's skin rippled in endless shudders. God, he had never thought anything could feel this good. His cock was so hard it pushed into his belly, smearing a copious amount of precome over him.

'Oh God, I'm gonna come.'

Jamie cried out in thwarted desire as Bryan removed

his fingers, then cried out again as Bryan roughly grabbed his hips and pulled him forward onto his lap. The rounded head of Bryan's dick pushed at his asshole. His cock felt so much bigger than his fingers as he steadily worked his way in. Holding onto Jamie's twitching hips, he pushed forward with inexorable pressure. Pain and pleasure warred within Jamie, and then suddenly melded into a sensation he had never felt before and would crave for the rest of his life.

'Are you OK?' Bryan's voice was strained.

'Yes. Now fuck me, Bryan. Fuck my arse hard.'

Bryan gasped and then slammed into Jamie.

Dropping his shoulders to the mattress and bracing his lower half on his feet, Jamie tilted his hips up as far they would go and opened himself even more to Bryan's prick. He felt so – full, not just from Bryan's cock up his arse, but with the pleasure that filled him to overflowing as Bryan fucked him. Shattered cries spilled from his lips as Bryan flexed his hips in a punishing rhythm, rubbing hard against that magic spot inside his rectum. He drove into him hard and deep, hammering with no control or finesse, only raw animal passion that set Jamie's own lust free. The beginnings of orgasm streaked up Jamie's spine and he grabbed his cock, pumping furiously to rush toward that shining edge with every atom of his being.

'Close. Close.' It was all he could gasp out.

Bryan pulled Jamie's buttocks further apart with hard fingers, pushing himself impossibly deeper as he pistoned into him. 'Me too,' he growled. 'I'm gonna come in you, Jamie. I'm gonna come in you so hard.'

Bryan's words pushed Jamie over the edge. He screamed, come shooting forcefully from his dick to splatter across his chest, body bucking against Bryan as he buried himself in him one last time in a brutal thrust.

The strong flex of Bryan's cock inside his arsehole as he came intensified Jamie's orgasm until his eyes rolled back and his head filled with white noise. Bryan's cry mingled with his, his body falling forward onto Jamie's as they both shuddered and writhed with the aftershocks of pleasure, until they both settled into limp satiation.

Beneath the hot press of Bryan's body, Jamie drank in every feeling. The naked skin of Bryan's chest and stomach against his own; his hot breath tickling his chest; his slowly softening dick still wedged deep inside him; the soft kisses he lazily scattered over his chest and shoulders. Jamie absorbed each sensation, drinking Bryan in until every cell was imprinted with him, altered for all time.

'I'm glad you asked me to come with you.' There was a smile in Bryan's voice.

Jamie's own lips curved. 'Me too.'

'Even if –' Bryan hesitated and then carried on, his words coming out in a rush. 'Even if this is the only time we ever do this, I want you to know that I'll never regret being with you.'

Opening his eyes was an effort, but Jamie did it to look up into Bryan's dark eyes. He could see him more clearly, dawn creeping in through the thin curtains. 'Let's clean up,' he said, 'and then go to sleep. I want to do that again when we wake up.'

'Really?'

Jamie smiled. 'Really.'

Happy New Year DJ Lawrence
by Graham Benedict

Back in the 1980s, when Lawrence had been 19, he'd managed to fulfil one of his childhood ambitions. He'd met Baz Taylor, the manager of a local music shop, at a party one weekend. He'd so impressed the guy with his knowledge of various music scenes that Baz had offered him the position of assistant manager, behind the counter of the local branch of Roddy's Records. He'd kept up his interests in most musical trends and, as a sideline, he had started running a little mobile disco and DJ business. It was nothing fancy, from a technical point of view, and nothing which couldn't be carried in the back of a small van. With easy access to a variety of playlists via the stock from the shop, he'd managed to work up a good business for weddings, birthdays, anniversaries, and almost any other social occasion. He'd even mix in the odd weekend rave session, provided it wasn't too heavy or hardcore underground.

After several years, his solid reputation had helped him to get regular gigs at several of the nearby naval training school. Junior rates, senior rates, even the wardroom, had often called on him to help provide some entertainment for the end-of-term parties and summer balls. So it had come as no surprise when he'd picked up the phone and heard the familiar voice of the social secretary for *HMS Kellywood* on the other end.

'Hi Lawrence, it's Chaz from the base. Any chance we could book the disco for New Year's Eve?'

'I thought you were going to be closed down until January next year?'

'Yeah, well, there's still a bit of money left in the social fund. Thought we'd use it up with a bit of a party for those left on base during the Christmas leave period. There's not going to be many people around – and most of those will be on various shifts or security patrols. We're probably looking at about 25 to 30, tops.'

Lawrence had thought about it for a couple of seconds. The Rose of England pub had cancelled due to a fire, so he'd been left without a booking that evening. What with them writing off their deposit and now this, things were starting to look pretty good.

'Yeah, I don't see why not. If you can sort out the passes and get me through the main gate, then that would be great.'

'Consider it done. If you can be here for seven, we can have the bar staff give you a bit of a hand, then we can open the doors at eight, and start the disco going at nine. We'll have to wait until the treasurer gets back from Christmas leave before we can pay you, though. That OK?'

'I don't think the navy is going to be bankrupt any time soon, is it?'

Chaz laughed. 'Not on the wages they pay us, mate! See you New Year's Eve at seven, then. 'Bye!'

Despite the old reputation for hard drinking, the navy gigs were some of the best he'd ever done, mainly because there were always the shore patrol guys to take care of any drunks before they'd got out of hand. People still enjoyed themselves, but the chances of someone crashing into the system, or messing around with the lights, was negligible. Weddings were a totally different story, and he never agreed to a booking for a wedding unless there was a substantial deposit for breakages paid up front.

New Year's Eve came round quick enough and, with the equipment and several boxes of vinyl and cassettes to help the general party atmosphere, he'd shut up Roddy's Records early and started on the drive out to the naval base as quickly as he could. The weather forecast had not been good, and before long conditions had started taking a turn for the worst – temperatures dropping to below freezing, and a late forecast of heavy snow. But the run out to the naval base hadn't been too difficult, given the winding country roads, and he'd managed to turn up on time. They'd helped unload his equipment at the back of the club, then he'd driven to a parking space around the back of the NAAFI, parking up in one of the delivery bays.

Inside the club it had taken him 20 minutes or so to thaw out and get warm again, and, after a cup of black coffee, he'd walked out across the dance floor and started the evening off with the first session of music.

The gig had been slow at first. In fact, it had almost felt as if he was dying on his feet up on stage, but after half an hour things started to liven up. The audience had been a mixture of navy and civilian staff, along with some of the families from the nearby married quarters. Most of the naval personnel were either going on the night shift, or coming off the previous one, which meant some of them were stopping off at the club without first going back to their barracks to get changed first.

Now, navy uniform had never been a turn-on for Lawrence. He kept strictly to his own set of rules: one –

friends are friends, but business is business, and two – you don't crap in your own nest. True, if some guy had taken a fancy to him, or vice versa, then he would've considered slipping them his phone number – usually on one of his neat business cards. But never while he was working, and certainly not while working the navy bases. The navy guys might well have had a reputation for camping it up, but, in those days, being involved with any gay activity in the armed forces was still a punishable offence. If any soldiers, sailors, or airmen were caught, then it was an almost instant dishonourable dismissal from the service.

However, just before 11 p.m., halfway through a Duran Duran medley, Lawrence had seen a guy walk in who had really made him stop and take notice! So much so, he almost forgot to back cue the next record.

The guy was what the navy called a leading rate. He had just come back from helping the local police, who were more than happy to let the shore patrol look after any drunken sailors. He was still dressed in his number one uniform, complete with boots, white gaiters, white belt, and an armband. He was about 6 foot tall, mid to late 20s, good-looking figure, and had a head of ginger blond hair, clipped down with a number three cutter so that it appeared to be a soft bristle rather than a stubbly crop. This was long before men started to colour their hair, let alone the navy guys, and from behind the decks Lawrence could not help but wonder as to just what the guy's cock would be like, snug in a pair of tight briefs, against a nest of golden blond pubic hair.

Then the guy had disappeared from view, despite Lawrence's repeated scanning of the crowd on the dance floor, or hanging around the edges of it. He eventually dismissed it as just a bit of fantasy – probably for the best, considering where he was, and the consequences if they were caught.

Still, the thoughts stayed at the back of his mind. He could quite easily picture it. The guy naked and asleep on top of his bed – on his back, with his cock soft and resting on top of his balls, his skin a golden brown, with the end of the wrinkled foreskin darker and more inviting. He had seen himself leaning over the guy, bringing his head down into the guy's crotch, and gently sucking up the limp cock into his mouth – feeling it grow against his tongue as he rolled it around, pushing it against his cheek and the roof of his mouth. Then sucking it fully erect – and hearing the pleasurable sounds as the guy woke to find himself …

'Oi, mate! Can you play that song by Wizzard again? It's for my mate over there with the antlers and bells on. Yeah! Dedicate it to Stevie, who looks like a right prick! Cheers!'

The evening progressed; Lawrence thought he could sometimes make out the guy he'd mentally christened Blondie, wandering around various groups of people. Laughing and joking, but never really settling anywhere. Then Lawrence had put on a slow mix tape, just four tracks, back to back, but it had given him an easy 20 minutes to work the room as well. He'd gone the opposite way to Blondie, still talking and chatting to people, and finally found himself up at the bar. Despite the offers, he got himself another pint of diet Coke. The last thing he needed was to be stopped and breathalysed on the way home – and the way for him not to end up losing his licence was to not drink at all.

Back up on stage again, getting everyone back into the New Year's Eve mood meant that Lawrence could keep looking out across the dance floor, encouraging the onlookers to get up and boogie with the dancers. The downside was that Blondie had actually caught Lawrence looking at him several times – and every time their eyes had met, Lawrence had been the one who had looked away first. He knew it never paid to build up any hopes, especially in view of where he was, but at least there was going to be some serious fantasy material the next time he decided to settle down and wank himself off.

Then Lawrence had cut the sound system and relayed the chimes from Big Ben. Not only had everyone cheered and celebrated, but quite a few had piled outside to listen to the nearby town bells – and that was when Lawrence found out it had been snowing heavily sometime during the evening.

Fearing the worst, he had trudged round the side of the NAAFI and discovered that that yes, where he'd parked his van under the loading bay overhang, it had become a pretty nasty snow trap – what with all the snow blown in, and the stuff which had dropped off the sloping back roof. Swearing and shaking his head, he'd blindly turned round, all his thoughts focused on who he'd need to talk to in order to get some help, because even he knew there was no way he was going to be able to dig the van out on his own. Let alone loading it up. But, as he swung round, he'd almost collided with Blondie.

The navy guy had grinned a little, in a friendly way. 'Looks like you're stuck good and proper.' He went around to the side of the van and gently rocked it from side to side, then he'd jumped back quickly when more piled snow cascaded down around him. 'I don't think you're going to be moving that until the morning. I'm pretty sure we could talk to the boson, explain what's happened, and maybe see if you can stay on camp for the night. I'm Gary, by the way.'

'Hi, I'm Lawrence. If the guy says yes, then what about the disco equipment?'

'The committee will be locking up shortly, and there's hardly anyone on base likely to try and walk off with anything.' His grin broadened. 'And with an armed guard on the gate, I don't think anyone's going to be stupid enough to try and burgle the place, do you?'

Relieved that he wasn't going to have to spend time on the van and then drive home falling asleep at the wheel, Lawrence had nodded his agreement. 'OK, you've talked me into it. Where do we go to find this boson bloke?'

Only afterwards, once he'd had a chance to sit down and really think about it, did Lawrence realise that the naval guy had probably followed him out when he'd left the club.

As it was, the boson eventually agreed to let Lawrence stay on the base for the night. From a massive board of keys, he had thrown Gary the key to one of the training billets.

'Almost everything's been shut down, so there's going to be no heating or lighting in that block. But there's plenty of blankets and spare mattresses, and the rooms are newly double glazed, so you'll just have to wrap up until the morning.'

Lawrence had silently groaned. He'd been having thoughts about crashing somewhere warm and cosy – but, given the choice, he'd take the accommodation rather than the van.

They had started to walk across the camp toward the accommodation area – Gary up front, Lawrence behind watching his arse as it moved and rolled in the dark wool serge material – when the navy guy stopped and turned to face him.

'Tell you what, I've a better idea. There's more than enough space over in the base staff blocks. Plus we've got all mod cons as well.' He grinned broadly. 'Well, if you consider the 1960s to be modern, that is. I'm sure we can find you some bunk space in one of the free cabins. How do you fancy that?'

'Are you serious? I would kill for some central heating and a warm cup of tea!' Then Lawrence looked serious. 'This isn't going to get you into any trouble, is it?'

'Don't see why it should. It's already gone midnight, everything will have shut down for the night.' He looked around casually. 'And given the weather I doubt if even the security patrols will be doing much but staying in and watching the security cameras.'

'Just so long as I'm not pulled out of bed and strip-searched at five o'clock in the morning by some guard, or whatever.'

Gary had cocked his head a little to one side. 'I could probably arrange that, if that's what you'd like?' He'd tried to keep a straight face, but the look of surprise on Lawrence's had been enough to set him off laughing.

Slightly miffed, Lawrence had just grumbled, 'Very funny. OK, lead me into the warmth, 'cos I'm fucking freezing standing here.'

Without changing direction, in a few moments they had walked over to one of several brick accommodation buildings. Once through the entrance, the warmth had hit him and Lawrence had seen a series of doors leading off the main passageway. At the far end were other doors which led off to the communal toilets and a separate shower area. Not quite all mod cons, but certainly friendlier than a cold barrack dormitory.

Gary led him down to the far door and opened it,

revealing a simple square room with four single beds – two by the door and two in the far corners, plus basic wardrobes, table in the middle, and four chairs around it. All very Spartan compared to home.

Behind him, Gary said, 'Don't worry, mate, I'm the only one here until Christmas leave is finished, so make yourself comfortable for the night.' He moved off to the wardrobe next to one of the beds furthest from the door, then pointed across to the other bed. 'You might want to take that one over there. It's away from the draught under the door, and you're near to the radiator as well. If that doesn't warm you up, nothing will.'

Gary had opened up his wardrobe and pulled out a large towel, which he threw on the bed beside Lawrence, along with a plastic bottle of shower gel.

'If you want to get a hot shower before you turn in, then you're going to have to be quick about it.'

Then, unselfconsciously, he had started to strip out of his uniform, almost in front of Lawrence – totally disregarding the DJ's presence in the room. He had unclipped the white belt, then sat down on his bed and removed his gaiters and boots before standing up again to put them safely in his locker. He'd unzipped his uniform jacket along with the attached blue and white sailor's collar, then rolled it off over his shoulders in one fluid movement. Giving it a shake, he'd carefully put on a coat hanger. Out of the corner of his eye, Lawrence could easily see the short-sleeved cotton white front was still crisp with starch, and beneath it Gary's biceps had flexed and twitched as he'd continued undressing.

Next had been the wide belt holding up his uniform trousers. It had been swiftly unbuckled, the waistband unclipped, and then the trousers had been taken off – Gary had to balance first on one leg, then the other, as he removed them. They had been folded carefully, then put on a hanger as well.

Try as he might, Lawrence found he just couldn't keep his eyes off him. Next off had been the cotton white front, pulled high up over his head. Besides revealing Gary's chest and shoulders, it had also allowed Lawrence an uninterrupted view of his cock, pinned sideways along his groin, beautifully encased in a pair of white briefs. Turning away slightly, Gary had held onto the wardrobe door as he took his socks off then, bending over, he'd slid his briefs down to his ankles, giving Lawrence a wonderful view of his round, firm arse. Stepping out of them, he'd picked up his towel, opened it out and then wrapped it around his waist – but not before giving Lawrence a brief but wonderful glimpse of his thick, swinging cock and his mass of golden pubic hair, before the material hid it from view.

Without saying a word Gary had left, and Lawrence, still completely unsure of the situation, waited until he'd heard the shower running before he stripped off, wrapped the towel around his waist to hide the raging stiff hard-on he had, then made his way to the shower room.

Inside, he'd hurriedly slipped into a shower cubicle in the hope that the hot water would take the lust away. It had little effect, and Lawrence had waited until Gary had finished, dried himself off and left, before turning off the shower and drying himself off.

When he finally got back into the room he had been first disappointed, then resigned to the fact that Gary had turned out the lights and was already curled up in bed.

Yeah. It never paid to build your hopes up too high.

Lawrence had given himself another once-over with the towel, sadly noticing his own deflated cock, and had just pulled back the sheet and blankets when he heard

Gary's voice in the darkness.

'If you drag that bed over alongside mine, you'll find it's much warmer if there's two in a bed ...'

Lawrence didn't have to be told twice. Within seconds he had wheeled and pushed the bed up against the opposite wall, jamming it between Gary's bed and the wardrobe. They had tugged and pulled the bedclothes so that they sort of overlapped, and although it wasn't the same as a double mattress, it meant they had more room and comfort than if they had tried it on just a single.

Lying on their sides, they had faced each other, and Lawrence had been more than prepared to let Gary take the lead. Just the simple nearness of him, his wonderful warm, clean smell and his obvious body heat had been enough to put the blood back into Lawrence's erection. The next thing he knew, one of Gary's rough but gentle hands had run down over his hip and thigh, cupping his balls and giving his hard cock a squeeze.

As Lawrence bit his lip in order to keep his excitement contained, he had reached up and slipped two fingers into Gary's mouth – feeling him eagerly suck on them as he flexed the hand still wrapped around Lawrence's cock.

Then Lawrence had pulled them away before drawing Gary close and replacing the fingers with his own mouth and tongue, instinctively wrapping his leg around Gary's and pressing hard against him – revelling in the sensation of heat as their cocks pressed up against each other.

Being versatile, Lawrence had waited to see what Gary might do, but when he didn't object to Lawrence's hand sliding down his back and kneading his arse, Lawrence had decided to take it further. His hand had moved across, working first his thumb, then another two fingers down into Gary's arse crack – teasing and tapping with his fingertips at Gary's hole.

Gary had wriggled and pushed back against his fingers, then gently taken hold of Lawrence's wrist and moved his hand away. Putting some space between them, he said, 'We can save that for later. Firstly, let's see how good you are at swallowing the anchor.'

Lawrence had been confused for a moment, but when Gary put a hand on his shoulder and slowly pushed him further down the makeshift bed, he'd finally understood.

Under the covers he had blindly found Gary's chest and then traced downward, following the trail of chest hair until his chin had found the hot, sticky tip of Gary's rigid cock. Even in the dark, Lawrence had no problem imagining the glorious length of meat surrounded by a mat of golden pubic hair. His mouth had opened wide and his hand had come up to help guide Gary's throbbing shaft between his lips. He had clamped down on it firmly, working his tongue over the top of it and savouring the salty-sweet taste of sticky precome where it had been pooling in and around the edges of Gary's foreskin.

It had been wonderful, but Lawrence had felt cramped down at the bottom of the bed. He'd swung his feel around and up so that they rested on his pillow. Not only did that give him better access to Gary's prick, it also gave Gary easy access to his own rock-hard shaft. No sooner had he settled back down to sucking on Gary's dick than he had felt Gary wrap his hand around his stiff shaft and slowly start to work his fist up and down. Gary had even caught Lawrence by surprise by slipping several fingers of his other hand between his thighs and starting to massage the very root of his cock, behind his tightening balls.

In reply, Lawrence had gently eased apart Gary's legs, holding one leg up before releasing the cock from his mouth. Moving down, he had sucked on Gary's balls, one at a time, and then worked his tongue further along, easing his shoulders and then his arms between Gary's legs as he continued to lick and probe at the base of Gary's arse. Lawrence had paused to catch his breath, then he had slipped his thumbs between Gary's cheeks, eased them apart, and had started to work his tongue over and around, circling inward, until he had finally speared the centre with several firm jabs of his tongue. Gary had slowly opened up and soon he had been breathing heavily as Lawrence continued to tongue-fuck him, working the saliva into his hole with his mouth and a helpful finger.

Finally pushing the sheets and blankets to one side, Lawrence had moved out from between Gary's legs, rolled him on his back, spread his legs wide and then knelt down in between them. Moments later, Gary's rigid cock was back in his mouth as Lawrence worked his tongue, lips, and even the back of his throat over the other man's shaft.

Gary had thrown back his head and bit at his hand to stop himself from shouting out, then he had reached out, grabbed a pillow, raised his hips and stuffed it under the small of his back. Lawrence, his own cock bobbing and twitching, had stopped sucking and taken hold of Gary's legs. Resting them on his shoulders, he shuffled forward so that his own cock was pushed hard up against Gary's upraised arse. Slipping his hands around Gary's hips and cupping his arse for support, Lawrence had lifted him higher and pulled him forward, lowering him down onto Lawrence's eager cock. There had been a little rough resistance as it had pushed its way into Gary's crack, but then it had found Lawrence's saliva and wedged itself up against Gary's puckered arsehole. In one movement, Gary had relaxed, pushing down against the bunched-up pillow, and Lawrence had felt the solid head of his cock slip past Gary's ring, closely followed by the hot joy of his shaft sliding into the muscular sailor beneath him.

What with all the mouth and hand action, and the dim sight of Gary's hand as it curled around his own proud cock, Lawrence knew he was near the point of no return. Pushing forward, he had felt Gary's arse come firmly up against his groin; working the two of them further up the makeshift bed, Lawrence had finally planted his hands on Gary's pillow, either side of his head. As he'd looked back down at the curled-over form beneath him he'd seen Gary's hand become a blur as it jumped up and down. The rushing feeling in Lawrence's balls had spurred him on to work his hips, pulling out so that only the head of his cock stayed in place, then pushing back down again, working the whole of his shaft into Gary, and feeling his balls bouncing against Gary's arse.

Moments later he had heard Gary grunting – the sound loud in the silence – then felt the guy jerking beneath him as Gary's ring clamped tightly down on Lawrence's shaft. Lawrence had even felt the wet splashes on his chest and arm as Gary shot his load between their interlocked bodies, and it had been the trigger for his own release. Pushing himself up on his toes, he had pounded into Gary, arching his back and thrusting himself deeper and deeper into Gary as he emptied his ball sack as far up the sailor's tight arse as he could get.

Finally, spent and worn out, Lawrence had carefully disentangled himself, then collapsed blissfully alongside the still panting Gary.

As he caught his breath he'd looked up at the ceiling. 'Now, that's what I call a Happy New Year!'

They had stayed in the makeshift double bed until early

the following morning, just dozing and cuddling. Then, after rearranging the room back to the way it had been, Gary had led Lawrence into the shower room again. This time they had showered together, kissing passionately and eventually wanking each other off under the strong jets of warm water.

Back in the room, they had dried and dressed, with Gary wearing his uniform again, only this time without the white belt, armband, and gaiters. Half a day off, then he was back on several night shifts. After a welcome breakfast, Gary had returned the keys to the boson's Store, and organised some of the duty watch to help dig Lawrence's van free.

With the disco kit loaded, Lawrence had driven off to get ready for another pub gig. In the rear view mirror, he'd seen Gary standing in the middle of the roadway, watching him leave. Sadly, despite going back to the navy camp many times, Lawrence never did find Gary again, but as he knew all too well, when it came to the armed forces it never paid to build your hopes up.

Lay-by
by L.A. Fields

Bruce still tips the scales at around 290 pounds. It was an event the day he fell under 300, albeit a low-key one, and it mostly took place in his head. He did not want his aunt, who he'd been living with since he started his first semester at college, to know that he had ever been over 300 pounds. She could probably tell regardless; she's incredibly weight conscious and measures out all of her food based on a large chart on the fridge. She makes Bruce feel helped and harassed at the same time, when nagging and reminding start to sound like the same thing.

Aunt Leena (short for Leeanna) keeps sugarless candy stashed around her apartment to curb her appetite. She knows how much food is in the fridge, and can usually tell if Bruce has eaten a portion of something, and how much, just by eyeballing it. This had once been part of the incentive to living with Leena as opposed to paying for a room on campus. No cruel city kids to room with, no lines for laundry machines, and Bruce would have someone around to keep him on his diet and monitor his exercise. He asked for all this. He moved in here especially, like it was a good thing.

But he's since learnt that the kids at college aren't even mean. In his computer classes, the ones only majors take, Bruce has actually found some friends. It isn't like high school at all; they don't make fun of him, and Bruce knows it isn't because he's skinnier, like Aunt Leena says. Bruce is still huge, he has a long way to go before he's not considered repulsive by many, but still the kids talk to him, and invite him to parties, and seem to genuinely like his personality.

In fact, Bruce has even met a lesbian at school. He only made it to Raleigh for college; he didn't make it out of North Carolina, and he didn't get out of the South at all, but something about the university culture made it OK, somehow, to be such a thing. *A gay*, as Aunt Leena says. One of them.

Bruce has told no one about himself, not even the lesbian, just in case it's some sort of trap. She might be a secret agent for the school, posing as a student, trying to trap Bruce into admitting what he is so they can throw him out. He tells Aunt Leena lies about all the pretty girls, and certainly they are very pretty at his school; not that it matters either way to Bruce. But Aunt Leena is still Aunt Leena: she already finds his fat disgusting; he can only imagine the look on her face if she found out he was gay on top of it. He'd be nothing more to her than a big fat, flabby faggot, and who wants to be that?

The guys are pretty on campus as well, though no one is so gorgeous that they're worth the risk of approaching. There were hot guys back in high school too, but Bruce wouldn't talk to them either. Even if by some strange chance those pretty guys were actually gay, they'd just fuck each other, wouldn't they? Or be celibate for a while. Bruce imagines most guys would rather abstain for the rest of their lives than have anything to do with him.

But that is not true about everyone. There was one guy, Wade Anderson from back in the Mile, as the town is nicknamed. He was interested in Bruce, or at least he had sex with him a few times. After months under the relentless attention of his aunt, Bruce feels sure that Wade was just desperately hard-up, that he only chose to be with him was because there truly was no one else around. Never mind that Wade was always kind to him, that his eyes would travel the great distances over Bruce's body without the critical wince that Aunt Leena and even perfect strangers get; but surely Bruce remembers it wrong. He didn't yet understand the subtleties of disgust. He knows them better now.

The last time he saw Wade, Bruce packed a bag to go with him on one of his hitchhiking adventures. Wade takes off all the time, no roots to hold him down, no money to carry him; he just goes out in the world and exists with no plans or support, every once in a while showing back up in town to crash on his mom's couch. He's her only son, and she lets him get away with all that. Bruce doesn't have anyone so tolerant in his family. He packed his bag one night to go with Wade, but he unpacked it the next morning, and starting planning for college instead. The idea of running away had grown like a bunch of grapes in his heart, each aspect of the fantasy branched out from the others like a plump, glistening opportunity. But Bruce let the ripeness pass. He thought he'd have to content himself with a handful of shrivelled dreams, the sensible raisin snack that wild imaginings age into. But, instead, his fantasies fermented. Something bloats in Bruce still, even as he is slimming down. Something buoys him.

The day Wade calls is a terrible one. Bruce is accused (fairly) of eating the last yogurt, a decision he made after nearly an hour of late-night agony, pacing next to the refrigerator, opening it over and over to stare at the tiny cup, pulling himself away, and then coming back again, until finally he just ate the thing in a rash attack with his spoon. It wasn't that he was hungry, or that a shot glass of yogurt is all that tempting, but once it occurred to him to eat it, he couldn't stop thinking about it. If he wants it, and it's right there, why shouldn't he eat it? His aunt says it's a question of his willpower, but if it takes that kind of gargantuan will to avoid eating one tiny snack, then his life must be a torture of longing and shame and obsession if he wants to be skinny. But hell, his life is like that already.

The phone rings in the middle of the fight, and Bruce runs to answer it as he would rush to an escape hatch.

'Hello?' he says, and it's Wade, calling from a pay phone, asking for directions, wondering if he can stop by. They haven't spoken in months, Wade has been MIA from his mother's house, and Bruce had been pining for him, or so he realises, as he tells Wade the way to his building. Aunt Leena perks up when she hears they'll have company. She enjoys showing off, though she probably won't like Wade, as he's not impressed by nice things or polite people. He's an underwhelmed sort of kid.

Wade comes to the door as Bruce is changing, trying to find some clothes that aren't too tight or too big. He can hear Aunt Leena falter in her greeting, which means Wade is not what she expected, and when she shows him into Bruce's room, Wade is not what he expected either.

His clothes are filthy, and there's a hole in his shirt with blood on it. There are burgeoning bruises on his face. His hair is matted to his neck with sweat, and his fingernails as he waves hi to Bruce are dark and ragged, like he just climbed out of his own grave.

'What happened to you?' Bruce asks as Aunt Leena snaps the door shut on them both, most likely wanting nothing to do with it all.

'Just some guy robbed me,' Wade says, sort of collapsing carefully against the wall. 'It was kind of funny actually. He only got about $20 off of me, and he seemed disappointed that I wasn't more scared.' He closes his eyes in a long blink, like it's a lot of trouble to open them back up again. 'Let me keep the wallet, though. Mind if I sit down?'

Bruce looks at his daily-made bed, then at Wade's clothes. 'Aunt Leena's really picky about stuff getting dirty. Maybe you better take off your clothes first.'

Wade snorts and starts yanking at his clothes. He is a little younger than Bruce, but has always seemed so much older, worldly from all his daring travels. Back in the Mile he was just the grandest thing around, at least to Bruce. He went where he wasn't supposed to, he'd had sex with strangers and lived to tell about it, though Bruce was the only one who cared to listen.

Wade gets down to his underwear and Bruce tells him that's good enough. He wanted to help Wade undress since it looked like a struggle, but he did not want to be too presumptuous. Wade might have met anyone, done anything, while he was gone. He always comes back so mysterious.

Wade sits down close to Bruce, too close, and lays his head on Bruce's abundant shoulder.

'You don't have a concussion or something, do you?' Bruce asks.

Wade rocks his head back and forth. 'All he did was pop me in the mouth a few times. I'm just tired. I had to bum change, and find a phone, and try to remember your aunt's name, and it's just been a long day.'

Wade puts an arm around Bruce, and kisses his sleeve, but Bruce tries to slide away. Wade picks up his eyelids heavily again.

'Sorry,' he says. 'You got a boyfriend or something?'

'No, it's not that,' Bruce starts to say, but his aunt's voice interrupts him from the living room.

'Bruce? Can I see you for a moment?'

Bruce makes a face in the direction of the door, hopefully communicating all of it: his aunt; his situation; his recurring fear that something is different between them now, too different to be comforting. He closes the door behind him and walks down the hall to find his aunt in a huff.

'I called your mother,' she says. 'I wanted to know just what kind of boy shows up looking like that.' She watches Bruce, her nostrils flaring, and he can only imagine what kind of gossip she's heard. Wade has a terrible name in their home town, and he earned it fair and square being such a loafing, conspicuous queer, but it still seems lame that his reputation should precede him, that his past should follow him here. 'Just what have you allowed into my house?' Aunt Leena asks.

Bruce cowers before her, mumbles, 'He's my friend.'

'Some friend! Your mother said he almost got you fired, hanging around all the time, being a useless leech.'

Bruce grimaces. Wade did almost get him fired from the McDonald's once, but not just for hanging around. Everyone hung around the McDonald's, there wasn't a lot else going on. Bruce thinks his manager suspected what they were up to, what Bruce and Wade did behind the dumpsters after close, on the nights that meant everything to Bruce.

'I can't ask him to leave, Aunt Leena. He's got nowhere to go.' Then the clincher. 'It would be rude.'

Aunt Leena swells at the very suggestion. 'Oh, don't worry about that!' She grabs her purse and heads to the door. 'I'm such a Christian I'll let you force me out of my own home, but he better not be here when I get back from Sue Ellen's.' Her friend Sue Ellen lives in the building. They sound like screechy birds when they get together, talking crap about everyone, including Bruce, knowing full well when he's in earshot but also knowing that they're untouchable. This latest event with Wade should fuel tons of gossip. She might be gone for hours.

'I better not even see the back of him going down the stairs,' she says, and sweeps from the room importantly, enjoying her own show.

When he gets back to his room, Bruce finds Wade fallen asleep in a slump on his bed. Mouth open, arms dangling, his feet still clad in socks. Bruce tucks him in, noting a scrape on his chest where the hole in the shirt was, which looks like it's from being shoved down on gravel and rocks. Wade's socks smell, and his hair isn't just dirty, but has actual dirt and sand in it, and even so, Bruce still sees something marvellously worth staring at. He wants to wake Wade up, not knowing how much time they will have at Aunt Leena's discretion, but he just can't do it. Wade looks too finished, and by now Bruce is used to this kind of yearning anyway; it's become sweet to him.

Wade doesn't wake up until evening, after Aunt Leena's called to say she will be spending the night with Sue Ellen. Bruce had been watching him sleep from the doorway, and he scurries away when Wade stirs, afraid of having his desperation exposed. He made Wade a sandwich anyway, which he holds up wordlessly as Wade emerges from the hallway.

Wade seems grateful for the food, like he just remembered he was painfully hungry and had been for a while. Bruce watches him build up his humanity again; eat, stretch, breathe deeply, like the tin man oiling hinges.

Wade takes a shower, and Bruce washes his sheets and remakes the bed, he thinks because of Aunt Leena, but maybe also to have clean sheets for something else. He meets Wade in the hallway, steam billowing out of the bathroom and crawling across the ceiling like smoke from a house fire. Wade is in a towel, suddenly clean, and pink with flush, and his eyes are awake finally, and it's good to see him again.

Wade smiles at Bruce, and leans suggestively against the wall. Bruce is slightly sweaty from wrestling with his bedding. He had meant to change his shirt, comb his hair, put on cologne, but Wade doesn't care about any of that. He takes Bruce's hand and tucks it between the panels of the towel. For a moment Bruce is able to palm Wade's soft, dangling cock, still moist and warm like the inside of a kiss, but the front door opens with a bang and Aunt Leena announces, 'I'm just here to pick up my things!'

Wade disappears quickly back into the bathroom, and Bruce is left standing in the hallway with a guppy face, his hand cupping thin air. Leena catches him just standing there, then notices all the steam.

'He in the bathroom?' she asks, her face pinched up around the question. Bruce nods stupidly. 'I guess we can disinfect it later.' She gets some pyjamas and her not-so-secret stash of booze and leaves again. Wade comes back out of the bathroom fully clothed, breaking Bruce's heart.

'I gotta go out for a while,' Wade says.

'No you don't.' Bruce follows him around as he finds his shoes and slicks his hair back in the reflection of the microwave. 'Leena's already gone again. You can at least stay the night.'

'Don't worry about it, I'll be back.' Wade smiles. 'I wouldn't say no to a bed, especially if you're in it. I gotta see about making some money, though.' He heads for the door, Bruce still trailing behind him.

'What can you do to get money?' he asks, but Wade just tips an imaginary hat and leaves. Bruce hurries to the window to see Wade emerge from the building, and he falls asleep on the couch waiting for him to return, which he does eventually, a few hours later, well after dark.

'How'd it go?' Bruce asks, wiping drool off his chin.

'Pretty good,' Wade says. 'I made almost 200 bucks.'

Bruce hesitates, wanting to know how, but he thinks he knows already. He's seen skinny kids like Wade hanging out on the bus line but never actually getting on the bus, and he knows what they do. He's thought about going to one of them before, he has plenty of money saved, but the thought that even they might reject him was too terrifying.

'Do you want to go straight to bed?' Bruce asks instead. 'I know it's still early and everything, but I figured you might be tired.'

'Yeah,' Wade says. 'Just let me clean up first, you know?' Bruce nods.

He follows Wade to the bathroom but continues past the door and into his bedroom with his mind purposefully blank as he listens to the sink run, to Wade swishing and spitting. He isn't in there long.

Wade comes to him. He stands in front of Bruce, his crotch at eye level since Bruce is sitting on his bed. Wade's wearing only jeans, but not for long as he unbuttons them. No underwear. Bruce puts his thick hands on Wade's skinny waist, assuming that he should start sucking, but Wade stops him by holding his chin.

'Don't do that,' he says, cocking his head. 'Kiss me.'

Bruce stands to obey. He holds Wade's face as he kisses him, his fingers exploring the bone structure and tucking back his hair. Wade keeps his hands at his side and allows himself to be felt, and it's a shift in their dynamic, as if Bruce has enough confidence now to act, rather than be acted upon.

He can see he's making Wade hard. He touches Wade's dick coaxingly, and feels Wade's hand describe the arch of his belly beneath his shirt. There is a moment of frenzied stripping, and they end on the bed, Bruce lying back on his pillows and Wade tearing a condom he must have pulled from his pocket. He rolls it on and works himself into Bruce, and it's like pressing a reset button, and suddenly Bruce feels just the way he wants to feel, comfortable in his body.

Even better, with all the weight he's lost, it's easier for Wade to kiss him while they're doing it, and Bruce gets to fulfil a small fantasy of his. First he comes while Wade is still inside him, and then Wade finishes off while they kiss, tongues pressed deep together, and the way Wade nearly chokes on his own orgasm is a thrill to feel.

They settle into a post-coital stupor, Bruce trying hard not to snuggle too much, under the strange impression that it would make him a nerd. They sort of nap and fuck throughout the night, not saying much until Wade sits up at dawn and starts getting dressed.

Bruce, miring in the two extreme emotions of panic and depression, puts on his clothes as well. Probably they don't fit like they used to, because Wade says, 'How much weight have you lost?'

'Thirty pounds,' Bruce says sheepishly.

Wade hmms, non-committal. 'Is that because of you, or because of your aunt's regime I saw on the fridge?'

'Both,' Bruce says, more than a little hurt. 'Don't I look better?'

'You looked fine before.' Wade pulls on his shirt,

covering up his skinny ribs, and it's easy for him to be so casual, since he doesn't even have so much as a single stretch mark. 'I don't know,' Wade continues. 'Your aunt just seems a little Reich-y, you know what I mean?'

'Oh. Yeah.' Bruce does know what he means, but he feels like anything must be worth it if it makes him thin. He has thought about moving onto campus sometimes, into the gay dorm, which they unofficially have over there. 'I can't really leave, though,' Bruce says, following his internal line of logic. 'Aunt Leena and my mom and everyone, they wouldn't let me.'

Wade snorts. 'Let you. Dude, you could have them make you leave. Just let your aunt walk in on us spooning on the couch. You'd hardly have time to pack.'

Bruce is still thinking. 'So you're saying I should come out?'

'I'm saying you should get out. If you want to.' Wade looks sagely at Bruce, his elbows resting on his knees, his hands folded together, and he reminds Bruce of Jesus right now, and a lot of the time, really. He seems so wise and doomed.

'Are you leaving?' Bruce asks.

Wade nods slowly. 'I should.' He gets up, starts moving with purpose. 'And you should think about it too,' Wade says, and to Bruce's questioning stare he adds, 'leaving.'

Bruce feels like they've had this conversation once before, when Wade offered Bruce the chance to go with him, to leave town and never come to college in Raleigh, but this is different. He isn't saying come with me out of pity. He's telling Bruce to go on his own, for his own sake.

And Wade's parting thoughts. 'This goes for both of us. If we don't get far enough away, we'll always be the same losers we were back in the Mile. That's why I keep moving.' He kisses Bruce on the cheek before opening the front door, and, grinning, says, 'I want to at least be a new kind of loser by the time I die, you know?'

Bruce laughs. He does know. He's always known what he wanted, and how to get it, but the problem was being brave enough to go for it. 'Maybe all I needed was a good poke in the ass to get moving,' he says, this time getting Wade to laugh. The sound of it makes the hope he's been holding in like intestinal gas burst and flood his body with resolve.

Bruce kisses Wade again, right in the hallway, knowing full well that his aunt might be coming around the corner any second, tongues and teeth and lips and everything. But for all that, it doesn't even wipe the smile off his face. In fact, he still has the same reckless grin when he walks into the housing office the next morning and asks them for a room on campus, any room at all, just so long as it's got enough room to grow.

April Showers
by Michael Wells

Through an hour of dawn drizzle I'd been running. A city fox had kept up with me along two streets on the opposite pavement, matching me step for step before it turned and disappeared through a corrugated iron fence. It was unusual for me to have company on my early morning runs. I keep away from people, taking to the streets in my well-worn trainers only when others are returning from nights out or before they drag their weary bodies out of bed wondering why they drank so much the night before.

Usually I only dodge tired-looking cleaners on their way to the big city offices or the newspaper delivery guy; sometimes I stumble on the occasional drunk still reeling from a big night out. I know these streets, know how they work and where to go. I never get into trouble; I run fast and am gone before any chance mugger or tramp wanting change can grab me. I am safe in a city where people fear to open their doors.

I like it like this; I like the anonymity that a big city brings. You're never more alone than when you're surrounded by millions of people just getting on with their lives. I've become less of a people person, and can't remember the last time I went out with friends – or on a date. I haven't always been like this, but over the five years since moving here to write I've kept myself more and more to myself, going out early to run, late nights at the gym and a few meetings with my editor.

My life follows much the same pattern – or it did. Today, things changed. A new life crashed into mine without any chance of me being able to control it.

Stretching and arching my shoulders, I leant back from the computer, took off my glasses and sighed. I quickly leant forward, back to the screen, clicked "save", and watched as a small clock on the screen span to save my document. There it was, three months' work, finished. I'd make a coffee, check through the kitchen window on what was happening on the busy street below, then come back and email my senior editor.

Looking at the clock, it was just after midday. I rose and stretched again. If I got everything emailed off this afternoon I could treat myself to an early visit to the gym, before the office workers filled it with so much coloured Lycra. I hated sitting at a computer all day. My muscles ached for action; to feel the power in my arms pushing against the weights was a real turn-on for me. There was nothing like building up a sweat and sending rivulets of healthy sweat running down the soft hairs of my chest and stomach. I was proud of my body and loved the admiring glances from strangers it attracted. Well, I'd worked hard enough for it, so why not show it off?

Running my fingers through my hair, brushing a blond curl from my forehead, I wandered to the kitchen, flicked the switch on the kettle, and grabbed a mug. I looked out of the second storey window to the busy street below. I love living in the city, ever changing, always buzzing. I know you have to put up with neighbours, the odd rude shopkeeper and shouting cycle couriers, but there's nothing like running through the streets early in the morning, before the commuters arrive, before you have to dodge taxis and tourists. It still gives me a thrill to walk through my front door and into an electric atmosphere that says "anything can happen".

Grabbing the now boiled kettle, I poured and stirred the instant coffee. I noticed the builder's van that had been outside all week was still there. The flat upstairs was being renovated, and I'd spent the last week listening to the knocking, crashing, and banging that comes with building work. The builder was cute, though. I'd spotted him dodging through the shoppers to get something from his van, packing up his tools and even running to move the van as a traffic warden came along. He was tall, maybe 6 foot 1 or 2, and looked powerfully muscular in a tight, sinewy way. When he took his boiler suit off before throwing it in the back of the van one evening, his T-shirt stretched where it barely covered his broad chest and arms. I'd passed him on the stairs once; he'd smiled. He had beautiful, naturally tanned skin and thick, short cut black hair. Greek, perhaps? On his forearms were small, dark hairs, which were, at the time, lightly dusted with white plaster dust. The smile, a flashing white smile that said in an instant "sorry about clogging the stairs", "sorry about the noise" and then "hello, you're cute". As he went up the stairs I turned and checked out his bum. In a boiler suit it showed nothing, but there's no harm in checking, is there!

I smiled to myself at the memory of him and turned and walked back to my desk. Just as I was about to click and check my emails a drop of water landed on my hand. I looked at it for a second, not quite believing what it was, and then another drip. 'What the …?' I looked around me, looked up, I could see nothing. Then another drip and another. From a tiny crevice around the ornate Victorian plasterwork of the light fitting water began steadily falling. I quickly moved my computer, pleased I had decided to buy a laptop rather than a tower, and moved the edits of my book I had spent so long working on. Grabbing my keys, I bounded to the front door and headed upstairs.

Taking the stairs two at a time, I hammered on the door of the next floor flat. Calling and banging with all my strength finally got a reaction. I heard hurried footsteps along the hall and the door was flung open.

Before me stood the gorgeous builder. He was soaking wet from head to toe. In an instant my eyes took him in. He was wearing nothing but jeans and trainers, and water, running down his body. His hair was plastered to his skull, the small fringe spiked down with numerous droplets of water. His face was beautiful, and he had a panicked look in his eye that made my heart skip a beat. With a flick of my eyes I watched his washboard stomach heave in and out as water ran down it in rivulets. He was breathing so heavily, his chest, bigger than I remembered from viewing him from my window, rose and fell rapidly. I just wanted to fall into that chest and have him wrap his arms around me.

'Thank God you're here,' he said. 'Quickly, this way.' Before I could even answer he had turned and darted down the hallway to the kitchen, literally dragging me behind him. The kitchen looked like a tropical rainforest. Water sprayed from one wall across the whole kitchen; it dripped from cupboards, ran down the walls, and was pooling across work surfaces and floor. On the floor I could make out his boiler suit and T-shirt, which he had used to try and soak up some of the water. They had been overpowered by the waves that headed their way.

'Grab me that wrench,' he commanded as I waded into the spray. Instantly my T-shirt became wet and stuck to me like a second skin. My nipples jutted out where they'd become instantly excited on seeing the half-naked Greek god; my stomach, taut from workouts, showed its hard-earned shape through the thin material. I hoped he hadn't noticed how excited I had become.

The mysterious wet man dived under a cupboard at the same time as commanding me to "try and stop the water spraying from the bloody wall!" Water poured on top of him and ran across his tanned body as if in a shower. From where I stood, hands against the wall, all I could see were his glistening wet jeans, hugging the cutest bubble butt I'd seen in ages. I held my hands over the jet of water coming from the hole in the wall; it seemed to make it worse and the water sprayed at different angles across the room. My hair became plastered to my head and I could feel water running down my back and chest and into my jeans, which were becoming heavy and waterlogged. I watched as the muscles tensed in the builder's back as he pulled at the wrench in the depths of the cupboard. A pool of water had gathered in the dip in his back, just above his arse. I wanted to get down on my knees and lick it all up. His twists and turns in that cupboard showed every muscle working, each in turn tightening, moving, and joining with another to combine strength. His back rippled with powerful movement. I now had the problem of hiding my erection in my wet and hugging jeans. Rubbing where I leant up against a kitchen work surface had made it worse, and I couldn't cover it with my hands as they were busy trying to stop the fountain of water shooting from the wall.

Then, as if by magic, the torrent stopped. The wet wrench-monkey fell backwards from the cupboard with a huge grunt of relief and landed in a pool of water, his back resting against one of the dripping cupboards. I felt the water pressure under my hands slow as the pressure in my jeans got worse. He sat there like a god, born from the sea, panting, his beautiful chest rising and falling rapidly, his muscles shining. He smiled at me, whistled a long, relieved note through hugely kissable lips and rubbed his hand down his chest and stomach as if suddenly seeing the water that was making it shine for the first time.

He looked around. 'Fuck,' he said, 'look at this place.' Looking up at me, his eyes taking me, and my jeans, in properly for the first time, he smiled. 'Thanks!' He held out his hand. 'I'm Alexi.'

'Tom,' I said taking his brown hand in mine. Despite the water I felt the warmth and power of his hand connect with me. I looked at him and smiled. 'Need a hand clearing up?' I asked.

'I think you've helped enough, you're soaked! No, honestly, I'll take it from here, I'll be fine.'

'Look,' I said, really not wanting to leave this beautiful Adonis, 'you're just as soaked as I am. When you've sorted out the plumbing here, come down to the flat below and dry off, OK? I've got some clothes you can wear, or we can dry yours …'

My words began to sound corny as they petered out. Still smiling, Alexi looked at me with the deepest brown eyes I'd ever seen, which began to knock against every emotional door in my mind that I'd closed since I've been in this city. 'You're a lifesaver,' he said, 'give me 20 minutes and I'll be down'.

Back in my flat I peeled off the wet T-shirt and pushed and pulled at the soaked jeans and trunks. Finally free, I flung them in the direction of the washing machine and naked went to check on any damage in my living room. The desk was wet, but there was no damage to anything else. Water was still dripping gently through the ceiling, but it wasn't the torrent I had dreaded. I placed a towel over the desk and stuck a pan under the drips, all the time thinking about Alexi. What am I doing? I thought to myself. I can't do anything with this guy. He's a burly Greek builder, he's probably got a wife and 12 perfectly tanned and beautiful children at home, he'll pulverise me.

Quickly, I went to the bedroom, grabbed a pair of joggers and a fresh T-shirt, and dressed. In the kitchen, I pushed my wet clothes into the washing machine and stood wondering whether I should wait for Alexi's wet clothes to join them.

In a slight daydream, I turned and there stood Alexi, his glorious chest dry now apart from a smear of water across his chest from the sopping T-shirt that hung over his broad shoulder. In one hand was his wet boiler suit, in the other some towels. 'Sorry,' he said, 'the door was ajar. Is it OK to come in?' Instantly I regretted putting on joggers with no underwear. I knew that Alexi had seen my dick twitch and bounce as I looked at him. His eyes took in my body and, as he looked at my face, he broke once again into his smile that just melted my heart.

'Sure, no problem,' I stuttered. 'Give me your stuff, I'm just about to dry mine …'

He took the one step toward me that brought me within touching distance and gently pulled the wet T-shirt from his shoulder. I grabbed the rest of the damp clothes and pushed them into the machine. Setting the dial, I stood and turned to find that Alexi was right behind me.

'Thank you for your help today.' His hand came up and was clamped on my shoulder. 'I don't know what I would have done without you. You saved my day, I owe you – big time.' My mouth opened to bat away the compliment, but before I could get the words out Alexi's lips were on mine. Soft, full, strong lips that entangled me in their warmth. He kissed with such tenderness and self-contained strength I could do nothing but stand there and slowly melt. Drawing away, he said, 'Sorry, I couldn't help myself, you're so stunning. I'm really sorry, you're probably not even …'

But before he could finish the sentence I wrapped my arms around him and was kissing him with passion I hadn't felt in years. Our bodies came together, warm skin against warm skin, muscle against muscle. It was like each of us was trying to hold the other tighter than the other. My hand went to the back of his head, fingers pushed into the thick, black hair and I pulled him in as close as I could. The warmth, the heat that was oozing from him was like power being transferred from his to my own body. We couldn't get enough. Alexi pulled away from me and bent slightly to kiss my neck. Soft, warm kisses that sent a shiver of electricity through me.

As he kissed me, his hands wandered around my back, discovering my muscles and stroking my skin. When his mouth met my nipple, I gasped. Taking the signal of pleasure, Alexi began to slowly trace the outline of it with his tongue. Round and round the wet tongue went before taking it gently in his teeth Alexi bit oh so softly at its erect end. I gasped again; my body bucked, bolts of electricity shooting across my skin. Biting harder, Alexi took the other erect nipple and squeezed it between his thumb and forefinger. I shuddered and grabbed at the back of Alexi's head and buried my face in his thick hair. With a twist of an arm I sent him down my body, giving no resistance, his tongue and lips never losing contact with my chest. He kissed his way down my stomach and, finally, to my groin. On his knees now, Alexi, chin on the waistband of my joggers, looked up at me with a passion I felt totally. I wanted to be connected to him; I wanted our bodies to be as one. Nimble hands grabbed at the waistband and pulled at them. His mouth was in my groin, greedily licking and sucking; my dick, harder than I can ever remember it being, was caught in the fabric, held by Alexi's chin, unable to escape. The feeling was exquisite. Hot hands grabbed my dick from its prison, fabric fell to the floor, and Alexi still looked at me. Then, drawing his eyes down to his prize, he parted his beautiful lips and swallowed me. The sensation of being inside his mouth almost felled me. My knees buckled and I grabbed at the kitchen counter to steady myself, drawing deep breaths to stop my head spinning. Heat pulsated from my dick and lifted years of coldness from my bones. With his tender mouth, he pulled from me loneliness and bitterness; playing with my dick, sucking my balls and eagerly discovering pleasures I knew had equally become mine.

I had to taste that passion on him, had to be sure that his beautiful lips were telling the truth. I gave up my position at the counter and let myself fall. Face to face with him, I looked into those deep, passionate eyes and silently begged him to take me. His smile replied; he had got the message. Lips on mine, tongue discovering mine, passion demanding more and more. Strong hands, muscles tensed, wrapped themselves around me and lifted me onto the work surface. Kissing as if we were never to see each other again, Alexi quickly unbuttoned his still-wet jeans. Tugging and pulling at them to ease them from his taut, hot skin, he kicked to release them. His dick, trapped until then, bounced and jumped, happy to be free, hard as stone in his dark triangle of hair. Somehow, from the wet jeans Alexi grabbed a condom. Pausing to rip the packaging with his teeth, he smiled at me. The smile said more than I thought possible ... "Is this OK? Are you sure? We're going to be together now, as one."

I smiled back at him and raised my legs, wrapped them around his waist and used my strong thighs to pull him toward me.

From the position I was in I hadn't even seen Alexi's dick. His chest, muscled and tight from physical work, was covered with hair, his nipples were large and tanned, darker than the rest of him. The chest hair, dark and tightly curled, led to a treasure trail of downy darkness crossing his rippling stomach. His dick, as yet unseen, the prize at the trail's end. I didn't know what it looked like or how big it was ...

I felt it before I ever saw it. Alexi looked intensely at me, watching my face for signs of pain as he slowly entered me. Taking a deep breath, I pushed toward him and felt the searing heat as he pushed his length gently into me. I gasped and clung to him. He hugged me tight and held me as I relaxed and allowed him deeper and deeper into me.

Passion, from where I don't know, hidden from everyone for all the years I lived in the city, erupted from my soul. Alexi looked in wonder as I released my wanton urges. Grabbing his arse, I pulled him into me, kissed him deeply as he started to push and thrust deeper into me. Sliding forward on the counter, I balanced on my arms and threw my legs over his shoulders. Alexi pushed into me, one hand pulling at my neck to bring me up to kiss him, the other exploring my chest, discovering muscles and making me gasp as he once again found and tweaked at my nipples. Never had I felt such instant passion; no one had ever discovered the depths of my physical emotions. Panting and thrusting harder, I pushed at Alexi's chest to slow him down. Pulling back slowly, he paused before pulling completely out of me, then pushed slowly back in, then again, completely out and back into me. With each thrust my emotions leapt higher; my dick jumped with each delicious movement and rubbed against my quivering stomach. Sensing we were both close to coming, Alexi grabbed my dick, lubed it with spit, and moved his hand in time with his own thrusting hips. Long strokes in my arse and long strokes on my dick sent me into a frenzy. He had total control of my body and mind right now, and I loved giving it to him. Faster and faster he moved, muscles pounding, our bodies glowing with the sweat of passion.

Alexi smiled at me. 'You ready?' he whispered. With one hand behind his head and one arm clinging to his back, he lifted me from where I had been seated. Stepping back and bracing himself against a wall, he tensed his arms to lift me up and down his long dick. I had never known what it was like to be in such strong arms, and so gave in fully to the feeling of being without control, both physically and passionately. Alexi thrust against me, lifting me, then pounding into me again. Faster and faster, harder and harder, again and again until I could control myself no longer and with a crescendo of panting cries my dick erupted, sending spunk shooting between us. Again I came, spreading hot juice on our chests and stomachs.

He pushed me to the counter again, pulled out, and peeled the rubber from his dick. Seeing his dick for the first time, I knew why it had felt so good inside. It was beautiful. Alexi's eyes were on me, feasting on my body and the ecstasy on my face. His hand threw a few long, powerful strokes as his dick. Throwing his head back, with a cry of pure joy he covered me with ropes of hot spunk. His body convulsed with the passion, and slowly the convulsions were replaced with the most beautiful, loving smile. I pulled Alexi down onto me and kissed him once again deeply. Our wet chests stuck to each other, sharing our juices as we had shared our passion.

Finally, when our kisses became short and the sweat of our bodies began to cool, we slowly pulled apart. Alexi looked down at our come-smeared chests. Raising his eyes, a cheeky smile on his beautiful lips, he took my hand and said, 'Come on, I think it's time we got wet again. Which way to the shower?'

A Queer Kind of Caring
by Eve Ray

I had just buried my first lover. I had had moments of great beauty with Eric but now he was gone. I was crying though he had told me not to be sad. In my pocket was his final letter to me, which I was forbidden to open until the day after his funeral. I turned it over and over in my hand, impatient to know what he had to say. Honour and my love for him meant that I must wait until tomorrow.

It had taken a long time for me to come out and accept who I am. As a teenager I knew I was not attracted to girls but I also knew that I loved being with them, loved to talk about fashion and make-up and girly things. When I left schools and looked for work I also knew that I was not after fame or wealth or power. I wanted to be a carer.

I was engaged as a care assistant at an old people's home. I was a solitary man in a workforce of women, and I adored their company. I adore women even though I am not sexually attracted to them. I didn't have a sense of being gay, although all the signs were there. Then I met Eric.

Eric was a new resident at the home, a single man in his early 70s. It had been suggested to me that he was gay and the thought had crossed my mind too as I bathed him and saw his penis become erect as I rubbed him and towelled him down. He had a fine body for his age and his penis was a sight to behold. I wished that I could be that firm and that big in my 70s.

As we sat in his room one day, and as I began to help him to undress for his bath, he said, 'You know I'm what they used to call queer?'

'I had thought you might be.'

'I'm not ashamed of it all,' said Eric. 'I've had some beautiful relationships with some lovely men.'

I nodded, unsure what to say.

He continued, 'When I was your age it was illegal. They called it gross indecency. Back in 1960 I had a married boyfriend. A lot of queers married. I suppose they hoped they might turn or something. It was a vain hope, I can tell you. His wife suspected something and found a bundle of my love letters to him. She went to the police and I was arrested, publicly humiliated as they led me away in full view of the neighbours. Six months' hard labour I got. They took me to Pentonville and the warders made sure everyone knew why I was there. Imagine the humiliation. Forced to strip, being examined, made to dress in hideous blue flannel. There were four prisoners there who made my life hell. They called me a "fucking bumbandit", and threatened to hold me down and have their way with me. I have never felt so worthless. I was nothing, the lowest of the low. When I came out I was branded, as it were. The queer, the pervert. I couldn't get a job, couldn't rent a room, and all for loving a man. And I had the constant memories of what happened to me in Pentonville; how the warders knew I was being bullied by these other prisoners and just stood by and let it happen.'

Eric broke down and began to sob uncontrollably. I instinctively took him in my arms and kissed him, forcing his lips apart and placing my tongue inside his mouth. He responded immediately, and soon we were rolling on the bed in a passionate embrace.

'Poor Eric,' I said, stroking his still full head of hair.

'You sweet boy,' he said wiping away the tears. 'Can you make an old man happy?'

I finished undressing him and took off my trousers.

'I've got a packet of condoms,' I said, looking with anticipation at his still magnificent penis.

Why had I done this? Maybe a sudden intuition that I was destined to love men just as he had done. The thought that in the face of Eric's courage and suffering it would be wrong to deny my feelings. The fact that Eric was 40 years older than me seemed not to matter at all.

Eric took a condom and rolled it onto his penis. I bent down over a chair and invited him to come and take me. I soon felt him around my anus, fumbling and fumbling again.

'I'm so sorry, you sweet little boy. I can't seem to get hard enough.'

I kissed him.

'I'm sorry. It's been some years.'

I kissed him again.

'Eric, you're still a beautiful man. You turn me on. Let me have you. '

And I did. With the condom on, he stroked my penis and then placed it gently in his mouth and began to suck and work with his tongue. I was about to come and gagging for it, and he said, 'I'll bend over for you and you can make this old man young again.'

I wasn't particularly skilled, and it took a while to find the opening, but I slipped inside and he was nice and tight and his back passage adapted to the size of my penis as I pushed the shaft in, and Eric emitted a squeal of delight. I began to move gently back and forth, back and forth, and Eric gasped and moaned as I did so. Then I came, ejaculating huge amounts of semen into the condom.

'Thank you, Eric!' I said pulling him up, turning him round, and kissing him.

'Thank you, sweet little boy. You've just made me 50 years younger.'

I thought that I couldn't feel properly gay until I had been penetrated, and if Eric wasn't quite hard enough to do it any more I would help him. After work that day I went to a sex shop and bought a couple of dildos.

When I saw Eric the following day he was crying.

'Punish me. Spank me. I've been a dirty boy and wet my pants.'

I undressed him and found he had indeed made a mess of himself. Maybe the excitement of the day before, his first anal penetration for many years, had been a bit much for him. He was ashamed. I cleaned him up not with the disgust that I felt for other patients but with a feeling that this was an act of love and devotion.

Eric sat in his clean underwear and began to rummage in his drawer. He took out a pair of leather ladies' gloves. They were cream, the backs decorated with lace.

'You've got dainty hands,' he said. 'These should fit. They were a present from a boyfriend back in the 60s. They were always too big for me.'

I did as Eric requested, put him over my knee, and spanked him hard 25 times.

'Thank you, my sweet,' he said. 'I haven't had a good thrashing for ages. Bring a cane next time and we'll do it properly.'

The following day I brought the dildo and a cane I had been using in the garden to hold up my runner beans. It had been all I could find at short notice and, cleaned up, it would do service.

'You've been a filthy boy and I'm going to punish you' I told Eric sternly. I could see him becoming visibly excited. 'What are you?'

'A filthy boy, sir.'

'Bend over.'

I forced down his underpants and gave him 30 strokes on the buttocks which went red, criss-crossed with the marks of the cane.

'My best lovers could all raise welts,' he said.

I then handed him a ream of paper and a pen.

'Your punishment is 100 lines. "I am a dirty little boy and must not wet my pants again".'

'Make it 200, please,' he asked.

'Very well. Two hundred lines to be handed in first thing tomorrow morning.'

That was Eric. On the one hand he was the grandfather I never had, telling me stories of his youth, the gay folklore that I was to pass on; on the other, the helpless child in need of discipline and punishment. There was a third Eric too. This was the passionate lover drawing from the well of youth that remained within him, a well that had not dried up and which, in fact, was being replenished by regular sex.

The following day, I found him kneeling on the floor by the bed. He held out to me the sheets of paper covered in his immaculate handwriting. Two hundred times he had written out "I am a dirty little boy. I must not wet my pants again".

'I sat up all night writing. I can't sleep. '

Eric remained on his knees as I read the lines then, without warning, he opened my flies, pulled out my penis, and began to pleasure me with his tongue. I came quickly in his mouth and he swallowed quickly and greedily.

'I love you, sweet little boy,' he said simply.

I reached into my bag and handed him the fat dildo I had bought. A harness and strap-on came with it. He beamed with delight at the sight of it.

'For me? Thanks you, you sweet little boy. I'm going to give you a treat you won't forget in a hurry.'

He strapped on the harness and placed the dildo inside it with surprising assurance.

'Bend over, sweet little boy. Uncle Eric's going to take you.'

He did, and he did it very gently, so I was hardly aware that he was inside me until he began to get deeper in and I let out an involuntary gasp.

'Is that too hard for you, sweetie?'

'No,' I said, 'it's perfect.'

And he moved in, back and forth, until he became tired and withdrew. I looked at him with tenderness and kissed him gently on the forehead. He looked faintly ridiculous, the implied power and violence of the strap-on forming a strange contrast with the frailness of his body, the parchment folds of his skin. Eric saw the ridiculousness of it himself and began to giggle.

'I enjoyed that,' he said.

It was Eric who suggested a day out. I knew he had studied in Oxford back in the 50s and he had told me about the male nudists at Parson's Pleasure by the River Cherwell. It was a glorious summer's day, and I packed a picnic and a bottle of Pimms, a bottle of lemonade, and some fresh mint, which I put in a cool box with the sandwiches.

Arriving at Parson's Pleasure, we laid out a blanket

and our picnic things, took off our clothes and set off for a walk.

'Are our things all right there?' I asked with a worried look on my face.

'They'll be fine,' replied Eric. 'You get a better class of person here, an altogether higher calibre queer.'

He laughed, a loud, throaty laugh.

We walked naked, hand in hand, and I compared my firm, 30-year-old body, so sexually inexperienced, with Eric's, turned 70, sagging in places, a little waxy but still firm and still a source of delight. Some might say our relationship was disgusting, sick even, but we both knew it was beautiful. I knew I was gay and proud to be gay. Above all, I was proud of this gentle and loving man.

We walked to the river bank and watched the punters negotiating the rollers that by pass a weir on the Cherwell. It was a beautiful summer's day in Oxford. Eric was already back in his student days.

'It wasn't all persecution, you know. A lot of people were quite tolerant and turned a blind eye. The colleges were all male in those days, full of public schoolboys who had only ever known all-male institutions. A lot of it went on and everybody knew. In any case, the police are not allowed into colleges, not without the dean's permission. And most deans were as queer as I am.' He chuckled at the thought. 'We had happy times. Most people who knew accepted us. Not like that vengeful bitch who was married to my boyfriend.'

Eric squeezed my hand as if for reassurance, as though the painful memories of 1960 were once again returning to haunt him.

We returned to the spot where we had laid out a blanket and I poured us a glass each of Pimms, with lemonade and fresh mint. I unpacked the sandwiches and we began our picnic.

Eric began to laugh.

'You're at work today; you're being paid for this. If only matron knew.' He was convulsed with laughter and barely able to hold his drink. 'And they're paying you overtime and expenses for something else.'

'What?' I asked.

'Old Eric reckons he can manage it today. Old Eric is going to bugger you.'

He began to giggle, before, taking a bite of an egg sandwich and a sip of Pimms, he said, 'Kneel up,' and I did. I put my face in the fragrant grass and Eric took a condom out of his bag and rolled it onto his penis.

'I haven't been this hard for years,' he said, and I could see the delight on his face. I felt him move in behind me as I knelt, thrusting my bottom into the air, exposing it as best I could to the delights that this old man had in store for me.

He began by kissing my buttocks, and I felt his stubble against my bottom as he moved his nose and tongue to my rectum.

'You've bathed today, you smell lovely.'

I felt his tongue against my opening, felt the quick movements like a snake putting out a sensor for prey. He moved in again and gave my anus an extended licking. I felt myself relax. Eric was hard enough to bugger me properly, and I had enough experience of the dildo now to know that I could take his penis.

The initial entry was a little uncomfortable, and I let out a gasp. Eric withdrew, and slid in again slowly and deliberately.

'I'm half in now,' he announced. He withdrew a little and pushed again, and I had the agonisingly pleasurable feeling of wanting but not wanting the toilet as he buried his penis a little further in me.

'I'll have one more go,' he said, 'and then you'll have all of me inside you.'

I felt him withdraw and push gently again until my widened rectum accommodated him completely.

'I'm all in now. I never thought I would be able do this again.'

He began to move back and forth with great delicacy and gentleness. This was a wonderful feeling. I was now used to taking dildos even bigger than his penis and I felt no pain, just the initial discomfort that turned to delight as he thrust, in and out, in and out.

As I knelt in the long grass of Parson's Pleasure I was suddenly overcome by a melancholy thought. How long would we still have to enjoy each other?

In and out, in and out, and he was keeping it up at his age; so stiff, so hard, and so full of youthful energy. This was not the same man who had been admitted to the home only a few weeks earlier, who had seemed resigned to a slow, lingering death. He had rediscovered youth and vitality. Eventually he did tire and, having ejaculated into the condom, withdrew to lie down next to me, breathing heavily.

I lay on top of him and kissed him as passionately as I could manage.

'Thank you, thank you.'

I knew how much it meant to him to be able to pleasure me. We lay beside each other for a while, saying nothing. I longed to return the favour but could see that the effort of pleasuring me had exhausted him. He had no energy left for lovemaking. So I gently kissed him all over his body, before making two glasses of Pimms, with lemonade and sprigs of mint that were starting to wilt in the hot sun. I wet Eric's penis with Pimms and sucked it off, pulling on it until he came again, and I swallowed his semen mixed with the Pimms and mint. This was the sweetest of cocktails for a summer's afternoon.

As we walked back to the car, Eric said, 'That was a lovely day. You have made an old queer very happy. I don't think I've been so happy since before Pentonville. That sort of thing leaves scars, you know. It blighted my life. But I can forget about it now and die a happy man.'

He kissed me very gently on the forehead.

On the drive back to the home he said nothing. I was nervous about broaching the issue of death. It's a difficult subject even when, as in the home, it's almost a daily event. But, as we pulled onto the driveway of the home, I suggested we could do the same again the following week.

'I don't think so,' said Eric softly. 'I'm getting too old for that sort of thing.'

Three days later, after a short spell of leave, I came to work again. I popped by Eric's room and, there being no answer to my knocking, I gently opened the door. His effects were still there but the bed had been stripped to the mattress. Clearly something was wrong. I stepped outside and saw a colleague hurrying past.

'Eric?' I asked.

'I'm sorry, hasn't anyone told you yet?'

'No ... What?'

'He died yesterday evening; just nodded off in his chair and drifted away. It was such a lovely, peaceful death.'

I froze. I let out a howl of anguish and began to cry bitter tears.

I was called into see the home manager, who said, 'I know that you and Mr Jackson became close and it is upsetting, but we need to keep some professional distance to avoid the emotional burnout that would stop us doing our jobs.'

I said nothing.

She leant across her desk and placed her hands on mine.

'I know you're a very caring young man,' she said, 'and I'm sure you'll learn from this. Mr Jackson left this on his table.' She handed me an envelope. 'It's a final letter but he also left instructions that you are not to open it until the day after the funeral. That will be next Tuesday. You may, of course, have time off to attend.'

She smiled and squeezed my hands, held them for seconds that seemed like hours before sitting back in her chair, which I took as the signal to leave. I went back to Eric's room and wept.

A week later, I could now open the letter. It was in Eric's copperplate handwriting and read,

My darling, darling boy,
I know now that I will not see you again. I am tired and want to pass on. You have made an old man's last few weeks the happiest of his life. But you have your life to live and you must live it without me. Do not weep for me I have had my life. Go out and find a young man to love you and make you happy. Do it today.
With all my love,
Eric

I followed his advice and went to a gay pub in the town that evening and drank and smiled and, even though I didn't pick anyone up I knew that Eric had been right in his advice to me. The following week, I went to Pride in

Birmingham. There I met Paul.

Paul appealed to me immediately with his shaven head, Gay Pride tattoo, and pink ballet outfit combined with Doc Martens in some kind of post-modern irony. I was amazed at how someone so young could be so confident in his sexuality, so at ease with himself. I fancied him, I vowed to seduce him and make him my lover.

And I did. He responded to my pass and soon we were on a leather sofa in the furthest recess of the pub, kissing deep and long and with my hand up his tutu to size up what he had to offer. Where it went from here I couldn't say. One thing I knew. I had so much to pass on to him. The riches of my all-too-brief relationship with Eric; the history of the suffering and torment of those who came before, those who suffered death, humiliation, and poverty so that we could express ourselves so freely. Eric was one of those. He had made me who I was. I owed him nothing less.

Valentine
by Beverly Langland

Some women you know are bad for you. You touch. They burn. Yet these women remain simply irresistible. Valentine was one such woman, and Jake knew from the outset that the busty redhead would be bad news. There was something lingering beneath her pale grey eyes that sent a cold shiver down his spine. Jake knew, yet he went rushing headlong toward disaster all the same. If the attraction was immediate, the recognition was not. She stood irritatingly close to Jake's table. He could see her broad hips, her stocking-clad thighs on the periphery of his vision, an unwanted distraction from his morning ritual. Jake enjoyed reading about the sporting exploits of Handsome Jake – so named for no one ever seriously touched him in the ring.

'May I?'

Jake quickly scanned the coffee house. There were plenty of empty tables, a comfortable armchair by the window. He shrugged and tried not to focus on the cleavage that slipped into view. His fascination for large breasts was an anomaly he could not reconcile with his sexuality. Jake was gay, or at least he had never had a woman. Thankfully, she drank her coffee in silence, though Jake could feel the scrutiny of the woman's stare. Eventually, seemingly by force of her will, Jake looked up. She had big piercing eyes, so inviting they instantly drew him in. This was the moment realisation took hold, the moment he should have made his excuses and left. He didn't, and she had Jake hooked.

The redhead smiled, showing perfect white teeth framed by ruby lips, the lipstick applied slightly too heavily; a little red smear on one tooth looking ominously like blood. Jake smiled back nervously and returned to the remaining article. The best of the morning, for this one described his first defeat in the kindest light. Not that losing was something Jake was proud of – or accepted graciously.

Another ten minutes passed and still the distraction hadn't moved. Jake was about to give up and leave when the woman finally spoke. 'You don't remember me, do you?'

Jake looked up, feigning interest. He gave her another cursory glance. Red hair, grey eyes, big tits. The rest didn't matter, or at least didn't register. Had she a cock, it would have been a different matter. 'Sorry. Should I?'

'We went to school together.' For the first time the woman had Jake's full attention. He studied her face for as long as he could before those crystal-cold eyes became almost painful to bear. She was not beautiful but he considered her attractive – in a rather mannish way. Jake prided himself on having a good memory despite years of opponents punching him in the head, and his schooldays were not that far behind him. He had vague memories of grey eyes like hers but he couldn't recollect the woman (girl, as she would have been).

'Sorry, I don't remember you.'

The grey eyes didn't falter. 'Of course, you knew me as Paul back then. Paul Grayson.'

Paul Grayson. *Faggy Paul Grayson*. Jake felt himself turning red as the name registered. Guilt welled inside his chest, clutching at his heart. He had been in a gang of boys who had unashamedly bullied Paul Grayson for being different, for being a raging poof, as Jake's father often alleged. Jake went through with the harassment even though he was struggling with his own sexual identity. Who wasn't at that age? Shifting the focus on to someone else was easier than suffering the taunts of the pack, and Paul had been an obvious target. Jake felt particularly guilty for he knew Paul had a *thing* for him. He knew what Jake was before Jake knew himself. Paul seemingly had an innate ability to seek out the different, and his constant presence around Jake had scared him. Jake didn't want to be different. Paul had reached out to him and all Paul got in return was a punch in the face. The slight kink in the nose was still there. Now, those grey eyes had him fixed. 'Still fighting, I see.' Jake felt himself burning with embarrassment for his past hypocrisy. 'That's some shiner.'

'Look, Paul –'

'Valentine. Paul died long ago.'

Valentine. What sort of name was Valentine? 'Well – *Valentine* – I'm deeply sorry if I caused you pain in the past.'

Valentine nodded gently. 'You know, I always fancied you at school. God knows why. We girls always fall for the bad boys. Oh well, *c'est la vie*. But let's not harp on about the past. Let's look forward to rekindling a lost friendship.' Valentine held out her manicured hand, touching Jake's with her fingertips. The red-painted nails matched her lipstick. Valentine's fingertips lingered until Jake pulled his hand away.

It's funny how two people can look back on past events and see them differently. He and Paul were never friends. They moved in different circles and even if he hadn't bullied Paul for his sexuality, Jake disliked him for other reasons. Paul was a swot. Paul was eloquent with words, with languages. Paul was good with numbers and maths. Paul understood science and especially (it seems) biology. The only thing Paul wasn't good at was sports, the subject where Jake was in his element. Paul Grayson was a walking cliché, a soft target for bullies like Jake.

'In fact, I'm having a little get-together tomorrow night. Why don't you come along and bring a *friend* with you?' Valentine rummaged in her purse and then handed Jake a business card.

Jake took the card and read the inscription, intrigued. One line written in red ink on a black background – *Hell Hath No Fury* – and beneath this a phone number. Valentine looked at Jake's puzzled face and explained that she was a professional dominatrix. Not once did her face break into a smile. Unlikely, but true. Jake watched the redhead walk away in her tight skirt, her pert bottom a stark contrast to her oversized breasts. Did Valentine still have her cock or had she gone all the way? Jake shook his head. What did it matter? He did not intend to meet the woman again; all the same, he slipped the card into his pocket.

'I think we should go. It'll be a bit of fun.' Jake had been attracted to his partner, Simon, for much the same reason he had rejected Paul years before. Simon's outgoing attitude to life, his effervescence, never failed to inspire Jake, who had a tendency toward melancholy. Although not outlandishly gay, Simon never hid his sexuality. Unlike Jake. To many they were a strange match, but for those in the know the signs were obvious. Simon a little submissive despite his exuberance, Jake the macho man, although these days he kept his bullying to the bedroom and the violence strictly for the boxing ring. As a couple, they had grown and fused; each had tempered the other's behaviour. Just as Simon had softened Jake, Jake knew that, over the years, he had unintentionally restricted Simon's enthusiasm for partying. This was why, after much deliberation, he agreed to go to Valentine's party.

To Jake's great surprise, he actually enjoyed the bustle of the occasion, though, a little to his irritation, Valentine and Simon hit it off famously. He had always had a jealous streak, which often manifested into something ugly and violent. But of whom was he jealous? Jake couldn't take his eyes off the redhead all night, though for the most part Valentine seemed deliberately to ignore him. The more she ignored Jake, the more intrigued he became. The way she walked in those outlandish heels. The way she bustled from person to person, making her presence felt, putting more than one overly boisterous guest in his place. Once, it seemed as if she sensed Jake ogling. She turned and caught him with that icy look. There was no smile this time, only a cold, penetrating stare that made his flesh tingle and his cock twitch.

On Valentine's insistence, the pair stayed over. Jake was in no condition to disagree.

'Isn't she great?' Simon lifted his head from Jake's hard cock. Jake, too cut to speak, could only focus on one thing – Simon's hot mouth, which, in his opinion, should be engaged in activities other than talking. Simon licked all the way down to Jake's hairy balls, taking them into his mouth. He sucked hard, stretching the loose skin of the scrotal sac away from Jake's body. Using one hand to lift them out of the way, he flicked his tongue against the sensitive area beneath. Wetting the index finger of his other hand, he teased Jake's anal opening, tapping his finger against the hair-ringed orifice. 'Shall I go in?'

Simon waited, but there was no answer from his lover, only the gentle sound of snoring. He lifted onto his elbows to find Jake half-asleep. 'You bastard.' Jake woke with a start, groaned and then edged Simon's head back into position. Another bout of bliss followed, and then nothing but cool air as Simon let Jake's balls slip from his mouth.

'Have you ever been with someone like Valentine – a transsexual?'

'What?' Jake grunted a no. The truth, but now wasn't the time to admit to Simon, was that while he had been busy, Jake had been imaging ruby-red lips wrapped around his cock. A handful of Simon's hair got Jake's lover focused. Simon moved his attention to the head of Jake's cock and set to work. Jake closed his eyes and slipped back into his fantasy. Valentine's sweet mouth felt so great, so fucking great …

Jake woke with the bitter taste of bile in his throat. He tried to touch his throbbing head only to discover that he couldn't. Someone had bound his hands together and his feet to a spreader bar, forcing his legs apart. Strong cuffs held him in position on a wooden frame. Jake was naked and vulnerable and his balls throbbed as if he had been kicked repeatedly. He looked down through bleary eyes and caught a glimpse of the leather ties that threatened to sever his balls from his manhood. Jake struggled but he hardly had the energy to move, let alone break free. As he became accustomed to the dim lighting, he saw the unfamiliar surroundings and snippets of recollection came flooding back. Valentine! The party, and now … Jake had entered another world. A dark, fantastical place. A world of wooden racks and rings set into concrete, of machines designed for torture. A world of whips. A world of pain.

The clatter of stiletto heels drew Jake's attention. A blinding shaft of light from an open doorway and then she was there. Valentine was Jake's fantasy-nightmare come to life. Her full, round breasts spilled over the top of a black satin corset; her legs, sheathed in sheer black nylon, were wrapped in black leather thigh-high boots. She touted a riding crop. Had she been dressed like this in his dreams? Jake's reaction to the sight of Valentine shocked him. Joy? Excitement? Arousal? Definitely arousal. Yet there was something else... Something stirring in the dark recesses within.

Jake was stunned into inaction when Valentine held out a studded collar and wrapped the leather around his neck, pulling a little too tight for comfort. A symbolic adornment of his status in her eyes. Valentine smiled from beneath her veil of heavy make-up. 'You want this, don't you, Jake?'

He shook his head. No. No, not this. 'Yes.' His mouth was so dry he could hardly speak. 'Where's Simon?'

'You can come in now, sweetie.'

Simon stepped through the doorway and into view. He was clothed in bra and panties and stumbled in his heeled shoes. Valentine had dressed him in women's underwear, had treated Jake's lover like a doll, a living plaything. Valentine had also bound Simon's hands. Jake watched Simon closely, his lover's eyes widening as he looked from Valentine to Jake and back again. Obviously, he had expected to see Jake. Had he helped Valentine? 'Show her she's safe.' Jake showed Simon that Valentine had bound his hands tightly at the wrists. 'The brute isn't going to hurt you, sweetie. I, on the other hand, make no such promise.'

Valentine took hold of Simon's hands and attached them to a hook on the end of a heavy chain hanging from the ceiling. He didn't fight or struggle. Simon seemed resigned to his fate. There was an awful moment of clanking as Valentine winched Simon upwards, leaving him suspended off the floor, swinging gently. Like a moment from a cheap horror movie. Simon's face blanched. He was clearly frightened of Valentine. How had he become so embroiled with this woman? Had they met before the party? How many times? Realisation dawned on Jake. His meeting with Valentine in the coffee house had not been by chance!

Jake wanted to gauge Simon's reaction. He didn't want to stare, couldn't bear to see the betrayal in Simon's eyes. Now Jake had fallen into their trap. He licked his lips unconsciously as Valentine bent close to his ear. 'My name is Valentine. From now on, you call me mistress. Isn't that right, Handsome Jake?'

Fuck you! Jake remained silent. He was starting to wish he had never met Valentine. He swallowed hard. He had let her collar him, but he wouldn't kowtow so easily.

'If you feel awkward saying the word, I'll be happy to whip you into a more cooperative mood.' Valentine raised the crop high, caught Jake squarely across his face. He barked in surprise at the pain. 'I see you like this game.' Valentine reached down and ran a fingertip around the ridge of Jake's cock. His back arched as he pressed against her hand, his body wanting more than his mind would admit. Valentine stroked Jake's growing erection, making him swallow again. 'There's no arguing with a hard-on, is there, Jake?'

'Bitch!' The whip caught Jake low on the stomach, dangerously close to his erection.

'Yes, Jake, all that and more.' Valentine continued to

whip him until his stomach was a raging mass of stinging flesh. 'Now, will you behave?'

This time the words came naturally. 'Yes, mistress.' Despite his reluctance, Jake found the phrase charged with sexual electricity. His pulse raced. His heart beat heavy in his chest. Oh, Valentine was good. Valentine was cruel. He could see now why people paid for her services. There was something in her demeanour, her tone of voice that put Jake down. She always made him feel small, and if words didn't work, there were always those pale grey eyes.

'Good. Then I'd like you to start.' Valentine untied Jake's left hand. 'Jerk off!'

Settling next to where Simon hung, she stroked his cheek, lifted his chin with her finger so that he would see more clearly. 'Jerk off, brute. We want to watch.'

'What?' Jerking off wasn't part of the scene. They were playing a game, a bit of rough stuff, and then he would get to fuck the redhead. Isn't that how these games worked? He would fuck the woman out of his system and then Simon and he would go home. That was Jake's plan. He suspected Valentine was having a field day, exacting revenge in the cruellest way imaginable. He wouldn't allow her to push him beyond a point he wanted to go. 'No way!'

'You mean "yes, mistress". It's simple enough – make yourself come.' Valentine pointed to a clock on the wall. 'I'm timing you. The longer it takes, the worse I will punish this bitch.'

'I wouldn't want to waste it.' A lame attempt to buy time to think, but Valentine would have none of Jake's delaying tactics. She stormed across the room, a face like thunder, and slapped him hard across the face.

'You pathetic creature!'

Jake's cock stiffened. He willed the bloody thing to go down, but as always, it wouldn't obey. The hard meat stood out proud, twitching, and aching for Valentine's touch. She kept well clear, tapping Jake's cock with the riding crop – teasing. 'Now, I'm counting...' She walked back to Simon, struck him once with the crop as a reminder of the penalty for Jake's failure. Simon howled.

Jake wrapped his hand around his cock and pumped furiously. A brave effort, though he didn't believe he could come – the leather strap pulled tight around his balls choked any hope of release. While Jake laboured, Valentine pulled down Simon's bra and began fondling his chest. Simon's eyes met Jake's briefly, then dropped to where Valentine was tugging at his nipple. Was that a moan of pleasure from Simon? How well did he know his lover? Was his humiliation turning Simon on? Valentine pulled at the front of Simon's panties and Jake thought he saw the answer – Simon had a raging hard-on.

Jake's eyes were wide now, his face flushed and red. Still he could not come. Valentine grew impatient, angry. 'Stupid cock! Can't you obey a simple instruction?' Jake felt the lash of the crop on his wrist. He moved instinctively and, as he did, Valentine grabbed Jake's free hand and retied it.

The redhead opened a storage chest and pulled out a short, stubby dildo. Simon hung impassive as Valentine parted his buttocks. She spat on the butt-plug, inserted the dildo into his anus. Simon's mouth worked noiselessly as Valentine took hold of his cock and stroked his erection. Satisfied, she went back to her chest and pulled out a red ball-gag with a leather harness. 'We wouldn't want the neighbours' complaining.'

She pressed the ball to Simon's lips. When he didn't accept it, Valentine grabbed a nipple and twisted hard.

He opened his mouth to cry out and Valentine expertly pushed the ball gag inside, pulling the straps tight around the back of his head. She ignored Simon's muffled protests, held the riding crop high. 'Twenty, I think.'

Simon shook his head, looked to Jake for help, but for once Jake had lost his fighting spirit. Perhaps his lover deserved a little punishment for his betrayal. Yet the sting of the lash across Simon's bare buttocks proved too much for him and he jerked on the chains, no doubt taken aback by the viciousness of Valentine's play. Only Valentine wasn't playing. She looked into Simon's eyes. 'I expect you enjoyed that, sweetie?' Simon shook his head, more vigorously this time. Valentine pointedly turned to look at Jake. 'Then you should find a cock that works.'

Jake had expected punishment for his past mistakes. He had accepted that possibility, wanted the cathartic release even, but it seemed evident that Valentine meant to vent her anger on Simon. The second lash was much harder, catching Simon across the nipple. It grew to an obscene size, bloated and red.

'So you do like it,' Valentine teased. Simon glared, throwing daggers with his eyes. His anger seemed to amuse Valentine. She aimed for the other nipple, but missed. All the same, she left an angry red weal across Simon's flesh and he let out another muffled cry. 'Hurts, doesn't it?'

Simon nodded, looking again to Jake for help. Jake was helpless. He felt like a gawking imbecile as Valentine abused his lover. He dreaded to think what the guys at the gym would say if they saw him now, stranded like a lost kitten. If only they knew how impotent he felt, bested by a woman, and not even a real woman at that. Valentine turned to face Jake again. 'Perhaps next time you'll think twice before hurting me.' She caught Simon again, and again, and again, leaving a criss-cross of stinging welts across his flesh. Tears welled to Simon's eyes, but only after 20 lashes did Valentine stop. A harsh thrashing; she was visibly shaking when she dropped the whip. Simon glared at her through bleary eyes, but Valentine wasn't paying attention to his sobbing.

Jake had been vocal while Valentine beat Simon. Not that his protests did any good. His blood boiled. He was furious with Valentine, with himself for falling into Valentine's trap, for letting this happen. Valentine smiled. 'Retribution is a bitch, Jake. Now, Simon tells me you don't go down on her. Is that right?' Jake tensed. He believed that real men didn't take it up the arse and didn't suck cock. 'You're not much of a lover, are you, Jake? Don't you think the little woman deserves better?'

Valentine took hold of Simon and pulled him toward Jake, the hoist he hung on traversing across the room freely. She left Simon dangling with his cock nudging Jake's face. 'Now, make it up to her. Suck! As for the other ...'

She unzipped her skirt, and let the material fall about her feet. Beneath, tight, elasticated briefs held her cock flat. These too came off and it sprang free. She curled her fingers around the elongating flesh, stroked her erection suggestively. Jake felt a tinge of anxiety as he saw the lust in Valentine's eyes. 'Your turn, Jake. This won't hurt too much.' Her eyes were blazing with desire. Something primeval reflected in her face.

That was the moment Jake fully realised he wasn't in control. Panic set in. His eyes grew wide in alarm. 'Now wait a minute!'

Valentine noticed the look immediately. 'Is Jake scared? You should be, brute. I'm going to fuck you good. Of course, I'll let you poke me in return. Don't deny you want to. I'll gladly be your woman, Jake. Afterwards. You see, I'm not quite a woman yet. I still have this monstrosity, and it seems a shame to waste a good hard-on. Consider this as a gift, a rite of passage. To think, all those years you've been missing out …'

Valentine manoeuvred behind him, and the wooden frame Jake was tied to tilted forward, pushing his face deep into Simon's crotch. He was helpless to resist, left this way by his own stupidity and acquiescence – ankles tied to the posts, arms tied forearm to forearm behind him, his bottom high and exposed.

'Raise your arse, sweetheart. Your girlfriend wants to fuck you.' Valentine slapped his thigh – hard. 'Open up!' She slipped a finger inside Jake's anus, lubricating and loosening his back channel with a cold jelly. Even this humiliation wasn't enough, for a second finger twisted inside him without too much trouble. Jake moaned and wiggled as Valentine's fingers worked inside his hole. This was nothing like he had imagined. He felt suddenly scared. Not of what Valentine might do – would do – but of his response to her dominance.

Valentine slapped Jake's buttocks sharply and pressed her cock against his puckered sphincter. 'Suck her, stupid. You don't come until she does.' Jake gave in and swirled his tongue around the silky skin of Simon's cock, taking more of Simon's length into his mouth. Slowly he moved his mouth, letting his teeth lightly scrape along Simon's hard flesh. His lover was excited. Jake gathered the precome leaking from the slit in Simon's cock. He let the bulbous head slip from between his lips, licking up and down the veins running the length of Simon's shaft.

'Good boy!' Valentine leant forward into Jake, the fat head of her cock edging past his fleshy barrier before withdrawing. A small movement that marked the start of a new journey for Jake. Jake groaned, and Simon groaned with him. 'I knew you'd like that.'

Jake had been prepared to let Valentine use him, but not like this. Valentine was marking her territory and she wanted him to know. Something had taken hold of her. The gentle Paul Jake once knew had transformed into a dominant, power-crazed monster. Had he and the gang been responsible?

Valentine was still taunting Jake as she slipped deeper between his buttocks. 'Ready to scream my name, Jake?' She paused, making Jake hold his breath in anticipation, wanting the deed to be over yet relishing his feeling of helplessness. Valentine slid her cock slowly past Jake's sphincter. She held her cock there, letting him feel her power, before pushing deep inside his arse with one sure thrust of her hips. Jake cried out and Valentine laughed – an insane laugh that echoed around the room. Her cock completely filled Jake. He felt stretched beyond limits, but he loved the pain, admitted so with every groan, every cry of pleasure.

As Valentine drove into Jake, Simon's cock grew more rigid than Jake had ever seen – the hard flesh throbbed in his mouth. Jake could taste the semen dribbling from the tip. He sucked furiously on Simon's cock, his inhibition suddenly lifted, his chin drenched with his own saliva. Simon pushed himself against Jake's mouth each time Jake tried to escape. There was no let up for Jake; Simon kept pushing until Jake could take no more.

Valentine's fucking grew more serious. Before long, Jake was moaning around Simon's cock, pushing this way and that to meet the dual thrusts. He rocked against the invading cocks as much as was possible in the restraints. Repeatedly Valentine's cock pounded into his arse. Jake felt her balls slapping against his flesh. If that wasn't real enough, Valentine dragged her long nails along his back, grabbed his buttocks as though with animal claws, pulling Jake close, holding tight. Obscenely wet sounds filled Jake's ears. He was certain Simon could hear them too.

'Scream for me! 'You want the brute to scream, don't you, Simon?'

Simon's affirmative came as a spurt of semen. He wanted Jake's humiliation as much as Valentine did. Jake cried out without inhibition, arching his back, drawing Valentine into him like a long-lost lover, not wanting to let go. Simon locked his legs around Jake's head, squeezing him tighter, drawing him deeper onto his cock, filling Jake's mouth with spunk. In the same instant, Valentine, spotting the signs of Simon's orgasm, buried her cock deep in Jake's rectum and hot sperm filled his arse. All Jake could do was cry out in ecstasy as Valentine reached beneath him to release the strap around his balls.

His orgasm was explosive. He came in huge torrents, showering his belly, Simon, everything with a spray of thick semen as Valentine milked him for every drop.

As his spasms ended, Jake collapsed against Simon, limp, drained – defeated. His face had lost its hard edge – the menace gone. Yet, in that moment of need, Valentine pushed Jake away, leaving him limp and wanting. She reset the frame so that Jake was upright. Semen dribbled from the corner of his mouth and ran down the crack of his bottom. Jake didn't know how Valentine stood the pain of her existence. How she maintained her hold on reality. All he knew was he was grateful for her strength. Grateful for the power of her presence. Grateful that she had claimed him and that he was no longer alone in this nightmare.

'This is my "anger room". The place I come to vent the built-up hurt and frustrations of the past. It works, though up until now there has been one thing missing – the infamous Handsome Jake Barrett. So, how about it, Jake? Has the hardships of the ring stopped easing your pain?' Valentine spread her arms wide. 'I am the solution. Love me, Jake, and I will take your pain away.' Jake looked toward Simon, his eyes pleading, but Simon already had the look of defeat about him. 'Don't worry about her, sweetie. She was just a distraction. You're home now, lover. You're home.'

Valentine was right, of course, just as Paul had known years before. She was putting on her skirt, acting as if having two men bound in her basement was the most natural of things. She kissed Jake briefly.

'Now, tomorrow night, you and I are going to the movies. *Belle de Jour* is playing at the Roxy, and I want you to meet a good friend of mine ...'

Jake wasn't listening. He was mesmerised by those ruby lips. He wanted to kiss them again, wanted so much to feel them slip around the end of his shrinking cock. Just thinking about the prospect hurt.

Some women you know are bad for you. You touch. They burn. Oh, how they burn!

Bustin' Our Balls
by Landon Dixon

It was a shitty hotel on the downtown fringe of Philly. There was nothing on the idiot box, less on the streets. So I was holed up in my room amusing myself – my dick in my hand. I was stroking quick and tight, cock hard and glistening with the gun oil I use.

When the door splintered open and a guy burst inside.

'Freeze, scumbag!' he yelled, levelling a rod at my head.

My hand did freeze on my dick, a scowl on my face. 'Jurgens!' I spat it out.

'*Agent* Jurgens to you, Kives.' He stepped over the broken wood and right into the room, slammed shut what was left of the door on its busted hinges. The rod stayed steady in his other mitt, .44-calibre black eye staring me down.

'So, you got the bum's rush out of Pittsburgh – rode out on a rail,' he crowed, sticking it in my craw, walking up to the lumpy bed and my long, tall cock. 'You're becoming small potatoes, Kives. Hardly worth the effort to chase after any more.'

'Like hell,' I snarled.

I started pumping heat back into my dick, nice and slow now, putting on a show, stroking all along the turgid length with my gripping paw, swirling blunt fingers over bloated hood real soft. I was bare-ass naked, my own rod sleeping under the pillow that propped up my back against the headboard. My hairy pecs popped as I dug my hairy balls out from between my muscled legs and squeezed the heavy pair, as I stroked my heavy dong.

Jurgens licked his lips, not looking so damn smug and authoritative any more. He cocked his rod up, giving the warm gaze to my hot genitals. Sure, he had me dead to rights, wanted on maybe 15 state-wide warrants and a few national ones. But his sworn duty couldn't stand up to the pulsating height and width of my passion prong, the sensuous heft and musk of my nuts. I knew the slot machine racket in Philly was over for me, but I wasn't going away without a suck-off send-off.

'You're a hard man to find, Kives,' Jurgens gritted. 'Harder to take.'

The big blond gorilla holstered his rod and unzipped his back-up piece, draping his own cock out into the open. It hung down long and wide even semi-erect, swelling fast. He laced a long-fingered hand around it, lifted, tugged, looming large next to me.

I pumped my cock and twisted my balls, staring at Jurgens' stiffening dong. We were on opposite sides of the law, sure, but he was built big as me, smooth and clean-cut like his profession, cock and balls pink and hairless. I was swarthier, my meat vein-piped. We each carried a load, and a lust.

'Yeah, so you got the drop on me. So what?'

'So this,' he said, sinking to his knees alongside me and grabbing onto my cock.

'Fuck!' I grunted, jerking. The man dealt a hot hand.

I planted my mitts on my pecs and mauled the humped pair, fingered the thick olive tips. Staring at Jurgens' strong, pale hand shifting up and down my straining pole, feeling it deep in my balls and the back of my skull. The guy knew how to take a man – and torque him but good. His technique was impeccable, pumping me even harder and longer, forging my fucking steel. He dipped his blond head down and slipped his red lips over my cap.

'Fuck! Yeah!' I bellowed, bucking into the guy's moist, velvet mouth.

I surged with juice and joy as Jurgens dropped his head down lower, his mouth, lips, and tongue inhaling my cock right to the boiling balls in one heady plunge. He kept me locked down in his craw, sealed tight and beating in the cauldron of his sensual mouth and silky, squeezing throat; a real-life sword swallower. His blues eyes rolled up into my glassy orbs, his wide nostrils flaring for air, flush lips kissing my pubes. And he kept right on fisting his own dick as he deep-throated mine.

Muscles quivered and bunched all over my burly body. I couldn't take the oral interrogation, the wet-satin pressure on my pulsing pipe too much for me. I thrust up, knocking Jurgens' head back. He started sucking on my throbbing prong full length and flat out.

I shifted down lower on the bed. His vaccing mouth never left my cock, his throat happily accommodating all the meat I had to offer. I rasped, 'Give *me* some of the good stuff.' And he crawled up onto the bed, swinging a leg over my melon, planting his kneecaps on either side. His dong hung down into my lips and I gulped up the beefstick like a starving man.

Jurgens' big, rounded buttocks spasmed in my gripping hands as I gobbled his swollen shaft deep as he'd taken mine on an erotic journey. His cock plugged my throat and filled my mouth. I rocked my noggin to and fro, sucking on his dick, matching his mouth-pumping motion on my cock. His hips moved like mine, feeding our hunger. I nosed his nuts with each upward gulp.

We hit the right notes, the high notes. His manly groans of delight vibrated all along my mouth-buried cock and through my rippling body. As I bucked, blasted ball-batter up against Jurgens' tonsils. As his cock spasmed and spray-painted my throat with hot, salty semen.

We jerked and jetted into each other's mouths, in each other's arms, jumping around on the creaking bed. Until our pipes were drained and we were sucking on spent.

I was out of town one half-hour later.

There was an alley that ran in back of the houses. It was a shitty section of Chicago, dilapidated drug dens and boozecans lining the dimly lit streets. There wasn't much light in that alley either, but I recognised those ass cheeks clenching and slamming cock into another man from behind, knew the grunting voice very well.

Jurgens had some punk up against the garage of a house. He was drilling into his chute, the big man's dimpled, glowing buttocks thrusting powerfully and rhythmically. I'd been in the firetrap two doors down, delivering some shine, found the fucking pair in the alley on my way back to my car.

'Keep that rod where I can't see it,' I growled, jamming my own iron into Jurgens' back.

He froze in the punk's anus, cheeks quivering. Then he twisted his hard, handsome mug around and scoped my rugged pan. 'Kives!' he hissed.

'Yeah. Looks like I got the drop on *you* this time, lawman.'

I pulled the steel mouth of my .45 out of the small of his back. I jerked my conk at the kid with his hands splayed up against the garage, pants down around his ankles, cute black ass packed full of Jurgens' huge club. 'Interrogating Drop-Down, huh? He tell you anything about me?'

'Plenty,' Jurgens gritted, his eyes flashing in the night. 'Seems you've muscled in on the illegal, tax-free liquor business in this area, set yourself up quite a string of stills and boozecans.'

Drop-Down squealed, 'No, Mr Kives! I didn't say nuthin' about –'

'Stow it, punk! Everyone knows you got a mouth that can't stay closed. Like you got a pair of pants that can't stay up.' I glanced from Drop-Down's frightened, pretty face to Jurgens' grimacing clock. 'That's why they call him Drop-Down this end of town, lawman.'

'So, what are you going to do, scumbag?'

I grinned, harshly. 'Plug you, what else?'

Drop-Down's big brown eyes almost popped right out of his Afro-ed head.

I stuffed the shooter into my jacket pocket, unbelted and unzipped my pants. Both men watched me, breathlessly, gulping at the sight of the solid length of hose I let loose in that alley. I gripped my dick with one hand and frisked lube out of Jurgens' pocket with the other. Then I greased my dong good and gleaming, busted my cap through the blond's bunched buttocks.

'Yes!' the dirty Fed groaned, thrust deeper into Drop-Down by the force of my hood splitting his ring, plugging into his ass.

I grasped his broad shoulders and ploughed inch after inch of bloated, vein-popped shaft into his hot, gripping anus, impaling the guy on my pole. Like he was already staking out Drop-Down's sweet ass. Both men breathed easy, breathed hard. I thumped up against Jurgens, stretching and stuffing and stoking his chute with my pipe. He drilled into Drop-Down in rhythm.

The night-shaded alley echoed with the combined grunts and groans of three men now, the crack of two sets of thighs smacking two sets of buttocks, the squelching of a pair of hard dicks fucking a pair of hot chutes. Sweat beaded my brow, rolled down my armpits. I dug my digits deep into Jurgens' flared traps and rammed his ass with a brutal intensity, feeling every heated plunge to the depth of my prick and my soul. He cocked the kid just as hard and as long and as heavy, pounding Drop-Down almost right through the wall.

'I should turn you in for fucking with a witness!' I rasped in Jurgens' ear, bouncing the big man back and forth on the end of my pumper.

'Yes, but you won't!' he snapped back, blasting Drop-Down's ass with his cock. 'Or I'll bust you like I could've for years!'

He had a point. I had a point. We'd been making it for, yeah, years – literally and figuratively.

I fucked Jurgens' ass in a frenzy. He caught the fever pitch, injected it into Drop-Down. The kid clawed at the wood, crying with abandon. He'd been hammered before, lots of times, but never this hard and this fast, by two old pros. He screamed, wildly shaking, going off against the wall.

Jurgens lurched against me, launching a sackful of hot sperm into Drop-Down's jumping black ass. I banged, blazed away, emptying my own rod into the sucking, tight tunnel of Jurgens' quivering ass. The three of us spouted off full bore, jerking together like the cars of a train shunting to a sudden and violent stop.

Me and the lawman were both out of town one hour later, headed in separate directions.

* * *

It was outside the jungle room in back of the sleazy strip club where Jurgens and I butted heads yet again. In fact, we just about ran face-first into one another, when his boss, Special Agent Carruthers, ducked into the room after my boss, Lucky Luigi Calabrese, had gone in a second before. The city was LA, a shitty section of town, the time dead of night.

'Slumming?' I jibed at the blond. 'Me too.'

His plush lips twisted in a grin. 'Scumbag bodyguard for a scumbag crime boss? You're nosing rock bottom, Kives.'

'I'm touching it,' I countered, looping a big mitt around and grabbing onto the guy's ass.

He shoved me up against the wall, fists clutching chest hairs. 'I'm on business, jerk-off!'

I kept my hand on his ass, kneading the hard, hilled flesh. 'Yeah, dirty business. Your boss is getting the big payoff from mine.'

'Bullshit! They're talking deal.'

I latched my other hand onto his other butt cheek, staring into Jurgens' stone-set mug. 'Yeah, that's what I said. Only the money's going from my guy to yours. You figure it out.'

His blue eyes were ice-cold marbles, his hard body burning against mine, hot breath scalding my lips. Then suddenly, savagely, he mashed his mouth into mine. Our throbbing cocks jammed together in the blowtorch heat of our passion. Fuck our bosses, we had our own private business to tend to!

The wall thumped with the bass of the stripper beat in the bar, men yelling and hollering. But there were just the two men in that breathless dark hallway in back, gorilla arms wrapped around one another, urgently thumping cocks into each other, excitedly sucking face, swiping tongue.

Our jackets were off, our shirts torn asunder. I ripped Jurgens' pants open and down. He returned the erotic favour. We blazed close to naked, muscle-bound, hugely cock-pumped.

Then we grappled again, pressing together in a torrid alliance of cock-skin and scrotum, kissing, frenching, pumping to our own frenzied beat. Our jobs, our duties, were abandoned along with our rods in the forge of our passion, our lust unleashed. We grabbed onto each other's heads and flogged tongues, frotted cocks, wantonly.

I dove my hands down onto Jurgens' mass-mounded ass, dug my blunt fingertips into the twin-heaped flesh. He grunted, spraying spit into my open mouth. His mitts followed my lead, locking onto my hairy buttocks, squeezing and groping the pair. We ground our cocks up and down, fucking foreskins.

The door popped open. Calabrese and Carruthers stared at us, the lawman slotting a thick envelope into his suit pocket as he gaped. Their dirty business was concluded, but ours had yet to be fully consummated.

'Kives! What the fuck?' Calabrese snarled.

'Agent Jurgens! Desist!' Carruthers chimed in with his paymaster.

But there was no stopping us now, no matter how many crooks gathered to watch. We'd worked ourselves too long and too hard. Our sweaty torsos stuck together, our cocks electra-gliding in flesh tones.

I pulled Jurgens' pert pucker open with my fingers, plunged his gaping pink anus with a pair of my digits. He did the same, pouring three fingers of poker into my hole, even deeper. We pumped each other's rectums as we surged the semen out of our kissing balls and up our rubbing cocks. We exploded together in another's mouths and arms and cocks and asses; shuddering, grunting, jetting juice in between us in geyserous gushes.

Our two bosses went for their rods, maybe disgusted by our reckless display of manly affection. Maybe turned on and too disgusted with themselves to admit it. Who knew? We knew what to do, though, breaking apart and slamming the men's gun hands down, setting the pair on ice with a couple of straight rights to the jaws.

Then we garbed our steaming physiques, held hands, made tracks for the exit.

We were out of town in 15 minutes, headed in the same direction, together at last.

Memories
by Michael Bracken

I lifted my wine glass and toasted my ten-year companion, a man I had met while completing graduate studies in English literature at a private university in Texas. We dated for a year before committing to one another, but marriages and civil unions didn't exist back then – and still don't in Texas – so we celebrated our anniversary on the day Daryl moved into my one-bedroom apartment. The ink was still wet on my diploma, I had just accepted a position teaching bonehead English at a community college, and we had no idea what a life together would entail.

The evening we met, Daryl was slinging drinks at a chain restaurant where all the employees were encouraged to cover their shirts with bling, and only a handful of drinkers occupied the bar. The first time I saw him he was bent over behind the bar retrieving a dropped towel, his black slacks stretched tight across his firm ass. I made some appreciative comment to my drinking companion – a lipstick lesbian who had asked me to beard for her at a dinner meeting earlier that Friday evening and who was picking up the tab that night – and she just shrugged. Her eye was on a rail-thin undergrad sitting alone in a back booth, a bottle of Shiner Bock at her elbow and a copy of *Madame Bovary* open on the table before her.

When Daryl straightened and turned to take our drink orders, I was smitten. His warm smile and glittering emerald eyes captivated me in a way I had not previously experienced, and I felt my pulse race.

Anita ordered a Cosmopolitan, but I kept it simple. After Daryl placed her cocktail and my Jack-and-Coke in front of us, my companion slid her Visa card across the bar, told Daryl to run a tab for both of us, and asked for a bottle of Shiner. He returned a moment later with her card and the Shiner.

My companion slid off the barstool and carried her drinks to the back booth where the rail-thin undergrad looked up, listened, and then closed her book. Anita slid into the booth opposite her and pushed the opened Shiner across the table.

Daryl said, 'Looks like your friend has her own agenda this evening.'

I shrugged. 'We don't play on the same team.'

He leant against the bar and placed his hand on my forearm. I could feel the weight of it through my jacket sleeve. Still gazing into my eyes, Daryl lowered his voice and asked, 'What team do you play for?'

He later told me he knew the answer long before he asked the question, having once seen me in the company of a mutual friend, and we were still talking when Anita left with the undergrad.

'There goes my ride,' I told Daryl when the two women walked out the front door. 'I might need you to call me a cab.'

'If you don't mind waiting until closing,' he suggested with a wink, 'I can give you a ride.'

I smiled and loosened my tie. I didn't mind a bit.

Less than an hour passed before last call, and soon I was sitting in the passenger seat of Daryl's Toyota, giving him directions to the apartment complex where my one-bedroom apartment was directly over the laundry room and often smelled of detergent and dirty clothes.

I invited him upstairs for a nightcap, but we both knew it was only an excuse to get him in my apartment, and I barely had the door closed behind us before we were in each other's arms. I had removed my tie during the ride and my jacket on the walk up the stairs. So I dropped them to the floor, pushed Daryl back against the door, and covered his mouth with mine.

He smelled of sweat and aftershave and alcohol but tasted of peppermint when our tongues met, as if he had sucked on one of the after-dinner mints the restaurant kept in a bowl by the exit. Our kisses were deep and hard, threatening to take my breath away. His turgid cock tented the front of his slacks and jabbed at me through our clothing. Mine did the same in return.

Our hands fumbled with buttons. I pulled his shirt free of his waistband and pushed it from his shoulders. It slid down his muscular arms and dropped to our feet, the bling clanking against the linoleum foyer floor. He wore a V-neck T beneath the shirt and I pulled it off him, finally revealing his thick, hairless chest and washboard abs.

My voice husky with desire, I told him how much I wanted him right then. 'Don't make me wait.'

Daryl grabbed my belt buckle. In a split second he had my pants around my ankles and was on his knees in front of me. I hadn't groomed because I had not expected an evening spent bearding for a lipstick lesbian to lead to a night of carnal delight, but the dark crotch forest didn't seem to bother Daryl.

He wrapped one fist around my cock, his thumb and forefinger tightly encircling the shaft just below the mushroom cap of my cockhead. I felt an unexpected rush of pain and pleasure that only increased when he bent forward and drew the head of my cock between his lips. He hooked his teeth behind my swollen, purple cockhead and painted it with broad tongue strokes, licking away the drops of precome that oozed out as his fist pumped up and down my shaft.

He grabbed my scrotum with his free hand and kneaded my balls, keeping both of his hands busy as he worked me ever closer to orgasm. My hips began to thrust forward and back, but Daryl never took more than the head of my cock in his mouth that first time. Before long, my balls began to tighten. I knew I couldn't restrain myself and I didn't try.

I came and came hard, firing a thick stream of warm spunk into Daryl's mouth. As I came, he squeezed my balls together so that I felt concurrent pleasure and pain. My eyelids fluttered and closed, and I had to press one hand against the door to support myself until my cock stopped spasming in Daryl's mouth.

When it did, he unwrapped his lips from my cockhead, released his vice grip on my scrotum, and stood. As he held my head between his hands and planted an open-mouth kiss on me, Daryl used his tongue to push a ball of my own come into my mouth, surprising me. No one had ever done that before, and I swallowed without thinking.

We stripped off the rest of our clothes, leaving a trail of discarded fabric from the front door of my apartment to the bed. I opened a new tube of lube that night, and I don't think we fell asleep until the sun began to peek through the curtains.

As we touched our wine glasses I asked Daryl if he remembered that first night as well as I did.

'How could I forget?' he replied with a wicked smile and a gleam in his eye. 'You were an insatiable dream come true. We didn't get out of your bed until you had to leave for class Monday morning.'

Despite a four-year age difference and a significant gap in education level, our relationship developed rapidly after that night. Soon Daryl and I found ourselves together more often than not, and even though lust brought us together, we discovered many mutual interests outside the bedroom.

'Remember what happened the night I moved in?' Daryl asked.

'Of course.' My cock had grown hard remembering our first night together, but now it became a steel beam in my pants, and I was thankful that the white tablecloth hid the physical evidence of my lust-filled memories of our ten years together.

Even though I had asked Daryl to move in and he had agreed nearly two months before his lease expired, we waited until the day after I graduated – the last day on his lease – to move most of his things. By the time we schlepped all of his stuff from his apartment to my second-floor walk-up, we had killed the entire day, had turned my apartment into a maze of poorly packed boxes and duplicate furniture, and were sweating like day labourers. The temperature outside had toyed with triple digits all afternoon and we had stripped down to cut-offs and running shoes.

We should have been tired after a day filled with serious physical exertion, but we were jazzed by the idea of finally living together, of not having to wonder which apartment housed our hiking boots, our favourite shirt, or that frozen pizza we planned to have for dinner. We were looking forward to waking each morning and not having one of us slip out early to return home.

I surprised Daryl with a bottle of champagne I had chilled to celebrate the moment, and Daryl popped the cork after he carried in the last box of his stuff. The plastic cork bounced off the kitchen ceiling and three cardboard boxes before coming to a rest under the kitchen table, and champagne sprayed my chest before Daryl turned the bottle toward the sink. I caught as much of the spillage as I could in a pair of champagne glasses, and then Daryl set the bottle on the counter.

'To us,' I toasted. And then, stealing a line from our favourite old television series, added, 'May we live long and prosper.'

Thirstier than we'd thought, we downed our drinks without hesitation. Then Daryl decided he hadn't had enough and began licking the spilled champagne from my chest. He didn't just lick away the fizz. He also sucked my nipples, bringing them to life and causing my cock to quickly rise to attention.

'I hope you realise what you started,' I whispered hoarsely as I pushed him away.

'You think you're up to it?' I reached out for him, but Daryl twisted away. 'You'll have to catch me.'

There really wasn't anywhere to run, but he managed to elude my grasp by dodging around the boxes that surrounded the kitchen table and were stacked throughout the living room. I finally caught him in the bedroom, where his box spring and mattress leant against the wall. We kicked off our running shoes and stripped away our cut-offs, revealing erections throbbing with anticipation.

He'd teased me enough and I was impatient. I grabbed Daryl's wrist and spun him around, face into the mattress leaning against the wall. I grabbed a half-used tube of lube from the nightstand, slathered it over my cock, and then took him from behind.

My slickened cockhead pressed against the tight pucker of his ass, and Daryl pushed back against me. Then he opened up and I buried my cock deep inside him. I drew back and pressed forward.

I reached around and took Daryl's cock in my hand,

my fist trapped between his mattress and his taut abdomen, and pumped my fist up and down twice as fast as I pumped my cock into his ass. He came first, spewing spunk all over my fist, his abdomen, and the mattress. His knees went wobbly and I grabbed his hips to steady him, my own pumping motions growing faster and harder until I couldn't hold back any longer.

With one last, firm thrust, I drove my cock deep inside Daryl, pressing him tight against the mattress as I emptied my balls inside his ass.

We leant against that mattress for the longest time, neither of us wanting to step away and end the moment. We had just consummated our couplehood, the closest thing to a wedding night we were likely to get.

But I had one surprise left. When I finally pulled away from Daryl and he turned to face me, I reached into the nightstand and retrieved a pair of gold bands I had purchased earlier that week.

We've been wearing them ever since.

Throughout the rest of our ten-year anniversary dinner we reminisced about some other memorable couplings, including the time he'd blown me in a movie theatre while watching a movie so bad we were the only people there, and the time we'd done it on a Florida beach during one of our summer vacations. By the time we finished our meal and left the restaurant, both our cocks were straining for release. We'd gotten a little old to be doing it in a parking lot, so I headed straight home.

On the ride, Daryl asked, 'So whatever happened to Anita?'

'The last time I heard from her,' I said as I pulled into the driveway of our home, 'she was writing PR copy for a beer company in St Louis and had finally met the love of her life.'

Then we went inside and made another memory.

Spanking the Stripper
by E.C. Cutler

When I got the booking to perform at the professor's house, I didn't think too much about it. Sure, it might have been unusual for a group of guys to request a male stripper, but what the client wants, the client always gets. And I knew I'd have absolutely no qualms about showing off everything I had to other men, teasing them, wondering if my grinding moves and muscular body were getting them hard.

Stripping might not be everyone's idea of earning a living, but I was never what you might call the studious type; I left school with barely any qualifications, just at the point where the economy had tanked and even the burger-flipping jobs were being taken by people with degrees. So I decided if I couldn't use my brain to earn a living, I'd use my body instead.

Two years later, I was working most nights of the week, mostly stripping out of a cop's uniform, or naval officer white, for a giggly bachelorette and her gal pals, or strutting my stuff at a divorce party where the air was thick with perfume and lust. I'd be lying if I said I didn't get offers from the girls at these parties – more than once I'd had a drunken bride-to-be come on to me, wanting one last fuck with another guy before she tied the knot, but I always turned them down. If I'd been straight – and not cared about the fact this woman wanted to cheat on the man she was about to promise to be faithful to for the rest of her life – I would have seen a hell of a lot of bedroom action.

I wasn't even considering getting any kind of action as I drove over to the professor's home early on Saturday evening. Professor Morgan lived a couple of miles out of town, well away from the busy campus where he taught. Following the winding coastal road, I took a moment to admire the spectacular sunset, the sky streaked with vivid shades of orange and purple as the sun slowly slipped below the horizon. How lucky the man was, I thought as I pulled my beat-up old Ford to a halt in the driveway of his beach house, to have such a view to come home to. Even luckier when you considered his nearest neighbour had to be a good half-mile back down the road.

A couple of cars already stood in front of the house, though it seemed like quite a sedate gathering. Normally when I rolled up at a party venue, lights were blazing and music pumping out, but only the glowing lantern over the porch door gave any clue that someone was home here.

Pausing only to slip on the helmet that completed my fireman's outfit – the friend of the professor's who'd made the booking had been very insistent they wanted me dressed this way – I rang the doorbell. It was answered almost at once, by a man who must have been somewhere in his 40s, in an outfit of T-shirt and baggy shorts better suited to a surfer type half his age, and clutching a glass of red wine in one meaty fist.

'You've gotta be Chase,' he said. 'Come right on in.'

He led me through to a small living room containing more books than I'd seen in any one place outside the public library. Three men sat in mismatched easy chairs, a coffee table between the three of them. A cheese board contained hunks of cheddar and brie, and a half-plucked bunch of grapes. Two wine bottles stood empty beside it, and a third, less than half full, was being used by a silver-haired guy to top up his own glass. He paused in the act, registering the sight of me in my uniform. His mouth gaped open, and it took him a moment to find his voice.

'Ray, just what the hell's going on?' He addressed the man who'd let me into the house, but this was my cue to speak up.

'I'm sorry, sir. We had a report of smoke coming from this property, so I came to check. I'm assuming you're the owner of the house.' He nodded and struggled to rise to his feet, pale blue eyes wide. Alarm had obviously killed whatever pleasant buzz the red wine had brought on. 'Well,' I continued, aware of Ray trying to stifle a laugh beside me, 'you'll be relieved to know that nothing's on fire, but it's definitely getting hot in here …'

With that, I whipped out the MP3 player I'd been holding behind my back and set it down, secure in its little dock with surprisingly powerful twin speakers, on the coffee table. When I pressed "play", music boomed out, its beat fast, insistent.

While the professor and his friends looked on, I started to undo my jacket. The dark-haired guy who'd been lounging in a wicker chair gave a delighted whoop, and the bespectacled blond sitting on the other side of the table from him yelled, 'Yeah, take it off!'

The professor seemed to take longest to work out what was actually going on. When realisation dawned – by which time the jacket was off, revealing that my uniform pants were held up by wide red suspenders, but my tanned torso was bare, he turned to Ray.

'You – you hired me a stripper?' I heard him ask over the music.

'Well, you're not 40 every year,' Ray replied with a grin. 'Happy birthday, Michael!'

Professor Morgan seemed to relax after that, as though he'd been given permission to enjoy my performance. Lost in the thrill of stripping for these four horny older guys, I slipped the suspenders off my shoulders, one strap at a time, teasing my audience with the promise of more to come. Their eyes seemed to burn into me as I undid my pants, which had been designed with Velcro fastenings at the sides, so I could rip them off while leaving my boots on. Call me picky, but the thought of dancing in bare feet on strange carpets has never appealed, not to mention that some people really get off on the sight of a guy in nothing but big, heavy boots.

Though I had a little way to go before I reached that point. The helmet went next; I tossed it to the blond, who gave me a saucy wink as he set it on his own head for a minute. These guys all seemed remarkably comfortable about the fact they had a man stripping himself bare in front of them, and for the first time I gave serious consideration to the thought they might all be gay. Of course they are, you dumbass, a small voice in the back of my head chirped, why else would they have asked for a guy to come here? They want to see you naked; they'll all be getting hard-ons in their pants at the thought of seeing your big, fat cock ...

Only my shorts remained now; turning my back so I faced away from them all, I eased the tight-fitting black garment down, gradually exposing my ass cheeks and showing them my all-over tan.

'Oh yeah, let's see those buns of steel,' someone – it might have been Ray – called out.

With the back of the shorts resting just below the bottom curve of my ass, I danced suggestively, moving my rear in slow circles, flexing my cheeks as I did. This move always drove the girls wild, building up the tension before the moment where I showed them what they really wanted to see, and I hoped it was having the same effect on the professor and his buddies.

At last, I hitched the underwear back up, and did a cheeky pirouette. Though I hadn't set out for it to happen, by this time, my cock had begun to rise, though in the tight confines of my jersey shorts it didn't have much room for manoeuvre. Stripping for women didn't usually get me hard, but as I have one of those cocks that looks big and meaty even when it's limp that tended not to be an issue. They got a lingering look at the goods in the moments before I slipped on my clothes, switched off my music and left, and they were happy. But tonight was a different matter. I knew that as soon as this last item of clothing came off, I'd be exposed in all my glory, my tool surging up full and proud.

Aware that I was on the clock and they'd only paid for a half-hour show, I couldn't delay proceedings any longer. Still keeping up the tease as long as I could, I hitched the shorts down, giving the guys first a glimpse of the pubic bush I keep trimmed real short to make my shaft look even longer, then going further, showing them what they'd been waiting so eagerly for.

When my dick bounced free, it was to a chorus of approving murmurs.

'Holy cow!' the dark-haired guy exclaimed. 'When you said you were gonna book a guy who was hung, you weren't joking, were you?'

Basking in their admiration and envy, I tossed my shorts to the floor and advanced on the professor with a gleam in my eye.

'OK, Prof, it's time for your birthday lap dance.'

His buddies guided him on to the love seat beneath the window. He didn't protest as I approached, still moving to the beat, and straddled his thighs as he sat back. I ground myself against him, feeling the heat of his groin through his pants, and all too aware of the bulge straining against the material. I doubted anyone had ever done anything quite like this to him, but he was clearly loving the feel of my body. His hands came round to cup the bare cheeks of my ass, and I reached to move them away. The rule with any lap dance was "look but don't touch", no matter how cute the person you're dancing for might be, and the longer I studied the professor at close quarters, I began to discover that, for a guy 20 years my senior, he was very cute indeed. Sure, he had crow's feet, but those deeply etched lines only added to his allure, and his lower lip was so deliciously full it almost cried out to be nibbled on. Shame that in a few minutes our time together would be up and I'd have to leave.

My musings were interrupted as someone grabbed hold of my wrists. I registered the feel of metal against my skin, and almost before I knew what was happening, heard a loud *snick*. When I tried to move my hands I realised they'd been cuffed together behind my back.

'Hey, what the hell –?' I began. I'd been in a few crazy situations while I'd been stripping, and on more than one occasion the police had arrived at a party, responding to complaints of noise from the neighbours – which can be pretty awkward when you're standing half-in and half-out of a cop's uniform. But I'd never actually thought I might be placing myself in danger. Suddenly, it struck me just how isolated the house was, how unlikely anyone would hear me if I called for help.

'It's OK, Chase.' Ray's soothing voice in my ear stilled my fears. 'Relax, we don't mean you any harm.

It's just that Michael told me something a while ago; said he had two fantasies he'd love to fulfil. The first was to have a lap dance from a gorgeous, naked hunk, and, if Michael's half as hard in his pants as I am right now then I guess you've more than brought that one to life. But the second fantasy was to spank the ass of a younger man. So I thought why not take the opportunity to combine the two?'

'You mean, let the professor spank me?' My voice came out as more of a squeak than I'd intended.

'Indeed. If you don't want to play, we'll let you go now. But we're willing to pay you an extra $100 on top of what you're earning tonight for your time. How does that sound?'

I had to admit it sounded good. I hadn't got another engagement booked tonight, and I could definitely use another hundred bucks. And all I had to do was take a couple of swats to my ass. How hard could it be?

'Sure, you're on.' I thought that once I'd agreed, they'd release me from the cuffs, but instead they remained firmly in place. My cocky self-assurance began to fade, but for some reason my erection stayed harder than ever. My head might have been full of doubts at the thought of still being chained up, but clearly my dick didn't feel the same way. Between them, the professor's buddies helped me up from his lap, taking every opportunity as they manhandled me to "accidentally" brush a hand against my rigid shaft and heavy balls.

They took me over to the sturdy, ladder-backed wooden chair the blond guy – I thought I heard Ray call him Brian at one point – had been sitting on. Ray undid the cuffs, but my relief was only temporary, as my hands were guided to clutch the top of the chair back, then Ray refastened one cuff around my wrist and the other around the chair. I might not have been restrained too securely, but I didn't need to be. I wasn't going anywhere, not naked and lugging a heavy piece of Shaker furniture behind me, at any rate.

And anyway, this was more than likely all part of the professor's fantasy. You could find any number of pornos where older, dominant men disciplined submissive young guys. Until now, such a scene hadn't ranked too high on my own personal fantasy list, but standing here stark naked and helpless in front of four fully dressed men, waiting for whatever might be about to happen with a pounding heart and a cock that stubbornly refused to deflate, I was beginning to change my mind.

'Such a gorgeous ass …' It was the professor who spoke, running his hand over my butt cheeks as he did. His palm was smooth, the hand of a man who'd never done any manual work in his life, and his touch relaxed me. He brushed his finger down my crack, daring to linger on the tight, hidden pucker. I couldn't stop a whimper slipping from my lips. The professor chuckled at this blatant expression of my need.

'OK, so this is how we're going to do this,' he continued. 'I thought that, seeing as I'm marking my 40th birthday, giving you 40 spanks would be appropriate.'

I swallowed, hard. This was way more than the light swatting I'd been counting on, but I didn't want to back out now. A hundred bucks was at stake here, after all. 'Of course,' I said at length.

'Of course what?'

It took me a while to realise what he was getting at. Dominant older man and all. 'Yes, sir.'

'Good boy.' Again that finger, tickling my asshole, threatening to push inside just a little way. 'So how we're going to do this is that each of us is going to give you ten spanks each. First Ray, then Brian, then Woodrow, and finally yours truly. Are you ready?'

Even broken down like that, it still sounded like a pretty heavy-duty spanking, but I was determined to get through it. 'Yes, sir.'

The professor withdrew his hand. 'Ray, he's all yours.'

Looking over my shoulder, I saw Ray take up a position to my right side. Just as the professor had done, he caressed my ass, as though acquainting himself with its size and shape. His hand was rougher than the professor's, with the little callouses on the fingertips you get when you play the guitar. As I was still registering this difference in feel, he started to spank me.

The swats were light, carrying little in the way of power, and I started to think 40 of these weren't going to be so bad at all. None of the other men said anything, and though I couldn't see their faces, I was sure they were all firmly turned in the direction of my ass as Ray peppered it with what were little more than love taps.

When he stepped aside, Bryan took his place. 'How's his ass looking?' the professor asked him.

I felt his fingers trace over my skin. 'Blushing nicely,' Brian reported. 'I'd compare the shade to a good white Zinfandel. Not much in the way of heat coming off it. Ray, you've gone easy on him.'

'Hey, you've always got to break a virgin in gently,' Ray retorted, and I found myself wondering about the dynamic between these guys. From what they'd said earlier, it sounded like the professor had never spanked anyone's ass, but Ray and Brian were swapping quips that suggested they'd done this before. I didn't have time to give it any serious consideration, as Brian delivered a sharp, stinging swat to my right cheek.

Unlike Ray, he spanked me with considerable force, and he varied his blows, making sure I didn't know when or where the next one was going to land. Glancing to my side, I saw that Ray, his part in the game over, had retired to the wicker chair and was stroking his dick through his shorts.

By the time Brian retreated, his ten swats delivered, a hot ache had spread through my ass, and if I could see it, I was certain it would be a couple of shades deeper than when he'd started. Two down, two to go.

Woodrow, the dark-haired guy who'd raved over the size of my endowment, hit me just as hard as Brian, but he spaced the slaps evenly, and between each one, he took the opportunity to fondle my dick and balls. I wasn't sure if this was part of the rules or not, but no one told him to stop, and his long, bony fingers kept me on edge throughout this portion of the spanking. Even though my ass was beginning to hurt like hell, I knew if he kept on jerking me, I'd spurt my come all over the place.

'Please, sir ...' Throughout the spanking I'd stayed silent, but as Woodrow smeared the juice that seeped from my cock-tip over and around the head, I had to speak up.

'What is it, boy?' he asked, not pausing in his action.

'If you keep doing that, you're going to make me come – sir.'

'Oh, he's gorgeous when he begs, isn't he, Woody?' Ray commented. I couldn't be sure, but it looked like he'd unzipped himself and had his cock openly in his hand. Whatever, the tension in the room had certainly gone up a few notches since Woodrow started spanking me.

With some reluctance, Woodrow let go of his hold on

my dick before delivering the last two swats.

'He's all yours, Michael. Primed and ready for the birthday boy.'

'But before you start,' Brian chimed in, 'we've got one last present for you.'

'Haven't you guys spoiled me enough already?' the professor asked, but he took the gift-wrapped package Brian produced from under his chair and tore the paper off it. 'Oh guys, that is beautiful. Thank you.'

He came round to hold his present up to my astonished gaze. 'What do you think, boy? Isn't that a wonderfully made paddle? Maple wood, if I'm not mistaken.' He made a show of examining the highly polished bat, giving me plenty of time to imagine how it would feel as it slammed against my already punished ass. After all, why else would Brian have given it to him now?

'It – it's very nice, sir.' I didn't know what else to say.

'Now, I'm going to give you ten with this, and at the end I want you to kiss the paddle and thank me.' It sounded like a speech he'd made many times in his head, and now here he was, getting the opportunity to utter these words for real. Part of me envied him for having the kind of friends who'd make such a cherished fantasy come true, but mostly I was still worrying about how much a paddling with that thing would hurt, compared to what I'd already endured.

'Bend over,' the professor instructed me, and meekly I got back into position. He tapped the paddle against each of my butt cheeks. Preparing myself as best I could, I gripped the thick wooden top of the chair back.

Silence came down on the room in the moment before the first blow fell. I couldn't even hear the fast, slapping sounds of Ray's hand working on his own dick.

Summoning all my courage, I mentally commanded the professor to do his worst. The paddle cracked against my ass. I'd never felt pain like it, and I lost all my composure. Jerking from foot to foot, I howled in agony. I almost begged him to stop, but thoughts of my payment, and the respect I'd earn from these guys if I took the whole punishment, made me hold my tongue.

Nine more agonising blows followed, each one piling fresh hurt on already sore flesh. But through it all, my hard-on barely wilted – helped in that regard by the professor's soft hands smoothing over my flaming hot ass and, just as Woodrow had done, toying with my dick.

When it was over, and the paddle was presented to my parched lips, I kissed it without hesitation. 'Thank you for punishing me, sir,' I said.

'You took that very well,' the professor replied, 'and they say every good boy deserves a reward, don't they?'

Setting the paddle aside, he took hold of my cock. His touches didn't tease any more; now he worked with purpose, jerking me off with fast, hard strokes. I'd had no idea my evening would play out this way – finding myself chained in place while four men I'd never met before spanked my ass, before being expertly wanked to a swift, unstoppable climax that had my come gushing out all over the professor's Shaker chair. Yet, as the professor unfastened the cuff that held me in place and Brian went to fetch me a glass of water which I drank from greedily, I didn't regret a moment of what I'd done.

While I dressed, they counted out my fee for the spanking, the professor sticking a couple of extra tens on top of the pile. 'Because that was everything I'd hoped it would be, and more,' he told me, as I tucked the money into my back pocket.

Driving home wasn't going to be easy, not when my

ass felt swollen to twice its usual size. But I reckoned I might stop off for a beer on the way, maybe offer up a silent toast to the professor and his buddies for booking me tonight.

'You can see yourself out, right?' the professor asked, taking his sweater off over his head. The last thing I saw before I shut the front door behind me was Brian pulling Woodrow into an embrace, their lips meeting in a kiss. Seemed like they intended to keep the party going long after I'd left. I only hoped the next time they had one of their get-togethers they had need for a stripper who was happy to take a spanking, and if they did, my name would be top of their list.

A Bear in the Woods
by Marcus Swannick

It was in one of those little gay bars you used to find down a side street in the Soho area, away from the likes of Old Compton Street. From the outside it didn't appear very inviting; in fact, it looked shabby and run down, which was probably part of its attraction, to be honest. It had been prophetically christened *The Queens Vaults* years ago, mainly as you had to walk down a dozen steps, then into what must have originally been the cellar, in order to get to the bar. That, and the fact it was a regular home from home to more than a few old queens. But back before the changes in UK licensing and alcohol laws, the old *QV* was one of those private, "members only" kind of clubs where you could get a drink after hours.

Down in the *Vaults* it was one of those uneventful Saturday nights, when everyone who was anyone was out doing someone somewhere else. And, to be perfectly frank, having survived the working week, for once I really couldn't be bothered to go chasing around the other clubs to find them. So I was just sitting there, on a stool at the end of the bar, bored from over-relaxing and casually watching the fluff go by.

I must have been distracted for a moment or two, because when I looked back over the tables again, I was surprised to see someone had alighted – as dear Noel

Coward was wont to say – at a table near the far end of the bar. He sat alone, sipping from a squat tumbler of what looked like whiskey and ice, and back then he really did look like a square dick in a round hole. At least he did to my trained eye. So obviously out of his element in this kind of piano bar, let alone Old Compton Street itself.

The crowd which had deigned to come out and grace us with its presence that night was overdressed, loud-mouthed, and bored. They sat around the tables clustered near the big ebony grand, or hovered around the bar, some on stools like myself, others just camping out wherever they saw fit.

The patrons were mostly older men in lounge suits and silk shirts, sitting opposite fresh-faced rent boys sipping pink martinis or "Penis Colliders" and laughing on cue.

I really didn't fit in there myself, but I have a love of piano music, so I occasionally found myself among the rabble in order to listen to Bobby Jackson, the jazz and cabaret star. Recordings are nice, but nothing beats the atmosphere of a live act.

But, try as I might, I couldn't help staring at the man sitting at the corner table. My eyes were drawn to him no matter how hard I tried to look in other directions. He looked damn good too. Around 40-ish give or take, 6 foot something tall and muscular, but not huge. Sort of like an athlete or an Olympic swimmer. He wore a Fred Perry shirt and a pair of faded but tidy black jeans – itself unusual – and when I glanced down I could see he was wearing them over what looked like riding boots. They weren't fresh, out-of-the-box new, but scuffed and scarred through years of hard use and wear. At the time I wasn't quite sure if the whole routine was some elaborate show, or whether it was an honest deal. Which then led me on to wondering what this interesting gentleman actually did for a living. His face was suntanned and rugged looking, with sweet green-and-gold eyes, thick brown hair – short, but not cropped – and he was sporting a light brown beard which was closely trimmed and neat, rather than the stubble fashion of the time.

With a large hand he lifted the whiskey tumbler and gulped down the last of his drink. Trying to look casual, and failing, he turned and nodded to Karl behind the bar. In that lazy way they have, the bartender poured him another. Tray, napkin, glass on top. Smooth, professional Karl. Frankie – one of the table waiters – picked it up and was about to deliver to it to the guy, but I reached over the bar top and put a hand on Frankie's arm.

'You might want to sit this one out, love. I'll take this over to handsome.'

Frankie smiled at me, chuckling warmly. 'He doesn't look your type, Danny boy. Too pure and innocent, for a start.'

Sliding the tray over to me, he went back to checking the rest of the tables for waiting punters. We had been friends for a long time, and Frankie knew exactly what was going through my mind. I had decided I had to meet this guy, one way or another, if only to find out more about the obviously lonely, but oh so attractive, mystery man.

I half walked, half sauntered and sashayed over and placed the drink down beside him. Without even looking up, he quietly muttered thanks and then offered me a five-pound note.

Not to be upstaged, I said, 'Thank you. But usually my clients leave it on the bedside cabinet.'

Too late, I realised my flip comment had caught him

off guard and he looked up at me. His expression appeared confused, startled and almost afraid, and I could clearly see the nervousness in his eyes for the first time. Rapidly trying to salvage the situation, I stuck out my hand.

'Hi, I'm Daniel, though friends usually call me Danny. And the whiskey's on me.'

Indecision replaced confusion, then he finally relaxed. 'I'm Michael. I heard the music as I was passing outside.'

I smiled. 'Ah. Well, it takes a special kind of person to appreciate the performers in this club. Mind if I join you?'

OK, so it wasn't the smoothest of lines, and for a moment he seemed a little surprised. 'Well, I, er ...' Then he grinned at me. 'You're more than welcome.' Without hesitating, I waved Frankie over, ordered a small bottle of Becks, then pulled out a chair beside him.

Later, I realised what it was that had initially attracted me to him. He always had a really beautiful smile. His rugged face became enchanting as his lips curled and little dimples formed on each tanned cheek, like apostrophes around his mouth.

I barely sipped at my bottle as we sat listening to Bobby coax jazz variations of Cole Porter and Gershwin standards from the old grand piano. Between sets, I discovered Michael lived out in the sticks, over in Norfolk somewhere, and actually owned a stable. That explained the boots: they were real, honest riding boots which saw the stirrup on a daily basis. Thank you, Miss Marple.

The more we small-talked the more his confidence seemed to grow, though I somehow managed to keep my curiosity in check in case my eagerness scared him off.

Which was just as well, as, when the evening came to a close, we left the bar together. Despite my offering an invitation for a nightcap at my flat, we ended up walking back to the hotel where Michael was staying.

I'll admit I'd been having little fantasies about him all night, and I knew there had been a frisson of sexual tension between us the more we got to know each other. Even so, heading back to his room at the Yarlborough, I felt a little cheap. Sex on the first date and in a hotel room no less? As Doris often said, "whatever will be, will be". But I didn't know if I would ever see him again and I just had to know what it was like to be with such a broad-shouldered and obviously virile country boy.

We entered his room and, by the time the door had shut, he'd surprised me a little by pulling me into his arms and impulsively pressing his mouth onto mine. It seemed a clumsy and awkward move, but I returned his kiss, exploring his mouth with my tongue, feeling his facial hair as he brushed his wiry beard on my chin and lips.

Pulling away from me, he seemed to become shy and embarrassed. 'I'm sorry. I didn't ... I've never been with another man like this before.'

I thought he was joking and started to laugh. 'Yes, dear heart, and I'm the Queen of She –' But the look of hurt on his face made me realise just how serious he was.

In a sort of mad rush he told me he had married young but, after 20 loveless years, he was finally getting a divorce and being true to himself.

At that time I wasn't sure if I believed him or not – he'd seemed so comfortable with me, showing intimacy so easily.

Bashfully, he looked me in the eye. 'I'm serious, Daniel. I've thought about it, and dreamt about it. I've even masturbated while fantasising about what it would be like. All I know is I really want you to spend the night with me and I want to make love to you but, honestly, I just don't know where to start or what to do next!'

Again I thought he was just messing with me, and then I started to feel the wonderful joy at discovering he really was utterly and completely genuine. And I knew that was the point when I fell in love with him.

With little encouragement from me, we undressed and stretched out together on the king-size bed. I felt the fresh hotel sheets under us as we started caressing, touching and exploring each other's bodies. To me his body was magnificent, and it was a new thrill to lie next to him and admire him in all his glory.

I let him wrap his muscular arms around me, then pushed him back down on the bed again as I ran my hands up his arms and over his wide, powerful shoulders. His chest was covered in a mat of coffee-coloured hair, which swirled in rings around his nipples, while his belly was flat and firm but not too ridged with muscle. With a gentle fingertip I lightly traced the trail of soft hair down over his stomach, then continued down into his thick bush of pubic hair, and moved myself closer to his delicious looking cock. He had been immediately erect from the moment we undressed, and his prick stood proudly in the air like a flagpole. I reached down to hold it, and Michael moaned softly.

My heart melted. The man was uncertain, but I knew he wanted me, wanted to share himself with me and finally experience what he had only dreamed about: sexual pleasure with another man.

I took control and slowly eased down his torso until my head lay on his fuzzy stomach, my face hovering just above his crotch. I teased the tip of his throbbing cock with my tongue, flicking lightly at the precome which glistened on the thick head. He reached down and slowly started stroking my hair and gently rubbing my neck and shoulders with his strong fingers. With slow and delicate moves I worked both him and his cock into a frenzy. His balls are still impressive, but back then they seemed huge, like chicken's eggs, moving of their own accord as I softly played with them. And all the time I kept working his cock with my tongue, lips, and hand.

Occasionally he would fondle my cock hesitantly, touching it as if it were some kind of live animal that he didn't want to hurt, and all the time I really wanted him to take hold of it firmly, squeeze and rub it. But I didn't push him. I just kept licking and flicking at the bulbous head of his cock, rolling his balls around in the palm of my hand and feeling them tighten up as I did so.

And then, to my total surprise, I felt a large, firm hand on my hip, followed by a hot mouth closing around my cock.

I have to admit I never saw it coming and I just didn't have any time to prepare myself for what happened next, because within seconds of feeling his firm lips encircling my shaft and his hot, wet tongue on my cock, I was firing off shot after shot of hot come – the first into this innocent virgin's mouth, then repeatedly onto myself as he pulled away in surprise!

But, even as I was spurting for the second or third time, I felt Michael's hips start to thrust up under my head, and then he started to explode – his massive balls emptying what tasted like pints of hot, salty come into my mouth and down my throat as if from the end of a fireman's hose.

Despite my best efforts I couldn't handle it all, and ended up gagging a little – which immediately upset

Michael, and it took quite a lot of reassurance for him to realise he hadn't hurt me at all. In fact, quite the opposite. It had been one of the most powerful ejaculations I had ever experienced.

Eventually we lay together, with me snuggled up against his big bear chest, and through the night we were just happy to touch, feel, and explore each other. Until, after smothering his cock in saliva, I straddled him – feeling the heat of his stomach against my thighs and groin. Gently moving backwards, I took hold of his wet shaft and gently placed it between my arse cheeks, the head firmly against my puckered ring. Very slowly, I started to work him inside me, sighing as his cockhead slipped past the muscle, then moaning quietly in pleasure as his shaft followed. Within minutes Michael was bucking and thrusting beneath me, all the time hitting my pleasure spot, then he was releasing his load inside me as I stroked myself off, feeling even more excitement as I watched my come splash across his panting, furry chest.

The following morning I woke early and slipped out of bed without waking him. I managed to give myself a quick cat-lick wash before dressing and then leaving him to his slumbers. On the desk I left my mobile number and a message explaining that I had a prior meeting arranged with family I just couldn't break. However, if he wanted to then he should call me and we would arrange another, proper, date and a night out.

Thankfully, he rang back.

'Way out in the country-ee-ee! Where the air is …'

We had been seeing each other, as best we could, for three or four weeks – mostly with Michael travelling down to London for short weekends – when we decided it was time I spent a holiday out in Norfolk.

'And Danny, no jokes about six fingers or webbed toes, OK?'

Spoilsport. But then he did seem to be getting to know me so well. So I accepted the invitation – and, to be honest, I was looking forward to seeing what country life was really all about.

But I hadn't really been prepared for the train journey from Liverpool Street to a strange place called Thetford. At first it seemed OK, quickly speeding through little commuter villages on the outskirts of London, then on into the country. But my excitement at this completely new adventure seemed to make the time drag, and even occasionally stopping at places with strange sounding names didn't help at all. Then, after what seemed like years, we finally arrived at Thetford and I saw Michael waiting for me outside the station exit.

He looked incredible. His beard and hair had been neatly combed and tidied, and he was wearing a nicely fitting pair of worn blue jeans over his scruffy black boots. The open lumberjack shirt revealed the top of a white cotton T-shirt, while his biceps pushed at the faded fabric of the rolled-up sleeves. He was a beautiful bear at home in his natural habitat. He was also standing next to a Triumph motorbike, and as I got closer I could see he held two helmets in his hand.

Oh my fucking good night! Are you really fucking serious about this, Josephine?

After a bit of coaxing I finally swung my leg over the beast of a machine and tried to settle down in the pillion seat behind him. Thankfully, he took my arms and wrapped them firmly around his waist before starting the bike up and slowly driving off. After a while it seemed we were off the regular roads and travelling down country lanes – passing the occasional farm or two – before suddenly turning off and disappearing down one of the dirt tracks which led off into the massive forest. The more I relaxed, the more secure I felt and, hugging tightly to him, I nuzzled my crotch up close to his arse and rested my head on his broad back.

We rounded a bend and slowed down, coming into a large clearing in the forest which was bounded by a white rail fence. That was when I first saw the horses. They were grazing, hoof deep in rich, green grass. For a moment I was captivated by a foal looking up as we arrived, then saw it move close to its mother as we got nearer.

The Triumph rumbled loudly as we "downshifted" – whatever that is – and moved onto another forest pathway which led to a stone and timber farmhouse. It's not really a log cabin but a mixture, which gave it more substance and style. I was, unashamedly, enchanted by it all and felt a tinge of jealousy for Michael, hidden away in the forest, with all the animals. It all seemed so wonderfully unreal and idyllic, even though I knew Michael had problems of his own.

Michael decided to postpone the grand tour until after we had eaten and, for the first time since we'd met, I finally got him to relax and start talking about himself. Over a light lunch he told me more about his soon-to-be ex-wife, and how miserable he'd been the last few years.

'I really need this divorce, Danny. I need to move on with my life and settle down without the pressures of a pointless and dead relationship.'

'But you've got all this, Michael. I still have to be a slave of the nine-to-five day, which is rapidly becoming more and more a seven-to-whenever routine. Plus you don't have people judging you all the time out here. At work, everything is performance related, even when you go to take a piss.'

But he had been brought up in the wilds of the country and a hardened townie such as me must have seemed like an alien to him.

We finished and took the dishes into the kitchen. I felt his arms wrap around me as I stacked them in the sink, his chest firm against my back and the bulge in his jeans pressed firmly against me as well. But I could see the horses through the window, and although I knew he wanted sex, I wanted to wait. To me this was all so different and exciting, and I asked if I could go and look at the horses. Michael smiled, took my hand, and we both walked out and over to the paddock.

The horses came to the gates as we entered the stable area. They were strong but gentle, and before long I'd plucked up the courage to actually stroke one on the neck. Michael just laughed, and then carefully stood back while I fed them and generally made a fuss of them.

Later, as twilight was falling, we started putting the horses into their stalls for the night, shaking out a little evening feed and some bedding where they needed it.

When we'd finished we both stood in the middle of the stables, a little out of breath and hot from the exertions. Purposefully, he turned me around to face him, and I could feel the sexual tension that had been building between us all afternoon start to bubble up to the surface. I looked up into his face as he drew me toward him and, reaching up, I carefully unbuttoned his shirt. I pulled it off his shoulders and dropped it to the stable floor, followed by his vest, marvelling at the mass of hair on his chest. I raised my arms above my head and when Michael had lifted my T-shirt off, I brought them back down and around his neck, letting my head rest on his chest and breathing in his wonderfully warm muskiness.

He put his arms around me, his hands in the small of my back, and pulled me in closer, kissing the top of my head, before moving to hold me away from him at arm's length.

Smiling at me, he said, 'I don't suppose you've ever ridden bareback before, have you?' I was about to make a sarcastic comment when he qualified things by adding, 'I'm talking about on a horse!'

'I've never even touched a horse before today, let alone gone anywhere near to sitting on top of one.'

The next thing I knew he was off, and in no time he'd strapped a bit and harness to a big black and white stallion called Lord Melton the Third. As I watched Michael at work I kept looking at the way his chest and arms tensed and flexed as he adjusted the straps and pulled the buckles tight. Then watched his whole body twist and move as he threw a thick blanket over the stallion's back. I was also thinking about the way his cock was being held in check between his legs by his close-fitting jeans. Even semi-erect was at least seven inches, growing a little more when he was fully hard, and I couldn't help remembering how incredible it had felt deep in my throat and also inside me.

Then my fantasy disappeared as Michael was lifting me effortlessly up and onto the horse's back. I really had no idea what to do, so just grabbed the stallion's mane as Michael hopped up on a side rail and mounted behind me. When his arms came around my sides and he took hold of the reins I felt myself starting to calm down, and with his body pressed against mine, along with the warm horse between my legs, the sensations were both relaxing and also very stimulating. In my jeans I could feel my own erection growing harder as my balls moved against the horse's back, and it was obvious that Michael's cock was hard again as I could feel it resting up against my arse. A quick word, followed by a tap of his heels, and we were then gently walking out into the evening and heading down one of the narrow forest paths.

Still holding me tightly, he urged the stallion on. As the horse picked up a little more speed, I found myself buzzing with excitement. Before long we were cantering along the edge of a stream, and I have to admit that I was getting more comfortable with the cadence of the horse. Not only that, but I trusted Michael enough for me to untangle my fingers from the horse's mane and rest my hands on the animal's sleek, black shoulders.

With the warm evening weather, and the exercise, the stallion was soon damp under my hands and I could feel his heat as Michael reined him in, slowing us down to a trot and then finally stopping under a large willow tree. It was cool and sheltered and, as the horse rested, I couldn't help but think more and more about Michael's hard cock pressing up against me.

That was why I sighed when he gently began to kiss the back of my neck, dropping the leather straps and stroking my chest with his large hands. I leant back into his hard body and felt his sweaty chest pressed into my back. I really wanted to have him penetrate me, to feel his hard, thick cock pushed firmly inside my body, but when I tried to move backwards I started to lose my balance. It was probably that involuntary jerking of my knees and legs against his sides which confused the poor horse, but at that moment he began to walk slowly along the river bank again.

Michael was laughing in my ear as he picked up the reins again and gently guided the horse around and back under the tree. 'I think it might be better if we got off and let Melton here rest for a while.'

'Just so long as he doesn't go off and leave us stranded out here.'

'He'll be OK. Anyway, I'm here to protect you from the wolves.'

'What bloody wolves?' But as soon as I said it I knew he was joking, and I tried to poke him in the ribs with my elbow as he slid to the ground. Moments later, he had helped me down from the beautiful animal. He took the blanket off its back, and laid it out by the trunk of the willow.

He knelt down on the blanket. Without saying a word, I knelt down in front of him, our breathing becoming quicker and deeper with promised excitement. He reached out and I felt him fumbling with my belt; in moments he was sliding my jeans and boxers down around my knees. I opened his jeans, knowing full well he always went commando style, slipping them over his firm arse and slowly down his thighs. Then he pulled me toward him and, with our cocks and chests warm against each other, he kissed me long and hard.

We broke apart and hurriedly finished undressing, rolling on our backs, kicking our boots and jeans off, then knelt back in front of each other. Eagerly, I slipped my hands down and around his strong, hard cock and large balls, while his hands brushed over my hips to fondle my arse cheeks – parting them and teasing my hole with his large fingertips. All the time I could feel the excitement building inside me; the more I played with his cock the more I knew I wanted it pushed firmly inside my arse.

I moved back a little and went down on all fours, eagerly slipping his damp and sweaty cock into my mouth and moving my tongue around to generate as much saliva as I could. When his cock was as drenched as I could get it, I let him go and turned round, presenting my arse to him.

Within moments, I felt the head of his cock tight up against my puckered arsehole. But the moment was too much, and as he pushed himself forward I eagerly pushed myself back onto him at the same time. In one movement his thick, hard cock slid fully into me, completely taking his shaft in up to his large, hairy balls. And I have to admit that I cried out. The sudden invasion of his thick cock was more than I could bear, and the pain of him withdrawing also made me gasp.

Seconds later I could hear his voice by my ear, telling me he was sorry, telling me that he had never done anything like this before and if he was doing it all wrong then to please tell him so he could make it all right! He was so genuinely upset and concerned about me that I was deeply touched, and I really knew then I had finally found someone I was actually in love with.

Reassuringly, I said, 'Just stay still for a while and let me do the work, until you get the hang of it. Now slip that wonderful cock of yours where it was before.'

Very slowly, he gently spread my arse cheeks and I felt the head of his cock resting up against my ring. As best I could I started to edge back, then forward, then back again, feeling the pressure build until I moved back onto him and felt the head of his wonderful cock slip through and wedge itself inside me.

The pressure eased and, as my sphincter adjusted to the intrusion, I worked more and more of his glorious shaft inside me, until I was grinding my arse against the base of his cock and feeling his balls on the backs of my thighs. Without any further encouragement, Michael began to slowly fuck my arse. Then, as he picked up speed with his thrusting hips, I felt the head of his cock finding my pleasure spot, and the sensation worked me up into a frenzy of lust. I hadn't been fucked from behind like that for a very long time.

I felt him start to shudder. Arching his back in time with his thrusts, he seemed to be pushing even more of his cock deep inside me than before. Then he was breathing heavily and crying out as he started to come, followed by the flooding heat and the incredible sensation of his balls emptying into me. The feeling was so intense that I came immediately – gripping hold of his cock with my arse I shot spurt after spurt before finally collapsing onto the blanket, completely drained and fully satisfied.

The following evening, going back to London, my arse had felt more than a little battered and bruised. But it was a welcome ache, reminding me of the magnificent man who'd been there, and who I was determined to see again.

And the Crowd Goes Wild!
by G.R. Richards

Like all great ideas, Bob stole this one from porn.

'Gay wrestling,' he told the guys.

Vijay and Desmond laughed their asses off. 'Is there such a thing as un-gay wrestling?'

Bob rolled his eyes. 'I'm serious, you dickwads. We tried the 24-hour gym route – that was a fail. We tried the foxy boxing, even though there are only, like, four straight guys in this neighbourhood …'

'And the dykes weren't filling the stands,' Vijay snorted.

With a curt nod, Desmond said, 'Whose bullshit idea was that anyway?'

Bob's stomach plunged six storeys. Yeah, the foxy boxing was all him. He was overdue for a quality moneymaking idea, and he was convinced wrestling would be their golden ticket. 'Listen to me,' he said. The impending failure of their little gym put a strain on his voice. 'Do you want to lose the business? Because that's where we're at if we don't start making real money soon.'

Vijay and Desmond exchanged subtle glances, and then shrugged. 'What do you have in mind?'

'I don't know,' Bob began, thinking back on all the wrestling porn he'd watched lately. 'As long as we put two hot guys in the ring, nobody'll give a fuck what they're doing.'

Crossing his arms in front of his chest, Vijay said, 'We need a plan, Bob.'

Bob bit the inside of his lip. He could see the action in his head. How to describe it? 'We've got a couple wrestling get-ups in the store, right? Put one guy in black, one guy in red. Have them tear the suits off to get the other guy naked.'

A grin grew on Desmond's lips as the image no doubt planted itself in his mind. 'Yeah,' he said. 'Lots of fake wrestling holds, two loose cocks swinging around, one guy sits on the other guy's face … This could be good.'

They looked to Vijay, who didn't appear convinced.

'Winner fucks loser,' Bob went on. 'How does that sound?'

'Like a live sex show,' Vijay answered. 'If the wrong people find out about this, we're screwed.'

'So we'll get the word out, but keep it on the DL.' Bob laughed. 'Because whatever kind of permit we need for this, we sure as shit ain't got it!'

Desmond laughed along. Vijay didn't, but he did mull the idea over and finally relent, 'You're right, Bob: we need the money. This'll bring it in. What choice do we have?'

'Next question,' Desmond said. 'Where do we get the wrestlers?'

Bob walked into the ring wearing a red spandex singlet, red wrestling shoes, and red ankle bands. He didn't so much want to be "the red guy", but Desmond insisted that the black spandex blended so well with his dark skin the crowd would take him for nude. And that was a good thing.

All three co-owners were pretty damn sure the guys

filling those seats weren't here for the love of sport. They wanted flesh, and that's what Desmond and Bob were set to give them. Vijay was better suited to the role of referee. No hard feelings. Anyway, Vijay the intense bodybuilder was in a weight class Bob and Desmond could barely see on the horizon. They were better suited to fighting each other – both were unmistakeably strong, but with the leaner musculature of a cyclist and runner, respectively. Bob had the kind of calves any man would be proud of, and he couldn't wait for Desmond to tear off his singlet so the crowd could get a good look at his abs.

'You ready for this, man?' Desmond reached out to shake Bob's hand in the centre of the mat.

When Bob pressed his palm to Desmond's, the crowd went wild. That was a good sign – they were obviously easy to impress! Or maybe the sizzle in the air excited the waiting masses. Either way, Bob said to Desmond, 'I'm as ready as I'll ever be.'

The fight was on!

The crowd roared as Bob dove at Desmond, but the moment his hands met those big, dark shoulders, he was at a loss. What the fuck should he do? And then a move from grade seventh gym class leapt into the foreground of his mind. Without thinking, Bob swept his foot behind Desmond's heel and brought him crashing down to the blue mat. Bob landed with his knees on either side of Desmond's body, straddling his middle.

A surge of sexual energy ran through Bob's core. His thighs tightened like crazy as he reached for the straps of Desmond's singlet. He wanted to get that black spandex off, and get this guy naked. That was his first task.

But Desmond worked faster, and by the time Bob finished contemplating his next move, Desmond had already flipped him over. Bob didn't realise what had happened until his face smashed against the mat. Hadn't they agreed to go easy on each other? *Motherfucker* – that move was not what Bob classified as taking it easy! Desmond's spandex front met Bob's tight ass. The big guy's weight crushed the hell out of Bob. Holding his wrists down against the mat, Desmond wrapped his feet around Bob's calves. *Shit!* Inside his red singlet, Bob's cock got stiff against the mat as Desmond's prick ploughed into his spandex-covered ass cheek. On instinct alone, he bucked up against that big boner. God, he hoped he'd lose the fight. He wanted that huge dick to destroy his hole.

A surge of adrenaline rushed Bob's body, from his fingers right down through his toes. With all his might, he flipped and landed with his back crushing Desmond's front. In this position, he could hardly call his opponent pinned. Desmond still had a hold on his wrists, and he forced Bob's hands to grab on to his red singlet and pull the straps down. When he got it down to Bob's waist, Desmond escaped from the bottom.

Desmond flipped Bob face-down on the blue mat and pressed his arm on Bob's naked shoulder. He tore off the red singlet in one stealth move, and smacked the fuck out of Bob's ass. Bob couldn't turn to see, but he was sure his cheeks glowed red. When he couldn't take any more pleasurably painful spankings, Bob realised his hands were now unhindered *and* Desmond's clothed hard-on was right there for the taking. When he locked his fingers around Desmond's firm shaft, the guy got so distracted he totally let his guard down. Or maybe he was just giving Bob the opportunity to strip off his black singlet. Either way, that's what Bob did – he flipped Desmond onto his back and tore off his bodysuit. Instead of grabbing the guy's raging boner, Bob sat on his face.

Now things were getting interesting!

The crowd had been silent for a while, the way masses went when they anticipated something big was about to happen and they didn't want to miss a second of it. Well, this was something to cheer for — Bob held down Desmond's upper arms with his shins and took that sneering, smiling head in both hands. He tried to shove his dick in Desmond's mouth, but the guy shook his head left to right. Bob tried to cram his cock in there, but Desmond wouldn't quit jostling. The crowd egged him on. How could he stop now? So Bob gave up on the idea of getting his prick inside Desmond's mouth. Instead, he shoved his shaved balls right down against Desmond's lips and sat heavy on his face.

Desmond struggled, but Bob kept moving his head in tight circles, and forcing him to eat sweaty ball sack. Damn, Bob felt good shoving his nads in that face he worked with every day. Desmond's irate breath sizzled against naked flesh, and his spit, his tongue, his lips, all brought out a whimper in Bob. Even as he shook his head and struggled to escape, Desmond drowned in balls. Bob's dick swung, bounced, rebounded off Desmond's eyelid, his nose, his forehead, wetting his dark hairline with gleaming liquid sex.

But this audience had paid to see a show, so Bob relented. He let Desmond's arms wriggle out, and the second they were free Desmond flipped him over one shoulder. Bob somehow ended up on both knees with Desmond behind him, exerting a furious hold on his neck. He didn't dare struggle, even when Desmond pinched on his titties and twisted them in circles.

The crowd moaned and hollered. They wanted Bob to fight back.

Spitting on his fingers, Bob reached around in search

of Desmond's asshole. If he could get his fingers in there, the crowd would go wild. Of course, he couldn't get at Desmond's hole from that angle, but his opponent let him spin out of the hold for the pleasure of the crowd. They wrestled –*really* wrestled – for supremacy. Desmond seemed to regret letting Bob out of that last hold, and now he fought with all his strength to get Bob back under his control. Grunting, Desmond flung Bob forward and he landed face down on the mat. Desmond slapped his ass before opening his thighs and then slapping his balls from behind. Bob hissed in intense pain. When he looked to Vijay, their unobtrusive referee, for help, Desmond slammed a large hand down flat against his back. Desmond's knees kept his legs in place. He was well and truly pinned.

Over the crowd's wild hooting, Bob heard Desmond spit. When hot liquid met his flesh and streamed down his ass crack, his cock surged against the blue mat. He let out a huge moan and writhed against the fingers following that gob of spit down his crack. Desmond got his ass good, rubbing that puckered little fuck hole so fast it seared. Now the crowd made a ruckus in the stands. Among the cries and cheers, Bob heard two distinct words repeated over and over again: "Fuck him! Fuck him! Fuck him! Fuck him!"

So much for Vijay – the crowd had chosen the winner! Even so, their co-owner referee stepped onto the mat to declare Desmond champion and grant him the grand prize of condoms, lube, and Bob.

'The winner is black!' Vijay told the audience.

Laughter rang out from the stands in conjunction with applause and all manner of hollers. These guys were restless and randy, and they wanted to see somebody get fucked up the ass.

Bob wasn't a sore loser, but he might have a sore something after Desmond unleashed that big cock of his. Desmond didn't even let Bob up from the mat. He got Vijay to fit the condom down his cock and douse Bob's butt with heaps of lube. The cool liquid felt so good against his sizzling asshole. God, he couldn't wait to get fucked.

'Is there anything you'd like to tell the audience,' Vijay asked, 'before your opponent conquers your ass?'

This was all for show. Still, Bob wanted to say something clever. The best he could come up with was, 'I'm a loser, baby, so why don't you fuck me?'

Desmond laughed as he smacked his erection against Bob's bunghole. 'Sounds good to me!'

When Desmond set his sheathed cockhead flush against Bob's slick crack, Bob gasped in anticipation. And then it really hit him: there was a whole crowd of guys assembled to watch them fuck. All those dozens of eyes were on him – they'd even paid money to watch him take it up the ass. Tomorrow, they'd put the video online and thousands more eyes would be on him. He'd better put on a damn good show!

Bob turned his head so the crowd could see his face. He was surprised to find them quiet and transfixed, like they found the sight of Desmond's big, black dick entering Bob's tight, white ass hypnotic. As he pushed that prick past Bob's assring, Bob rocked his hips. 'Yeah, come on,' he hissed. 'Fuck me. Fuck me good.' He wanted Desmond's wood to fill him all the way up, and boy, did it ever!

The pressure in Bob's body mounted. As Desmond's cock tore through him, he bucked back. The champion held him flush to the mat. He couldn't move if he wanted to. He didn't want to, but it looked like Desmond was restless already. That powerful motherfucker drew his dick out, picked up Bob's ankles, and flipped him onto his back. He landed with a thud against the mat while Desmond held his legs up in the air like a big V. All over again, Desmond pierced Bob's asshole with his stellar dong. And then, with an ankle in each hand, Desmond held Bob's feet far apart and fucked the hell out of him.

Vijay led the crowd's cheers until the audience was louder than the sound of Desmond's front slapping against Bob's butt. Desmond didn't let up – Bob knew he wouldn't. He hung like a rag doll in the hands of a cruel brother and he took the fucking like he resented the whole affair.

Bob held his feet aloft even as Desmond pulled out of his ass and tore off his condom. Desmond's lips twitched as he wrapped his big fist around his cock and jerked on that stiff shaft with fluid but furious emotion. His dark brow furled. The crowd grew so quiet Bob could hear the change falling from their pockets as they shifted in their seats. He watched the creases in Desmond's brow deepen as those intense eyes closed tight shut. Desmond pounded his meat until a rumble roused from deep in his throat. 'Aw, yeah!' he growled as a torrent of come shot from his dickhead. Hot cream landed across Bob's chest. Brings a whole new meaning to the term "revenue stream", he thought. Spurt after white spurt soaked his stomach, his spread thighs, his dick, and his shaved balls while an audience of awestruck men looked on.

And the crowd goes wild!

The Gamekeeper's Lodge
by JY

Adam stood at the end of the gravel driveway and tempered the butterflies in his stomach with a deep, deliberate breath. He couldn't see the house that was his destination; the driveway curled away from him and was entirely consumed by a copse of gnarled, intimidating trees that hung darkly over the gravel like parted waves about to crash. He wasn't nervous, as such. A man as imposing as him has little to be nervous about in such situations. Instead, his butterflies were caused by a sense of betrayal, a betrayal of his partner, Kaye, and perhaps, more pointedly, a betrayal of himself.

He set his boot down on the gravel and began to follow the grooves cut into it by the car that left and arrived in the morning and evening. The crunch of the grit beneath his weight became an indistinct rhythm of white noise that helped soothe his uncertainty, populating the pauses otherwise filled with silence, and, as he was swallowed into the maw of the wooded copse, the intimidation of these ancient trees began to evolve into a sense of profound privacy. That was useful. Adam wanted privacy more than anything else right now, and he was buoyed by its comfort.

Adam followed the bend and a redbrick house drifted into view at the end of the gravel track, the top floor peeking above a black wooden fence and brick walls, which marked the perimeter of the property. It seemed like an old building; Adam could scarcely believe such a place existed this close to London. The first line of the address he'd been given read "Gamekeeper's Lodge", but he'd assumed it was the artistic license of property developers, who have a habit of ascribing archaic and lofty names to new buildings that don't deserve them.

Adam saw a curtain twitch in a window on the top floor, and guessed that his arrival was already known. Hesitation now would be a mistake, so he marched decisively toward the only gated section he could see – a large, heavy wooden door set into a break in the wall. A shining aluminium dial pad was fixed to the crumbling brick next to the gate and a camera stared rudely down at him. The dial pad looked anachronistically out of place against the red brick and black wood so, on a whim, he knocked on the gate instead of pressing the buzzer.

Adam listened as the crunch of feet on gravel approached from the other side, and he felt a pang of excitement, the first one he'd felt since he'd left his own house an hour ago. His breathing quickened a little as he heard the disembodied footsteps stop just inches away from him, on the other side of the heavy gate. He heard a jangle of keys, metal against metal, the turn of a lock, the slide and clunk of a deadlock, and he smiled a little as he watched the gate's handle turn to permit him entry. The gate squealed open as though in pain, offering a growing vista of the land it protected and, finally, of the house it defended.

The garden was perfectly maintained, a stunning spectrum of perfectly coordinated colour and shape and unsettlingly realistic human-shaped topiary. The gravel driveway swept from an unseen – though certainly heavily gated – entrance, ringing its way around a large circle of grass, looping right up to the front door of the house and continuing on to meet itself again at the unseen entrance. An expensive-looking car sat patiently before the front door of the house, the shining metal and modern curves of its bodywork giving an impression far grander than the house itself. The house seemed modest by comparison.

'Adam? Welcome. Come this way,' said a voice from behind the open gate. A slight, teenaged boy, of 18 or 19, in scruffy clothes, followed the voice out into plain view.

Adam hadn't been expecting the Northern Irish accent in which the brief introduction had been delivered. He hadn't been expecting an accent at all; he had never spoken verbally to the people on the end of the emails, and he wondered how this diffident young man could have been behind the rigid, confident, efficient words in the correspondence they had exchanged. But before Adam could think, the slight Northern Irishman was scuttling toward the front door of the house and Adam pursued, noticing with interest the mud on the young man's hands and the grass stains on his white linen trousers.

The boy deftly opened the front door and held it open, so that Adam could pass in front of him into the wooded interior. The young Irishman looked away as Adam passed; they had not yet made eye contact, and Adam registered a look of embarrassment on the slender face.

He muttered, 'Come through,' as he flitted anxiously, like a startled sparrow, past Adam and continued down the hallway, into what Adam would correctly assume was the kitchen. Adam followed slower this time, absorbing the black-and-white hunting photos that lined the walls of the hallway on both sides. The old sepia photos showed men with outrageous moustaches holding blunderbusses triumphantly over various vanquished mammals.

Adam ambled into the kitchen after the awkwardly nimble Northern Irishman, and took a second to let his eyes adjust from the darkness of the hallway into the brilliant brightness of the kitchen. A few feet in front of him, the young man stood with his back against the door that led to the remarkably well-manicured back garden, with his hands clasped nervously in front of him and his head bowed.

Adam waited a few moments, and began to feel a little uncomfortable in the Irishman's silence. He noticed with a little irritation that the teenager moved in stillness, clearly agitated. For a fraction of a second, Adam noticed him glance to his right, and he followed the Irishman's glance.

Adam's eyes were met by someone else's. An elderly man was sitting on a wooden stool, in a richly beautiful double-breasted suit, leaning on the breakfast bar that overlooked the gardens through the kitchen window, watching Adam closely. Despite the man's age, the eyes were sharp and ferocious. A glass of whiskey sat next to him. There was a quiet smile on his face that spoke of dark intentions.

Slowly, and in flawless received pronunciation, the man's cavernous mouth cracked apart like ancient earth dried in the sun, and he spoke.

'Hello, Adam. It's a pleasure to finally meet you. You've met Kieran?'

The old man gestured to the Northern Irishman, who remained in agitated stillness.

'Yes,' was all Adam could reply.

The old man offered out his hand to shake, and Adam had to shuffle uncomfortably across the kitchen to reciprocate, those eyes looking fiercer with every step closer. Adam took the old man's hand and slowly shook it, all the time feeling like he was being judged and inspected in the way an experienced trainer inspects a horse.

'Adam …,' the old man mused, never breaking his gaze from Adam's. 'Adam… Do you know what "Adam" means, Adam?'

'Formed from the earth.'

'That's right, that's quite right. It rather suits you,' said the old man, quietly. Then, with his tone suddenly edged with malice, he asked, 'Do you know why you're here, Adam?'

Adam nodded, looking away.

'Good …,' whispered the old man. He gently pulled Adam's hand down into the crotch of his exquisitely tailored trousers, wrapped his free hand around the back of Adam's head, drawing his face close enough to kiss, and then licked his tongue in one slow, smooth motion across Adam's lips.

'Are you going to be a good little slut for me?' the man whispered into Adam's mouth. 'Are you going to do everything you are told? Are you going to impress me?'

Adam faltered as he recalled the countless times he had used identical phrases on his partner, Kaye, as he bound her, or as he held her throat, or just before he warmed her backside with the palm of his hand for some imagined or exaggerated misdemeanour. This was how she must have felt. She could have said "no" and struggled away at any time but she didn't, and so could Adam in that moment, but he didn't. He needed to destroy himself, just once; he needed to tear down his walls as he had torn down Kaye's. He needed to look into the mirror and see if the reflection was still his own. He needed to stare into the abyss and see if the abyss stared back. That was why he was here.

But he was scared now. He knew that with his height, his youth, his build, and his strength, he could easily overpower these two men, and scale the gate through which he'd entered if necessary. He could forget he had ever arrived here, and pray that the two men would at least pretend to forget it too. Adam was a dominant man, but his dominance was youthful and heated; this man's was cold and controlled. Adam was chilled by the old man's authority, so different from his own, and he felt small next to the old man's easy confidence, his fearlessness, and his absolute lack of self-doubt. Adam knew that his dominance was impotent here, with this elderly man, in this elderly building, set in its elderly wood. In that instant, Adam realised that the only reason he didn't turn and flee was because the old man had not instructed him to.

'Yes, sir,' replied Adam eventually, unable to look the man in the eye despite their faces still only kissing distance apart.

The old man croaked condescendingly, 'There's a good boy. Now turn around.'

Adam did so, and his vision faded to black as the old man fastened a silk blindfold, scented like pine, around his head.

'Now kneel, Adam,' demanded the impeccable old man, and Adam knelt with his pulse quickening in his ears. He was virtually between the old man's knees but with his back to him, so he was facing out into the kitchen, toward the door through which he'd entered.

'Are you hungry, my boy?'

Adam shook his head, and the old man ignored it.

'Keiran, Adam is hungry. Feed him.'

'Yes, sir,' came the Northern Irish accent in reply, and

Adam listened to Kieran's footfall approach, wondering what it was he was about to be fed.

The sudden smell of soil and worked earth informed Adam that Kieran was right in front of him, then the sound of a belt being unbuckled and zip being undone told Adam exactly what he was about to eat.

With no ceremony, Adam felt Kieran's hand on the top of his head, and his mouth with was filled with a soft, fleshy warmth that could only have been a flaccid cock. Kieran's movements were wiry, uncoordinated, betraying a lack of sexual experience, so the flesh of his cock flapped hastily around Adam's mouth, causing him to gag softly.

'How does that feel, Kieran?' enquired the old man objectively. Adam heard the whiskey glass being lifted from the breakfast bar.

'It feels good, sir,' breathed Kieran, his cock beginning to stiffen in Adam's mouth.

Adam could feel the old man smiling at the scene: the inexperienced teen boy fucking the fully clothed, strongly built Adam, kneeling between his legs, blindfolded on the kitchen floor. Adam felt pathetic and, despite himself, he was enjoying it.

Kieran's cock had hardened fully by now, and he was holding Adam's head in place with both hands, probing the depths of his mouth and causing him to splutter as he jabbed it imprecisely into Adam's throat. Adam could feel the saliva building in his mouth, coating Kieran's impatient erection all the way down to the balls that, from time to time, slapped his chin. Kieran's youthful thrusts were energetic, as though he was unused to his own body and too keen to enjoy all of the sensations all at once. He wasn't pacing himself as he fucked Adam's mouth, so the old man, who definitely was pacing himself, intervened.

Kieran reluctantly retracted his erection from Adam's mouth, and Adam gasped for air and wiped a trail of saliva from his chin.

'Mmmmmm…' The old man moaned at the sight. 'Did that taste good, slut?'

Adam registered the smell of whiskey on the flawless old man's breath as he nodded meekly.

'Yes, sir.'

'You're pathetic. You disgust me.'

'… I'm sorry, sir.'

'You greedy little slut. Take your clothes off.' The old man's tone was just as cold and slow as it had ever been.

Adam unbuttoned his shirt and slipped out of it, then unfastened his jeans and slid them, along with his underwear, down to his ankles, where he encountered his boots. He struggled for some time trying to get them off, still blindfolded, and at one point he heard the old man quietly demand "don't help him" to Kieran, who must have tried to assist. For a few minutes Adam sat on the cold kitchen floor, fighting inelegantly to satisfy the old man's order to strip. Eventually, and with a tangible sense of embarrassment, he worked himself out of his clothes.

The old man hissed his approval. 'Good slut, that's better.'

Adam knelt blindly and obediently, like the old man's whiskey, waiting for the next demand. He could hear Kieran stroking his cock just to the right of his face. The demand came quickly, and this time with venom.

'You caused dust to land on my shoes while you were stripping, you worthless little hole. Clean them. With your face.'

'Yes, sir.'

Adam swivelled round quickly and placed himself on all fours, keen to appease this man, who seemed to know instinctively how Adam wanted to be disgraced. He immediately began lapping at the luxurious shoe leather, and rubbing his face into the resulting wetness, using the blindfold as a makeshift chamois.

'Kieran, be a dear and feed this meathole again, won't you? And use this.'

Use what? Adam, unsighted, had no idea what was happening. Nor did he care. The fact it was happening in that moment was all that mattered, the "why" and the "what" were peripheral. He understood now why Kaye had no sense of time when he punished her: nothing else matters but the moment. When you are in the moment, there is no past and no future. There is no before the moment, and there is no after it. The moment is now, and it is all eternity. Because like a dream, the moment is only real while you are in it, and like a dream, it is only real as long as it lasts.

Adam heard the old man pass the whiskey glass to Kieran, and then heard Kieran shuffle round behind him.

The old man's voice snapped Adam's attention back.

'Don't for any reason stop cleaning my shoes, boy. I will tell you when they are clean.'

Adam went back to licking the old man's leather shoes with renewed energy, rubbing his saliva into their surface with his face. As he did so, he felt Kieran rubbing his erection between the cheeks of his backside, searching with clumsy hands for a point of entry. Soon he found it, and Kieran began to press himself dryly and impatiently into Adam.

Kieran's cock mirrored the rest of his frame; narrow and slight. He was certainly not a large young man, but even so he struggled to ease himself in. There must have been frustration on his face, because it caused the old man to speak once again.

'Use what I gave you, Kieran.'

There was a pause, and Adam could sense Kieran wanted to protest. But he didn't.

'Yes, sir.'

Adam, without pausing from his duties as shoe-slut, felt a wetness rolling down between his cheeks – and it stung. It was the whiskey. The old man had instructed Kieran to lubricate Adam with what felt like 60 per cent 30-year-old whiskey, and the burn was almost intolerable.

In that moment, as Adam was already wincing, Kieran pushed his cock inside, as deep as it would go, filling his entire body with fire. Adam let out a long, anguished "nnnnnnnnggg" as Kieran began his irregular and all too eager fucking, holding him by the hips and thrusting unpredictably. It must have been painful for him too, though Adam could only interpret his little moans and murmurs as pleasure.

'Good boys, good boys,' muttered the old man from high up on his pedestal, watching the disgraceful scene play out like Yahweh regarding Sodom. He watched patiently as Adam was inexpertly fucked while lapping pathetically at his shoes. Adam could feel the old man's eyes on him.

'Uh … uh …,' interrupted Kieran. 'Uhhhhh, uhhhh, sir? Sir?'

'Yes, Kieran, you may.'

With this simple permission, Kieran's unpredictable thrusting turned into long, deep strokes as his orgasm swelled over him and enveloped him. With his eyes closed and his head thrown back, he drained himself into Adam, who found himself groaning in empathy, and his powerful teenage orgasm was long and satisfying. Adam felt every convulsion of Kieran's cock throughout his entire body. Keiran shuddered inside Adam as his orgasm gripped him, until his entire body slumped forward and, like a wave crashing on a breakwater before receding, his orgasm subsided.

Kieran caught his breath, slipped out of Adam, and slumped to the cold, hard floor behind him with a fulfilled smile stretching his flushed cheeks.

'Now, Adam,' said the old man, 'don't you spill a drip of the filth that's in you, do you understand? Not a drop. I've given you a gift; I wouldn't want to think you ungrateful. Now follow me. Crawl, slut.'

The old man stood slowly from his stool, took a handful of Adam's hair, and led him toward the garden.

A Year of Waiting
by Andy McGreggor

Dominique looked wistfully at the wet boy who had just emerged, dolphin-like, from the clear water of Lake Geneva. The boy was muscular and athletic, his upper body hairless and bronzed. Dominique noted how the lad's black hair was matted to his forehead. He lazily swatted a fly with his newspaper, and relaxed into his deckchair. The day was too hot to move quickly.

The boy had recently turned 19. He was struggling to fix the stern of a small wooden boat, its side having been clipped by a passing motor craft earlier that week. Such accidents happened, even in the demure environs of Lake Geneva. Dominique's eyes were drawn to the lad's butt, to the two heavenly jellies, shrink-wrapped into a soaked and tight pair of yellow briefs. The crack of the lad's arse beckoned.

Dominique sipped his glass of chilled white wine, a Swiss Pinot Gris, and drew on his first and only cigarette of the day. He was sitting in his garden, the prettiest garden on the shore. He loved his garden dearly, and today it looked particularly enchanted. Ferns and roses fought for space, a cedar tree offered shade, and a small stream trickled down to the shore. The day was getting tired, the golden light softening at the edges of the horizon, and the distant Alps turning dark and mysterious. Even the bees seemed languorous.

His cock was hard. Dominique had a big beast of a cock, that filled up the crotch of his fine linen suit at work, or his cargo shorts at home. Wherever Dominique went, his cock grew hard. He was cursed that way.

From the rambling old house came the smell of baking cheese, a fine *tartiflette* bubbling away gently in the oven. There would be a crisp salad too, and of course more wine; lots more wine. It was Saturday, after all.

Dominique stretched out happily. The boy waded back up to the mossy steps, and emerged dripping and shivering onto the lawn. 'Done it,' he said with a cheeky, devilish grin, a grin that melted Dominique's heart and stirred his cock afresh.

'Bravo,' replied Dominique, studying the young man's perfect body. Yanis had a classical body, the sort of body at which a man might marvel when set in stone at the Musée des Arts. 'You are hard,' remarked Dominique, noticing how the boy's cock reared up against his wet, yellow briefs. Dominique sipped his wine seductively.

'I know.' Yanis grinned, displaying a mouthful of pearly white teeth. His cheeks dimpled; the soft brown eyes that blessed his face sparkled impishly. 'Wanna see?' he offered, his tone cheeky and provocative.

'Later,' replied Dominique. 'First we eat, we drink, we relax, maybe we have some cake. We can play cards. There is no hurry.' He drew on his cigarette and winked, his middle-aged face soft and shadowed in the fading light.

'Are you hard?' asked Yanis, his girlish Mediterranean eyelashes fluttering softly. Yanis' mouth was moist with lust. Yanis adored Dominique, the young Greek lad having fallen in love hard. Dominique was strong, he was wise, and he was successful. Dominique knew how to live, and how to work. Yanis had always wanted a man like Dominique. He had wanted a man who was centred and strong, not someone with baggage and hang-ups.

Dominique and Yanis had met by chance, as is often the way with great love. One evening, tired and stressed, Dominique had been passing a luggage carousel at Geneva Airport. He was intent only on reaching the nearby rail station quickly. Dominique had just arrived from London City, his small, cabin-friendly bag on his back. As he passed the carousel, he had noticed a young man, a handsome man, a man of astounding, pulse-raising beauty. Dominique had glanced at the provenance of the boy's flight. It was a budget airline, arriving from Greece. On a whim, he had stood next to the young man and waited. He had glanced at the lad with eyes of fiery lust.

'Have you just got in from Athens?' asked the boy, his voice soft and honeyed, a delicious Greek accent adding to his many charms.

'Yes,' Dominique had said, mendaciously.

'Me too,' replied Yanis. He had smiled.

'Are you on holiday?' asked Dominique.

'Work,' sighed Yanis.

'Where?' Dominique enquired.

'At a hotel kitchen.'

'Do you want to work there?' asked Dominique.

'No,' replied the young Greek man. 'No, I do not want to work there.'

'You can work for me. I need someone to run my house.'

'Will you pay me?'

'Yes.'

'Can I live there?'

'Yes. I have a big house. You can live there.'

And so Yanis had taken the train with Dominique, and then a taxi all the way out to the lakeside villa, which was covered in bougainvillea and ivy. Yanis had looked at his new home with childlike delight, like a puppy rescued from the pound. Dominique's heart had leapt with joy at the sight of Yanis' face. Then they had kissed with smouldering passion. They had kissed for hours. They had sat side by side on the antique, damask-covered sofa in Dominique's living room, their mouths moist, their hands slowly exploring each other's chests and torsos. Slowly, they had become naked, their clothes fluttering like leaves, one by one, to the small pile on the Persian rug. At last, they had sucked each other's cocks, their bodies slick with sweat. Dominique had sucked the teenage Greek's cock with reverence, gently warming the fat, spongy shaft, tormenting the boy's olive brown glans with his tongue until he was rewarded with a mouthful of nectar-flavoured precome. He had felt Yanis begin to tremble.

In turn, Yanis had explored Dominique's equine cock with awe, and with a hint of fear. It was the biggest Yanis had ever seen, the king of cocks. Yanis wept softly as he sucked. He was bewitched. At that moment, he lived only to suck Dominique's cock, the scented cock of a master.

They had come together. Then they had come again. Kissing and sucking, they had passed a whole night, eventually falling asleep as the sun rose. 'Will you fuck me?' the young Greek had begged, that first morning as sunlight filled the white room, and the birds began their chorus.

'No,' replied Dominique. 'I will fuck you, but one year from today.'

* * *

That had been a year ago. A whole year, Dominique sighed. How time flew. Life was short.

Yanis pulled on a thick, white bathrobe, and went indoors to finish dinner.

Dominique was 40, and he looked stunning. He worked out, he ate well, and he dressed well. Yanis knew he had hit the jackpot when he had met Dominique. At first, the arrangement had felt odd. Yanis worked for the man whom he adored and with whom he slept. Yet it had worked well, and Yanis was in heaven. The young Greek loved the old house, built over four floors. Each day he cleaned and cooked. He lovingly polished the wooden floorboards, dusted the shelves and the rows of books, and put freshly picked flowers in the jug, on the huge dining room table. Yanis then swam in the deliciously cool lake in summer, or walked through the crisp woods in winter. When Dominique came home Yanis had a hot meal ready for him, and the two men would settle down to enjoy their evening.

Sex was a weekly event, not daily, Dominique preferring to keep things fresher through abstinence. Each Saturday Dominique and Yanis both looked forward to their night of prolonged and unhurried sex. The two men like to explore each other's bodies, and to push their sexual boundaries, but on one point had Dominique been adamant. He would not fuck Yanis for a year. 'Why not?' Yanis had asked repeatedly.

'Because when I fuck you, it will be special,' replied Dominique in a voice that allowed no discussion.

A whole year had passed. It was their anniversary, and they spent the morning in Geneva, visiting the art gallery, sipping sinfully thick hot chocolate at a favourite café, and enjoying a light lunch of salad and quiche in the old town. 'So tonight is the night,' said Dominique, sipping his chilled white wine.

'Yes,' replied Yanis, suddenly nervous. 'Tonight is the night.'

'Are you excited?' asked Dominique.

'Very,' replied the young Greek. Yanis' eight-inch, uncut cock was hard, throbbing, tearing through his skinny briefs. His penis ached. It was the centre of his universe.

'It's been a long time since a man fucked you, has it?' asked Dominique, eying the boy evenly.

'Actually, Dominique, my darling, no man has ever fucked me.' Yanis held Dominique's gaze.

'You are kidding me?' exclaimed Dominique, looking at his young lover intently.

'No, I have never been fucked.'

'You never told me.'

'You never asked.'

'Oh,' said Dominique after a pause. This was a great honour. He was privileged, Dominique realised.

It was getting dark. The lights on the far side of Lake Geneva glimmered in the pink dusk. Across that lake had lived Shelley and other romantic writers, and Dominique could see why they had been drawn here. It was pretty. Dominique could live nowhere else. The two men sat with their drinks on deck chairs, in the cool of the garden. A sweet tension buzzed between them, deliciously naughty.

'Shall we go in?' asked Yanis, his cock straining and engorged.

'In a minute,' replied Dominique, his tone wistful.

'I'm dying to suck your cock,' said Yanis impatiently.

'No-one's stopping you,' grinned Dominique. His

beautiful Swiss cock was lying half-hard in his lap, nine inches of uncut meat topped with a knot of foreskin. Yanis couched on the damp grass, his face obscured by shadow. 'Go on, suck it hard,' teased Dominique. 'Taste me.' Yanis took the lovely cock in his mouth, marvelling at its silky texture. Dominique was fully hard within seconds. He looked at the young man kneeling between his legs. What a handsome boy he was; so sweet, so bronzed, and so eager. Yanis' eyes were smiling, his soft mouth full of cock. Dominique lit his cigar, a weekly treat, and lay back in his deckchair. Beyond the garden came the sound of a solitary owl. Yanis was doing a good job fellating the older man, and Dominique began to moan in appreciation. The cigar sat unfinished in the ashtray. Dominique clutched Yanis' dark hair, grinding the teenager's head onto his cock. Yanis gagged softly, his drool coating Dominique's pendulous balls.

'Tonight you won't taste my come,' whispered Dominique. 'Tonight my sperm will be inside you.' Yanis nodded, and closed his eyes.

The two men stumbled through the open French windows, their cocks free and erect, their trousers awkwardly dropped around their ankles. They were kissing deeply. Inside the living room, lit by standard lamps, Dominique pushed Yanis onto the old sofa, pushing aside a financial newspaper. He pulled off Yanis' tight jeans, and the boy lay back. He was wearing a tight, navy blue T-shirt, and white sports socks.

'You wanna taste my young Greek cock, Daddy?' teased Yanis.

'You know I do, you little bastard.' Dominique laughed. Yanis waved his engorged, vascular cock in his lover's face.

'Smell it first,' taunted the 19-year old. 'Smell my teenage cock, Daddy.'

Dominique sniffed the tip of the lad's thick cock. It was slick with precome. It had a delicious scent that he had grown to love. Dominique had never smelt a cock quite like Yanis'. It was rich, feral, and musky. 'Oh fuck,' he groaned. 'Daddy likes that.'

'You gonna suck me, Daddy?' asked Yanis with a challenge in his voice.

Dominique took the young man's cock in his mouth, savouring its familiar yet exotic tang.

Yanis growled. 'Fuck,' he hissed. Dominique sucked for ten minutes or so, soaking Yanis' long cock, coating it in his spit, licking the tip until Yanis wanted to scream out. Normally in their lovemaking, Yanis would come first, and then Dominique would ejaculate on the lad's chest or in his willing mouth. But not tonight. Tonight would be different. It would be special.

'I'm scared,' confessed Yanis in a whisper.

'Don't be,' replied Dominique. Truthfully, he was as nervous as the young Greek lad.

'Will it hurt?' asked Yanis, his brown eyes soft and wide.

'No, my sweet, I promise I won't hurt you,' replied Dominique. 'I would never hurt you.'

'Then I am ready,' said Yanis, who stretched out on the sofa. He lifted his hairy legs, supporting his thighs with his strong, smooth arms. His fat cock was half-hard, lolling gently over his heavy, spunk-filled balls. A thick tuft of black, curly hair gave off an enticing scent of grease and shower gel. A single thread of precome hung like gossamer from the tip of Yanis' cock. But it was not that swollen member which Dominique craved that night. His eyes gazed longingly at the soft lump of muscle between Yanis' buns. Despite having hairy legs, Yanis' buttocks and his torso were hairless, smooth, and athletic.

'Oh, son,' whistled Dominique softly. 'How I have craved this.'

'Me too,' replied Yanis hoarsely. 'Lick me, Daddy,' he begged. 'Lick me good.'

'You got it,' replied his older lover. Dominique sniffed the lad's firm, tiny boypussy. Christ, it was good; meaty, manly, a hint of soap, and so pretty it was sinful. He gave Yanis' anus another appreciative sniff, like a wine connoisseur savouring a long-awaited vintage. Dominique had rimmed the young man many times before, but this time there was a purpose. Fuck, Yanis tasted good. The teenager was purring now, wiggling his butt in order to get Dominique to lick deeper and harder. Yanis was in heaven. Dominique introduced his finger, pushing it second knuckle deep. Inside his cavity, the young Greek was hot, moist, and hollow. Yanis moaned. 'Oh, Daddy,' he whispered.

'You OK?' asked Dominique. Yanis nodded. He was smiling, his pearly white teeth radiant in his dark face.

'Can I do more?' asked Dominique. Yanis nodded again, and moved his butt like a little, dirty whore.

Yanis was smiling no longer. His mouth was open in an intense and novel pleasure. Dominique had three of his fingers inside Yanis' boycunt. 'You gonna open up for Daddy?' asked Dominique. Dominique was sweating, his brow dripping. 'You gonna be a good boy for Daddy, and take his cock?'

'Yeah!' replied Yanis. The teenager was beaming.

Dominique reached for the lubricant. He generously coated his fat, Swiss cock. Dominique was harder than he could ever remember. His cock was bloated, pulsating, as volatile as a firecracker. He touched the tip of Yanis' anus with his cockhead.

'I love you,' whispered Dominique.

'I love you too,' smiled Yanis.

'This is going to be special,' said Dominique.

'I know,' replied the Greek teenager, his brown eyes wet with emotion.

Yanis felt the pressure. It was a hard knot, and the lubricant felt cold. There was more pressure. It was an odd sensation. Yanis looked into Dominique's eyes. The older man was flushed, his mouth open, his gold pendant swaying. Dominique stopped pushing. 'Tell me when you are ready for more,' he said. Yanis nodded, concentrating. There was no pain, just a certain discomfort. He wiggled his butt, and another inch of hard flesh slid inside his colon. It felt good – hard, but good. It felt intimate.

'More?' mouthed the older man. Yanis nodded. His sphincter was being prised inexorably open. Dominique's beautiful cock was inside him, breaking his boyhymen forever. Yanis surrendered and, with a quick gasp of pain, the last inches of Dominique's cock glided home.

Dominique groaned with the most intense pleasure. It was as though the entire length of his vascular shaft were wrapped in ermine. 'Oh God,' cried Dominique. 'Oh, it is so beautiful.'

Yanis felt the tip of Dominique's cock rubbing his swollen, tender boyclit, each thrust sending shockwaves of pleasure through his core, intense, deep, and hard. 'It's so good,' Yanis cried out. 'Fuck me hard, Daddy. Fuck me as hard as you can.'

Dominique fucked ruthlessly now; there was no more holding back. He jabbed his thick cock deep inside his lover's virgin colon, ploughing it mercilessly. Dominique was panting, his breath rapid. He felt the spread of a tense glow, beginning in his stomach, and spreading like a forest fire. Soon his loins were tingling, hypersensitive to touch, his whole being concentrated in his incandescent cock.

Dominique ejaculated with a roar. He whimpered as he pumped his jizz into the boy's barely legal anus. Yanis grabbed Dominique hard, hugging and caressing him. He soothed his older lover with his strong young hands, kissing Dominique's forehead.

'I love you so much,' panted Dominique.

'I love you too,' grinned Yanis, staring into his lover's flushed face and then kissing him hard.

Dominique pulled out his softening cock. It glistened with spent come, threads of mucus stretching like the moorings of a ship. He sat back on the sofa, catching his breath, and wiping his forehead with his hand.

Yanis sank to the floor and took Dominique's cock in his mouth, cradling it softly between his lips. It tasted wonderful, full of forbidden flavours Yanis had never experienced. Dominique laughed, panting, trying to brush the young Greek away.

'No! Please!' Dominique cried beseechingly, laughing as Yanis took the full length of his softening, tender cock in his mouth and sucked hard. 'OK,' Dominique relented. 'If you stop sucking me, I'll suck you.' Yanis, his mouth stuffed with cock, shook his head, his eyes full of mirth. Dominique gave in bravely, and stoically let his young lover suck him, his cock tingling, then growing. 'Fuck,' he moaned, his tone now serious and intense. 'Fuck, it feels good.'

'Fuck me again,' the boy pleaded. 'Fuck me now.'

'Are you sure?' asked Dominique, who seldom came twice.

'Yes, fuck me, Daddy.' Yanis crawled on all fours, his plump, light brown buttocks wobbling, his smooth perineum dripping with come. So Dominique fucked him again. His cock sank inside Yanis easily, his own come lubricating his entry. Yanis' anus was hot, tight, and sweet. He fucked Yanis hard, each thrust pushing against the teenager's prostate until he felt he would pass out.

'Don't touch your cock,' whispered Dominique, biting

Yanis' ear.

'Why not?' panted Yanis.

'I'm gonna make you come just by fucking you.' Dominique pushed hard against the young man's boyclit.

'Shit, yeah!' agreed Yanis. His cock was flapping as Dominique fucked. The room was silent except for their breathing, and the sound of fucking. Sweet odours surrounded their lovemaking, rich and male and beautiful. Yanis felt his balls swell. He was close. He became emotional, vulnerable. He wanted to weep with joy. 'Oh God, I am gonna shoot,' he protested.

'Just let yourself go,' panted Dominique. 'I'm gonna come too!'

Yanis shot his load into the palm of his hand, not wanting to ruin the rug. Dominique shot a second load into Yanis' virginal colon. They both collapsed and lay still, breathing softly.

'Wow,' muttered Yanis.

'I know,' replied Dominique.

'Why exactly did we wait a year to do this?' asked Yanis.

'I don't know,' admitted Dominique. 'It seemed like a good idea at the time.' He rolled over. 'Shall we open a bottle of champagne?'

'Yeah!' cried Yanis. 'Let's get drunk and have cheese on toast.'

'We just ate.'

'I know, but I am hungry.'

Outside the lake was still, and Dominique walked over to close the French windows. A golden light was escaping from the house onto the damp, dewy lawn. From the lake came the sounds of a solitary heron fishing. A plane was landing several miles away, and the dull rumble of a passing train echoed on the water. From inside, came the sound of laughter, then the popping of a champagne cork. Two men were celebrating their lives together.